BREEDS 2

Also by Keith C. Blackmore

Mountain Man
Mountain Man
Safari
Hellifax
Well Fed
Make Me King
Mindless
Skull Road
Mountain Man Prequel
Mountain Man 2nd Prequel: Them Early Days
The Hospital: A Mountain Man Story
Mountain Man Omnibus: Books 1–3

131 Days
131 Days
House of Pain
Spikes and Edges
About the Blood
To Thunderous Applause
131 Days Omnibus: Books 1–3

Breeds
Breeds
Breeds 2
Breeds 3
Breeds: The Complete Trilogy

Isosceles Moon
Isosceles Moon
Isosceles Moon 2

The Bear That Fell from the Stars
Bones and Needles
Cauldron Gristle
Flight of the Cookie Dough Mansion
The Majestic 311
The Missing Boatman
Private Property
The Troll Hunter
White Sands, Red Steel

BREEDS 2

Keith C. Blackmore

Podium

ISBN: 978-1-0394-8348-4

Published in 2024 by Podium Publishing
www.podiumaudio.com

BREEDS 2

Prologue

For some strange reason, Kirk didn't want to make the call.

Alone in one of Ross Kelly's spare bedrooms, he stared at the crude splints fixed to his broken legs. A brown telephone with a cord resembling a mutated strand of DNA lay in his lap. Kirk placed a hand on the receiver and took a breath.

Punched in the number. Waited.

It rang, jingling in that great emptiness, summoning forces best left undisturbed. Kirk waited, every second begging him to break the connection.

An automated voice suddenly answered. "We'll get back to you."

Kirk hung up. Waited again. The elders employed techs on their side. Communications sorcerers who could secure lines and scramble conversations. Part of the wait, but only from their end.

When the phone in his lap rang, he grabbed the receiver.

"Yeah," Kirk said. "It's me."

"What happened?" whispered a voice.

"It's done. Borland's dead."

"Good."

"There were problems."

"What kind of problems?" the voice asked with a dangerous note of curiosity.

Kirk took a breath. His report took over ten minutes, and the presence on the other end of the connection sucked up every sick syllable. Kirk could sense a growing unease on the other side, but he plunged forward, omitting nothing, purging himself.

"Dogs," the voice said after Kirk had finished.

"Yeah," the Halifax warden confirmed, waiting for a ridiculing blast, a warning reprimand. *Something.*

"And none of them survived?"

"We made sure."

"You're positive?"

"Yeah, but we'll hang on here for a bit. Heal up."

"Why didn't you kill the man called Ross?"

That one question reeked of suspicion. It paralyzed Kirk. Why didn't he kill Ross? It would have been the easy thing to do.

"We needed him," Kirk finally said, stalling.

"We needed him," the voice repeated neutrally.

"We need a new warden over here. The island doesn't have anyone now. Morris and I can't be expected to watch over it anymore."

"So you arbitrarily selected a man… an unbirthed man… for a duty that would ordinarily be assigned to an accepted and proven individual?"

A weary Kirk winced into the receiver, feeling hammers

at his temples. At the time, he'd believed he had it all thought out. He didn't want to kill another innocent bystander in that one-day war. He had struggled with the possibility for so long—actually *dreaded* making such a decision. He couldn't kill an innocent person. Kirk would have become the monster he swore he wasn't, the monster he'd rejected for years but recently questioned. He believed he'd taken the high road, reasoned that the island needed a new warden familiar with the territory, and convinced himself that the elders would see the logic behind sparing Ross.

The voice on the other end made Kirk's reasoning sound like amateur hour.

"Yeah," Kirk answered.

The silence was the worst.

"How did you manage to heal so quickly?" the voice probed, changing topics.

A fearful chill bloomed within Kirk's chest. "I… ate the *weres*."

A menacing silence followed that admission.

"You what?"

"I ate the *weres*. What I needed, anyway."

"You ate… a *were*."

Kirk stared off at the eggshell white of the wall and licked a tooth. "Yeah."

The voice said nothing.

This non-response terrified Kirk. "It was *war*, man," he blurted. "There was nothing else I could do. I was facing a pack of those fuckers and if I hadn't chowed down on one of them, the others would've killed me. And the *weres* would've ripped the throat out of this place. The only way you would've known—" Kirk stopped short. "I'm… I'm fine now. Don't worry. I feel fine. I'm not going to start feeding on *weres* any time soon."

The grim silence informed him that the joke was not appreciated.

"Hello?" Kirk asked.

Nothing on the other end.

"You still there?"

"…Yes."

"Anything wrong?"

"No," said the voice. "We'll be in touch."

The connection ended.

Kirk stared at the receiver, dubious of the curtness in those last few words. He sighed. *Great.* Just wonderful. The elders probably thought he was a goddamned cannibal, given the definite weird vibe from the conversation. He hung his head between his shoulder blades and massaged the back of his neck. The unnerving conversation replayed itself in his head. He'd told the truth and knew he couldn't have done anything differently. So why did he feel as if he'd just damned himself?

Dark thoughts seeped into his mind. He settled back on the bed and regarded his mending legs. He never should have answered his phone back in Halifax two days ago.

He nearly hurled the phone across the room when it rang loudly in his lap.

He snatched up the receiver. "Hello?"

"Put Morris on." The same voice as before.

Kirk blinked, his thoughts scrambling. "Yeah. Sure. *Morris!*"

A loud thumping grew louder in the hallway, and Moses Morris opened the door. Mucus filled the exposed portholes of his raw nasal cavities where Brutus had taken off his nose. Morris was also missing a hand from that fight, and looked as if a truck had run him down before dragging his ass halfway to Clarenville. Kirk handed the phone over and shooed him out of the room. Morris frowned and backed out, the phone cord skittering along the linoleum. He fumbled with closing the door, grunted in exasperation, and opened it again to yank the cord through. He scowled at Kirk and disappeared with a door slam.

Kirk sat back in the bed, eyes narrowed. He pawed at his beard and waited. After a few minutes, he heard Morris grunt affirmatives.

Seconds later, the door opened and the Pictou warden tossed the telephone into Kirk's lap.

"Wait," Kirk said, halting the *were*. "What did you tell them?"

"Probably the same as you. Can I go now?"

"You, ah, get any weird vibes off that call?"

Morris stared. "Like what?"

"Like he was pissed?"

"Yeah."

That disturbed Kirk. "What do you think that means?"

Morris shrugged. "That he was pissed. I dunno. I'm in pain here."

"Yeah, but… I got a bad feeling about this."

"Says the guy who turned a civvie," Morris pointed out, making Kirk squirm all the more. "Whatever. It's your banana boat. Not mine."

"We decided on Ross together."

"You put it out there and I agreed, yeah, but it wasn't my idea. I just want to get out of here."

Kirk shook his head in disbelief, color rising in his bearded cheeks. "You bastard."

"Can I go now?"

"We'll talk later," Kirk promised.

As an answer, Morris closed the door.

Not a second later, Kirk heard him swear on the lengthy telephone cord.

1

Clouds ruled the late October sky, blotting out a sun that Morris hadn't seen for most of the week. He leaned back in a chair on his cabin porch, his boots fixed on the railing, dark eyes staring from underneath a thick head of hair. A heavy black sweater covered his torso as well as an open hunting jacket of plaid blue, something which he only wore around his front door. Morris pinched at his new nose, feeling the contours of the fresh cartilage, and then scratched at a beard wired with silver. He relaxed with a mug of coffee in hand and listened to squawking blue jays. The morning was tech-free and simple, just the way he liked them. The view wasn't much, but he didn't mind. The privacy was priceless, and the single biggest reason he lived in the countryside. The clean air purified him, and the clear nights were every bit as spectacular as a summer's firework show. Out here, it was just him. Not another neighbor within a thirty-kilometer radius.

If there was, he would've known it.

Morris sipped his coffee. Three sugars and a generous

dollop of milk. Some would say he polluted the drink. He'd tell them to fuck off—without the sugar.

A thick fence of birch and fir ringed his property. Bright leaves drizzled his lawn. Morris intended to rake them later that day, whisk them into a beach rock fire pit, and burn the lot. In his mind, October was the finest month. It was the most colorful, the most pleasantly fragrant, and the most comfortable time of year.

October relaxed him.

Morris was all about relaxing.

The September Harvest Moon had passed without trouble in his part of the woods, and he hadn't heard a thing from Halifax, which was also good. As much as Morris enjoyed life as a *were*, he didn't like dealing with others of his kind. Didn't like the posturing, the attitude, or the arrogance. He rarely heard from Douglas Kirk down in the city, and that was a good thing.

Doug Kirk.

Borland. Newfoundland.

Christ and twelve monkeys, that had been a clusterfuck of epic proportions. The closest Morris had ever come to dying in all of his eighty-five years on the planet. The horrors he and Kirk had survived brought a smile to his bearded jowls these days, but the smile always frosted over when he really got down to remembering what had happened over there.

What had happened and what he'd done.

What he'd eaten.

Steam smoked from Morris's coffee, disturbed by the

faintest of breezes. He switched the mug to his other hand so he could rub at his left shoulder. A line of scar tissue ran under his fingers like a profane line of braille. Walt Borland, the ancient bastard, had stabbed a silver blade there and sunk it deep, as if he'd been staking a claim in Morris's flesh. And that had been only the beginning. The episodes with Borland and the *were*-breed called Brutus had been two of the most damaging claw fights he'd ever participated in. He'd sustained wounds and forced speedy changes upon himself which, at the time, he knew, just *knew*, he'd have to endure for the rest of his days.

Silver had cut his shoulder. *Weres* abhorred the lethal substance, the only element known to inhibit the regenerative ability of a werewolf. Wounds made by silver, be it bullet or blade, never healed. Morris had heard a few stories concerning old *weres* wearing shirts to hide baseball-sized holes in their torsos, using canes to walk on legs missing whole sections of the femur.

And yet…

He rubbed his shoulder, knowing there should be a slit wide enough to slip three fingers into, and felt the sealed edges of the scar. Nor did he have the burning, arthritic ache that came with a silver-induced wound. Those items weren't the only surprises of note. When Borland had blasted him with a shotgun and left him for dead in a snowbank, Morris forced the transformation from man to wolf. It took about three minutes, if one allowed the magic to naturally flow, to shift internal organs about, to enlarge musculature and reform bone. To push the change—to speedball through it—risked considerable damage, both internal and out. Damage that might not be corrected upon successive transformations.

Three minutes to safely morph.

In the fight with Borland, Morris had morphed in perhaps two minutes. Maybe even a few seconds less. And though his lungs and heart had made it through that rush job, he suspected his digestive tract, kidneys and liver might've been moved around and compressed into interesting places and shapes. And he'd been pretty sure his pecker and balls had been reassigned somewhere behind his asshole.

A guy never really appreciated how things hung until they'd been jammed into one's spleen.

In the aftermath of the Borland struggle, however, perhaps a day or two after that little war, Morris realized he felt fine. Matter of fact, he'd felt great. His hand even regrew faster than he had originally expected, but, having never lost a hand before, he wasn't sure exactly how quick it was supposed to sprout. He did know—with a chilling realization that tingled his spine—he owed his speedy recovery to his diet. What he'd eaten in Newfoundland. He'd talked it over with Kirk, who was up and limping around on a pair of shattered legs in two days. Walking tall on the third. Halifax, as Morris often referred to the only other Nova Scotian warden, had never sustained such crippling injuries before, and asking the elders for guidance on the wounds seemed unwise after a decidedly frigid Q&A on the telephone.

The elders. Morris sighed and took another mouthful of coffee.

They had wanted his report of what had gone down in Amherst Cove almost immediately after speaking with Kirk. Like a good little doggie, when they'd asked him how he'd healed so quickly, he'd given them an honest answer. A pause later, the elders had hung up on him.

Morris hadn't heard from them since.

The Pictou warden wasn't one to worry about much, but he was worried about the elders. Their silence bothered him. Bothered Kirk as well, but Morris hadn't talked to the man since leaving Newfoundland this past May, nearly five months ago, after helping Ross Kelly transition to the ranks of *weres*. As a warden, no less. Not that the promotion disturbed Morris. He didn't care who filled the vacant position as long as it wasn't him. He wasn't one for island life.

Then there was the other thing…

Where Morris broke down and fed upon the flesh of another *were*, and willingly became a cannibal.

A year later and he still remembered the taste of the *were* breed. God as his witness, he remembered. And the disturbing thing was… he missed it. Even craved it.

Kirk had kinda sorta done the same, feasting upon Borland's breeds, doing so because his life depended on it. Morris had replayed the events of that hellish day and night in his head until his eyes crossed. He came to the same conclusion every time. He and Kirk had done what was necessary to survive Amherst Cove. And survive they had.

So why did he feel like he was fucking quarantined, for lack of a better word?

And though he and Kirk had talked at length about their surprising rate of recovery, Morris wondered if the warden remembered the taste of *were* flesh like he did.

That notion made him shiver.

The orange and yellow leaves covering the lawn rippled in a haunting breeze. Soft rustles of movement became whispers of paranoia. Morris didn't like that. He finished his coffee in three quick gulps and put his mind to other things. Better things. The world would sort it all out eventually.

The telephone buzzed inside the house.

Not many had his phone number. Matter of fact, he could count them on one hand.

Morris considered not answering it, but that wouldn't do. It might be the elders. If it was the elders, maybe he could ask if he should be worried about last winter's forbidden dining experience.

He stood and went back into the house. Found the flip phone vibrating on the kitchen countertop.

Not the elders.

"Yeah?" Morris answered, scanning the ceiling.

"Morris?"

"Yeah."

"This is Bailey."

Morris didn't know a Bailey. "And?"

"I'm from Alberta. Heading your way. Looking to do a little outdoor hiking."

Outdoor hiking. He meant a hunt.

"That so."

"Yeah, how about some directions?"

"You're a long way from Alberta."

"Never been to your neck of the woods, either," Bailey explained, his voice grainy over the connection. "Anyway, I'm on the 104 driving east. How do I find you?"

Morris supplied directions.

"I'm on my bike so I'll be there in an hour." Bailey hung up.

The Pictou warden lowered his phone and stared out into the wooded backyard. His first hunt of the year. Deer and moose were still ongoing.

He hoped Bailey wasn't a freak.

By late afternoon, just as the sky paled around the edges and turned into gold, Morris heard the sputtering of a motorcycle. The machine could be heard a kilometer away, giving the warden plenty of time to become good and pissed off as the racket utterly ruined the countryside's spell of tranquility.

The road leading to Morris's cabin home was old and grown over. A grassy rise divided two sunken ruts salted with rocks, squeezed from the earth by a long, cold winter. For the intrepid snoopers who couldn't take a hint, Morris had dug potholes in the road, some of them deep enough to give some serious whiplash if drivers decided to proceed. Unless the visitor was a motocross specialist, the first hellish drop was enough to make most turn back.

But not Bailey.

The headlight jumped and jigged as it came into sight at the far end of the forest road. Morris, decked out in a new leather duster and a black special-op sweater, stood at the mouth of the old track and watched. He stared down the length of his nose, projecting a very willing disposition to stomp on any stupid bastard dumb enough to try fucking with him. *Were* or cattle.

Didn't make any difference to Moses Morris.

Dying sunlight fluted the figure as it sped along the road, growing in size and volume. The bike was a Japanese crotch rocket meant for the highways, not that it bothered the rider. Bailey wore unimaginative black leather and matching jeans. The bike revved repeatedly, needlessly even, as if the man were stricken with palsy. Even better, Bailey let loose a yodel of a shriek. A high-pitched goose of a war cry that didn't impress the warden in the least. The motorcycle was bad enough.

Morris didn't like Bailey a klick out.

He absolutely hated the man's guts by the time he pulled up in front of the Pictou warden and killed the engine.

"Hey chief," Bailey said and popped the helmet from his head, revealing an interesting haircut. The sides had been buzzed down to a five o'clock shade, while the top remained untouched and grown quite thick, resembling an artist's paintbrush dipped in tar. The man from Alberta groomed himself as if in a spotlight.

The egregious display caused one corner of Morris's mouth to twitch.

"That's some road you got there," Bailey exclaimed, baring a perfect set of teeth. "My shit's gonna just squirt after all that. Jesus! That was like buzzing over the fuckin' surface of the moon! Twice I damn near flipped over the front. *Eeeyow*! How ya doin'?"

Morris didn't answer. Didn't like the *were's* enthusiastic smile. It was too buddy-buddy.

"Uh…" Bailey hesitated, the headlights of his eyes dimming. "You're Morris, right?"

"Mm-hm."

"So why are you making eyes at me?"

"You're not a warden, are you?" Morris asked, knowing Bailey wasn't, but he'd make sure all the same.

"And if I wasn't?" Bailey asked, smooth features hitching into a smirk.

"Answer the fucking question, cocksucker."

Bailey's smile dissolved. "What did you say to me?"

"Cock," Morris stepped forward, invading the man's personal space and projecting war. "Sucker."

For a brief second, Morris thought—no, he *knew*—Bailey was going to try something. He didn't know what exactly, but something, and something bad. Because Bailey was crazy. Bailey was a homicidal wingnut a long way from home, and looking to have some destructive fun. Why else would he travel all the way out east on a pickle and ball buster? Morris knew all of that in the fleeting seconds of standing in the man's company and waited for the worst, *expected* the worst.

However, giving the airbrushed metrosexual fuckwad his

due, Bailey didn't do anything.

Which showed intelligence.

"No," Bailey answered with a soft leer. "I'm not a warden."

"I am," Morris reported. "And I like quiet. So when you leave my territory, you walk that goddamn bicycle of yours to the highway."

"Or what?"

Morris tilted his head and stared serrated daggers. "Don't question me, dogshit. You just fucking do. Understood?"

Bailey took his time in answering, but he backed down. "Yeah."

"When I'm in your rodeo neck of the woods, whoopin' my ass off like a glue-sniffing savage and disturbing the peace on a plastic piece of shit, then, *maybe*, if you're wearing metal that is, maybe our roles might be reversed. But since I sure as fuck don't plan on heading out west…"

That time, Bailey wisely kept his mouth shut.

"You still want to hunt?" Morris asked gruffly.

"Yeah."

"Didn't get enough this Harvest Moon?"

"Nope," Bailey said, unwilling to engage in any conversation.

"That's funny. Guy like you probably left dead things behind him every klick of the way out here."

Bailey shook his head, clearly not impressed.

"Here are the rules," Morris said. "You stay within a twenty-klick radius of my cabin. You hunt deer. No bear. No goddamn people. Ordinarily, I wouldn't remind folks of that last one, but you look batshit crazy to me. Crazy enough to try and slip one by. You try that and there'll be fuckin' consequences, understand?"

"Yeah."

That was good, but as God was Morris's witness, he didn't like the vibe exuding from this man.

"You can control yourself?" Morris asked.

Bailey flipped the warden a dry *please* look.

Morris didn't give a shit. "Whatever you take down, you leave. No trophies. Eat your fill, leave the rest, and get back to the cabin. One kill and that's it. Nothing else. So make it count. Don't need you clearing out the countryside in one night. And I don't think I need to remind you to stay the sweet fuck away from other cabins. Hear me? You leave the natives be. Make your kill, get back here, and ride out in the morning like your ball sack got hooked to a meteor. But you do so quietly, until you're well and away out of my territory, and you can safely mouth off to your redneck buddies out in Cowtown about how you pissed on an east coast warden. Got all that?"

"Yeah."

"Then say it, fucker."

"I got all that."

Morris turned away and strolled to his cabin, showing the *were* his back.

"Where you going?" Bailey called after him.

"Get some supper. Got a feeling it'll be a long night."

The notion of being hospitable was lost on Morris. He didn't offer anything to the Albertan. Didn't want to and didn't have to. His job in this situation was just to be an observer, to allow the *were* to hunt an animal, and generally see to it that things didn't get crazy.

He wasn't running a bed and breakfast.

2

It had become too quiet outside, and the fact that Bailey was out there wasn't lost upon Morris. He went to the fridge, retrieved a slab of hamburger meat, and dumped it into a metal bowl which he filled with water. Standing over the sink, he turned around and thought more about Bailey. Thought about the past Harvest Moon. Wondered about other things, things that had happened in the frozen hellscape of Newfoundland, just when a blizzard attempted to power-sand a little village off the face of the world.

Borland returned to Morris's memory. That ancient war dog who'd fought as dirty as anyone the warden had ever come across. Used a shotgun on him, a weapon which was frowned upon by *weres*. Morris had to hand it to the old bastard though, because if the elders were coming after him, he'd probably do the same.

The urge to have a drink took him, so he went to the fridge for a beer.

Wait, y'fuckin'… peckerheads. Them I'se killed?

Borland's voice hooked a tender spot in the dark fabric

of Morris's mind, causing every one of his bodily sphincters to clench. The warden's eyes narrowed. He forgot the cold can in his hand as the fridge door gently tapped his side. A sub-zero swell of suspicion erupted from his core and raced along his nerve endings, leaving frost embers of disbelief.

The first one. Weren't no warden.

Borland. To say Borland was crazy was an understatement. If the word could be applied with ink stamp, then the old codger had CRAZY stamped to his forehead with a rubber mallet.

Morris remembered Borland's final warning, just before the wardens killed him.

The first one. Weren't no *warden.*

That turned Morris around.

Right there, standing before the wall of picture windows, was Bailey, smiling as if he had a great big fat secret he was dying to tell. Morris stared back, his blood suddenly thumping in his temples. It took effort but he kept his features neutral. The chill of the beer reminded him he still held the can, so he opened it. The sound broke the spell.

Bailey's brow arched, indicating that a friendly beer wasn't a bad idea at all. His eyebrows almost disappeared under that low-hanging bang of hair that looked more and more like buffalo shit on his head.

No fucking way, Morris projected back at the visitor as Borland's voice disappeared in his head. He raised the can and drank, keeping one narrowed eye on his visitor.

Realizing a social beer wasn't about to happen, Bailey frowned and considered the sky before wandering away.

Morris drank deeply and ran a hand over his whiskers when he was done.

Old man Borland and his final warning from the grave. Who'd a thought?

His boots clicking off the hardwood, Morris went outside and sat on his porch for a bit. Bailey turned around from his bike and squinted at the warden.

"Be neighborly if you offered me a beer," he said with a friendly snarl.

"It would," Morris agreed darkly and left it at that.

"So how about it?"

"About what?"

"The beer?"

"You still talking about that?"

Bailey chuckled with a shake of his head. He dropped to the grass and sat cross-legged. He glanced at Morris every now and again, smile still in place, as bright and waxy and unnatural as those molded on a mannequin.

Morris finished his beer.

Birdsong rose and Bailey's bright demeanor dimmed, replaced by a disconcerting expression of satisfaction.

"You look pretty fucking happy over there," Morris remarked.

"I am pretty fucking happy."

"Yeah, well, just so you know, I wipe my ass in the same place you're sitting."

That uneased Bailey and made him look. "You got me," the man said, but didn't move.

"Got something," Morris agreed. "But I'm wondering

why a person is looking to do some hunting so soon after a Harvest Moon. Especially someone like you. I mean, you look like the type who probably got his share that night and then some."

"You get your quota this past Moon?"

Morris didn't answer that right away. He didn't participate in the hunt. Some wardens did, but not him. He still remembered the first time he participated in the Harvest Moon, and the kills he made—or rather, the kill. And the sweet taste of the meat.

"Ohhh, that hit a nerve," Bailey said slyly, the words oozing out of him. "What? Too busy with the others? Or you just yap about it, but never partake? Or maybe you're a fucking vegan?"

"Let's just say I choose my hunts."

"I choose them, too," Bailey said, not breaking eye contact. "Like this past moon, I got four."

Morris's features tightened in a frown.

"Yeah, that's right. Four. Call me a glutton."

"Call you a goddamn dingbat."

Bailey snickered. "You worry too much. None of it ever made the news. Well, maybe one or two did, but fuck it. Anyway, listen. I want to tell you about those kills. Really outdid myself. Four of them. All after midnight but fuck it, right? The night comes only once a year. You know the number four in Korean means death? No shit. It represents death. If you get into an elevator in Seoul and want to go to the fourth floor, you won't see a fourth floor button. Just two, three, five, and then all the others. Somethin', eh? I always go for four kills. Every harvest. It's a tradition with me. This year was no different. The first ones were a homeless kid and his mom. Can you believe it? In Calgary. Don't think they'd washed in a week. I caught them under an overpass just outta town, a ways away from the other homeless. Sleeping in rolled-up winter coats. Empty sandwich wrappers in a reusable shopping bag. The mom was good. The boy was better. Couldn't have been more than eleven. Just like veal. Cracked open the head of the third one. A guy who had camped out in his backyard. Just went in his tent after him and—"

Bailey snapped his all-too-white teeth.

"Then there was a meth-head in a softball pitch, passed out in right field. Love the drunks and the druggies. They think I'm a nightmare and start willing themselves to sober up. It's *great*. So fucking great. Best part? Their blood tastes like fizzy candy."

Morris said nothing.

"Only once a year," Bailey said with remorse. "That's not right. Not enough. Not *ever* enough for me. Can't see how it's enough for anyone. It's like comparing potato chips to steak. You can eat it, maybe even live off it, but it's not real food. This, now…"

At this point, he made a sweeping gesture at the surrounding outdoors.

"This is real."

And that bright feral smile returned to Bailey's boy-band features. "Seems odd you've forgotten all that."

Morris declined to comment. "You haven't been doing

anything out of season, have you?"

Bailey appeared to think deeply. "Oh, no sir. I respect the laws. Obey them. But sometimes… the urge takes you. Y'know? Like a smoker craving a cigarette. You know smokers who quit and even stay quit for twenty years still get nicotine cravings? Twenty. Years. Could eat them unlit. Sideways. Powerful stuff, which is why it's so damn hard to stop smoking. Me, now, I can wait for the Harvest Moon. Just got to do something in between is all. Take the edge off."

Bailey's little speech reaffirmed the warden's earlier opinion. The *were* was batshit crazy.

"So here I am," Bailey continued. "Never been out east before. What can I say? I love to hunt. Any kind of hunt. Any kind of meat. I'm there. Moose, deer, bear. Even goddamn Easter bunnies. The fluffier the better. You name the animal and I'm so fucking there. I think after tonight I'll head down the coast and make my way over the border. See what's happening down in Maine. Maybe carry on down the coast. Hit up Florida for a bit. Then head on back west."

"Might be better game down that way."

"The best game is riiiiight here," Bailey corrected in a sly voice. "Well, second-best game. *Man* is the top of the order. I mean, seriously… what else is there?"

In the ominous wake of the question, the two *weres* locked gazes and didn't flinch.

They'll be after ya, Borland's warning rustled in the back of Morris's mind. *One day.*

The warden's lips barely moved. "Sounds like you got it all planned out."

"I do."

The plastic smile emerged once again.

Morris summoned a lesser version of his own.

3

Night eased over the cabin and within its depths, Morris measured the darkening of his living room in long, quiet minutes. The kind of time when aging parents appreciated clear evenings and setting suns, where the waters of the bay shone like silver and the absence of children stirred up thoughts of the passing of years. People got a lot of thinking done in such moments, and this one was no different. Every so often, Morris would get up, easy chair creaking, and glance out his picture window at the Albertan. When Morris went to put on a cup of coffee, he'd turn his back and watch the visitor from a mirror. At suppertime, after frying up three custom burgers and then devouring them, he'd look up to check on the whereabouts of the biker.

The guy never moved from where he sat on the grass, cross-legged, bent forward as if picking at the soles of his boots.

Morris never could sit like that. It looked fucking unnatural to him, anyway.

Not to mention a pain on the old taint.

In between bites and gulps of the burgers, Morris passed judgement upon his not-so-welcomed guest. Bailey was as weird and disturbing as green shit on white porcelain. After his meal, the warden opened up another can of beer and drank half in three gulps that hurt. He belched mightily and finished the rest. The empty can he crushed and dropped in a blue bin.

A dog he might be, but he fuckin' recycled.

When Bailey was nothing more than an outline on the front lawn, Morris returned to his easy chair and dropped into it with a grunt. He faced the picture window, and Bailey remained in sight, still sitting in that punishing position. Unmoving. A torso blotting out his bike's chrome. Morris marveled at the resiliency of the oily rider hick, knowing his own legs and ass would be screaming after five seconds of being planted in such a way.

Uninterested, Morris sniffed, scratched at his balls, his beard, and settled into his easy chair for the wait. Thoughts of Borland and his warning circled the boundaries of his consciousness, whispering. Morris had already decided upon what he would do later this night, and it concerned a hunt of his own.

Sometime after eight, Bailey unfolded his legs and rose as if levitating. The soundless movement brought Morris to full attention. Bailey took off his jacket and threw it over his bike. He stripped off his sweater, revealing a pale but well-built body. It was bad enough seeing the guy dressed. Morris stopped watching when the Albertan went to work taking off his jeans, not needing to see any more. His hearing was just fine, however, and Morris heard every garment being slapped over the motorcycle's saddlebags through the wood and glass of his cabin walls.

Looked like Bailey was making his move.

Morris rose, making an effort to remain quiet, and backed into the shadows of his home.

*

The glossy smile Bailey used to charm folks waned as he kept his back to the warden's cabin. Warden. He scoffed at the title, actually chuckled at Morris's thumping chest. The warden actually considered himself a badass. A true badass. That amused Bailey. He knew something had long chewed that lawman's balls off. Bailey wasn't sure what, but straight-talking, hard-looking Moses Morris was all shell and gooey interior. Bailey could smell it on him like a child's fruity perfume.

Warden. *Badass.*

He smirked at the notion.

With night upon him, Bailey's thoughts turned to why he came out east in the first place.

Ignoring the chill, he undressed and heaved his clothing onto the bike. There was no rain on the air so he wasn't worried about showers. At times he could feel the warden's eyes upon him. That didn't bother Bailey either. If Morris was watching, it meant Morris was close by, and that only made Bailey's job easier.

The real reason why he came out to Nova Scotia.

To partake in that most elusive of hunts, the rarest of game.

The deadliest of hunts.

Stars filled the sky, a couple unnaturally bright. There would be no full moon this night but that didn't bother Bailey. He didn't need it to make the change, long since having mastered control over his lunar urges. Once naked, he knelt upon damp grass, relishing the contact, and placed both hands on his thighs, samurai style.

That's what Bailey thought of himself as, despite whatever name the elders might use refer to him. After nearly a thousand years upon this earth, he didn't really consider the elders as his keepers anymore. He existed beyond them, upon a different plane. A separate entity that honored ancient traditions when it entertained or benefited him. Borrowing from current pop culture, Bailey thought of himself as Ronin. Masterless. With the side profession of being an executioner within a very, very old order. A native of the Montenegro region in southeastern Europe, Balsa Milutin had adopted several names over the years and went by the singular name of Bailey since the 1920s. He'd well earned his reputation for taking lives. He'd feasted on Roman soldiers at the earliest age, gutted minions of the Ottoman Scourge during the twelfth and thirteenth centuries, and even wrought havoc amongst British infantry in the Boer Wars of Africa.

During quiet times, Balsa—Bailey—would close his eyes and recall history as it happened. He'd *made* history that had never been recorded by mortal hands.

And here he was.

Pretending to be an insolent pup. With teeth.

The act taxed his patience these days. He'd grown jaded with the role but still performed it with all the skill of a consummate professional, especially when his target was a warden.

As centuries cranked forward, Bailey discovered he preferred the earlier times over the current tech-focused era. The human cattle were more fearful back then, and infinitely more superstitious. Concerning *weres*, the newborns had been far more respectful, including the appointed wardens. These years, the law bringers had become increasingly full of their own self-important shit, believing themselves to be formidable. Dangerous.

Moses Morris, in Bailey's mind, was nothing more than a chained runt growling at his betters. Bailey had encountered many like him throughout the years. He'd even accepted assignments from the elders to kill a few, removing them when necessary. In his early years, he reveled in killing, tearing flesh with claws, crushing the throats and bones of *weres* and humans alike. Some of the world's bloodiest conflicts, sheer spectacles of carnage, had been conceived by his hand. He'd killed with thunderbolt necessity if the situation demanded such, tortured his victims for days if the mood came upon him. He'd participated in hunts that lasted almost entire weeks. In his mind, life itself was a gift. To undergo the change was a gift. Taking a life while as a wolf, well, Bailey didn't know if a word existed to truly encapsulate that emotion, that moment, that event. Having delivered all manner of death upon his victims, it presently amused him to kill as quickly, as *explosively* as possible. All life could end in an instant by whatever means, and he rather fancied the idea of a creature living, thinking idle or important thoughts (or not thinking at all) in one instant and then dead the next. A startling transition from life to death in a slice of a second, taking no more time than it took for a person flipping through TV channels. Life–death–life–death–life… death.

Bailey enjoyed that there were a lot of folks arriving on the other side, all by his hand, exclaiming, *"What the* hell *was that?"*

Was he being merciful? Not really. The truth was, Bailey just got off on it. Envisioning all those bewildered ghosts made him chuckle every time. And when you reached his age—one best counted in centuries—finding quality entertainment grew increasingly difficult with every passing year.

Until he'd been asked to hunt that rarest of creatures— one of his own kind.

That was something special.

An experience he wished would happen more often. As it was, whenever he was assigned to put down one of the pack, he preferred to take as much time as possible. Killing a fellow *were* was the highest, most secretive of honors—an extravagant indulgence.

Bailey's heart quickened as he gave himself over to the transformation, allowing it to flow its course. Skin tightened and stretched as if pulled by hooks. Bones shifted. Joints crackled. His eyes bulged, the whites disappearing, fading into orbs of black. His jaws popped and unhinged, widened, then snapped with grim eagerness. Blood spattered grass, the sound a drumbeat as flesh burst apart at invisible seams. Fluid flowed, splits mended, fur sprouted and thickened. Power thrummed, crackling through his spine. Bailey simpered madly during the scorching, acetylene burn of the change. He retained all sense of self as his limbs lengthened, as his muscles thickened. Claws fastened into the earth, drawing deep furrows, uprooting sinewy chunks.

The pain subsided, replaced by a God-like euphoric rush. Bailey growled and directed his glittering attention to the warden's cabin. He sniffed the October air.

Badass.

The little warden shit knew *nothing* of being a badass.

The monstrous werewolf, measuring nearly ten feet from nose to tail, crept toward the front door. His sense of smell led him while his ears twitched. The creature paused for a heartbeat, switching from the entrance to the window. Bailey fully expected Morris to have captured his scent.

For all the good it would do him.

Glass exploded as Bailey launched himself through the picture window. Shards and slivers cascaded upon hardwood flooring. He landed amidst it all with a *wuff,* front paws stopping in an empty easy chair.

No Morris.

Bailey's enormous head swung left and right before he pulled the chair onto its side, claws slicing deep into the fabric and releasing great gouts of white sponge. When he moved, sleek fur the color of midnight rippled, displaying a powerful chest, shoulders and limbs. Glass tinkled underfoot. Fangs bared and eyes narrowed, Bailey plodded into the kitchen area.

Again, no warden.

The werewolf executioner treaded down a short hallway, following the scent as pungent as fresh shit. A bathroom lay empty, as did a single bedroom. Upon entering the bedroom, however, Bailey's jaws ached and shivered like a diving rod.

Silver.

The warden's dagger. A foot-long saber of edged silver, left unguarded underneath the foot of the bed. Morris had left his authoritative badge. That was fine. Bailey would collect it later.

Puzzled, the werewolf retreated and sniffed his way back to the kitchen.

Back door, not entirely closed.

Bailey shoved his way through with a violent slap of wood on wood and stopped in his tracks.

Clothes. Morris's clothes, discarded in clumps along the rear deck and back lawn—everything including a pair of boxer briefs clinging to the neck of a discarded motorcycle boot. Morris had stripped a blatant trail to the tree line. Bailey studied the eerie curtain of Pictou forest not twenty feet away. The warden had changed. Interesting. Bailey licked his jaws and listened, hearing the buzzing absence of noise.

That Morris had transformed didn't bother or concern him. Wardens sometimes changed with the wolves to better supervise the hunt, but Morris would have known something was wrong when Bailey crashed through the window. He might've even confronted Bailey in the living room.

Instead, the warden had vanished into the woods. Perhaps Morris had sensed Bailey's true intentions. In his experience, the soon-to-be-dead occasionally developed that ability.

Locating the warden's trail, Bailey crept forward with nose to the ground, the air redolent of spicy wood, blood blots, and animal musk. His prey had *rushed* a change and fled, through a forest hallway where dark birch peels curled off the trees. Bailey stopped and sniffed, listened. The ground was unknown to him, this much he understood. Did the warden suspect him? The werewolf decided it would be wise to assume as much. Probably not the best idea to hunt Morris in his own territory. Bailey might have been a tad overconfident in his approach, but he wasn't about to pursue the warden across unfamiliar woods. A warden—a careful warden—might have any number of surprises waiting within the forest. Bailey approved. The hunt was about to become that much more interesting.

Fortunately for Bailey, he knew what to do.

He retraced his steps back to his bike—one of the previous century's best inventions in his opinion—and plunged into the woods facing east.

Bailey would not follow his prey. He would not play his prey's game. He would bring his prey to him. He'd force Morris to emerge from the shadows and act upon Bailey's yet-to-come transgressions.

Then, Bailey would murder him.

Envisioning scenes of the imminent slaughter, the smell of melted cheese hooked the killer's ultra-sensitive nose and pulled him deeper into the woods.

4

Deer hunting in Pictou County was a tradition in Dale Hutchinson's family. His grandfather had taken his father out on hunts when he was a boy, and some of Dale's fondest childhood memories were spent crouching in the bush with his dad and grandfather, enjoying the solitude of the Nova Scotian wild. Things had changed to a degree over the years. The hunts were a little more regulated, his grandfather had long since passed away, his dad no longer accompanied him, and Dale had a daughter who was more interested in apps and boy bands than trudging over woodland seeking wild game. Not that any of that bothered him. The yearly hunt had become an excursion for the boys anyway, a weekend retreat from their various jobs. An escape to the country cabin where they drank and played poker until passing out before dawn, only to rise a few scant hours later, bleary-eyed and hungover, to track down deer.

Dale's cabin was not so distant, at least not anymore. Claymore Lake was located about three klicks from the coastline, off a dirt road branching away from the 104.

When he was a kid, the area was untouched by townspeople. Unspoiled. His father had the foresight to buy whatever crown land he could afford, but he didn't anticipate the full magnitude of the property boom around Claymore Lake. Over the years, more and more cabins went up around the shoreline. Traditional one-story bunkers, two-story homes away from homes, and the not-so-odd but coveted A-frames that rose majestically above all others and somehow heralded the end of an age. The area had become a familiar, not-so-quiet getaway for several families. Loud parties were the norm on summer weekends. Speedboats cut waves across the lake's broad surface. Fresh air and other earthy scents had been replaced by wafting barbeques—not that Dale had a problem with barbecuing, but it did sadden him at times when he remembered hiking around the lake with his father, over hills and through bush that had since been cleared and developed.

There were perks, however, as Dale remembered the sight of four women jogging along the main dirt road. Four young ladies dressed in tight exercise suits and everything just a' bouncing. Trade-offs. Dale didn't mind trade-offs. The good Lord tooketh the reclusive feel of the lake, but he gaveth weekend boobs. No sir, Dale didn't mind trades like that at all. And his father had managed to buy up several acres of crown land. A thick, undeveloped barrier of timberland hid and protected the family cabin, acting as a natural defense to hikers from the back roads, and still half a kilometer away from party central situated along the eastern part of the lake. A system of old trails led west, away from the cabin, into deep forest. The land there was crown land but nowhere near a lake, thus undesirable to people looking to build more weekend retreats. Two kilometers into backcountry, the place was filled with wild game.

Even though the game had retreated from the growing human presence around the lake, Dale could still access it by all-terrain quads. His cabin was his base camp, a bastion of mountain men holding out against the recent rise in development, and a gateway to some prime hunting.

For a while, anyway, as Dale suspected the nine acres his father had managed to snap up had grown considerably in value, perhaps even surpassing two or three million dollars. When the advancement of cabins, marked by festive patio lanterns and fire pits, stopped on his property line, Dale intended to call in a real estate professional and sell the land off in huge bountiful chunks.

Tonight, however, Dale decided to forget it all and have some fun with his friends.

Well past a quarter to shit-faced, they sat around the old family table that Dale's grandfather and father had fashioned from oak. Five friends ringed a table covered in discarded playing cards, individual bastions of beer bottles, and snacks of gut-widening goodness. Nachos, cheese dip, chili dip, sour cream, salsa, cured beef strips, and potato chips. As the night wore on, the remaining friends would decide to play cribbage. They played with bottle caps for markers, each one valued at a nickel. The lads had decided long ago that the stakes would be cheap but the laughs and sense of camaraderie … priceless.

"Whaddaya got there, Johnny?" Cory LeBlanc asked of John Willis. Both men wore heavy-metal T-shirts already stained with various dips, the cotton material resembling the messy palette of a chemically enhanced artist.

"Ain't got nuthin'," Johnny Willis replied, his face covered in a graying shroud of a beard best suited for scrawny sorcerers. His belly touched the table's edge, even though he had leaned back.

"Whaddaya got?" Cory asked again. He sniffed hard enough to clear all the dust collected by his brain over the years. He then regarded Johnny with a wholly sober expression that seemed borderline miraculous, given his present orbit amongst imaginary stars. His bald head gleamed with sweat against the overhead incandescent light.

"Told ya, I ain't got nothin'.'" Johnny plucked a nacho shard out of his beard and ate it immediately.

"I said whaddaya *got*, y'fuckin' chunky-assed monkey."

"Y'wanna know what I got? I got this," and Johnny proceeded to scratch at his junk below the table, same fingers he'd been feeding himself with all night. "Got some for your wife too, if she wants it. Plenty to go around. Chunky-assed monkey style with a complimentary serving of dick cheese and taint-tickling. Butter up them giblets too while I'm at it. Give 'em a moo-cow squeeze guaranteed to please. Make her dairy white go all chocolate."

Those still conscious around the table exchanged looks of *what the hell?* No one knew where Johnny came up with his lines. They suspected it was frustration from his job finally bubbling to the surface, like the magma underneath

Keystone National Park. They did know that the reserved banker usually delivered his odd euphemisms and metaphors after his eighth beer. When the dead soldiers ran into double digits, *anything* came out of that furry mouth.

"Don't know where you get your muse, man," Dale said. "But that woman is fuckin' unstable."

"Don't know where she came from," Johnny said and tossed out two cards. "But I hope she sits on my face." He motor-boated. Spit flew. "We do our best work them times."

Heads shook around the table.

"How many, Cyrus?" Dale asked, correcting his listing to the left. He was smoking some of Pictou's finest pickled shit along with his beer and while he dealt out cards he suddenly knew, just fucking *knew*, that the recently discovered monster black hole at the galaxy's center was a cosmic pipeline to some serious undiscovered civilizations. He also wondered what aliens did to get high.

Cyrus didn't answer. The middle-aged mechanic studied his cards at arm's length, one eye widening while the other narrowed to a slit in a continuing, alternating pattern. Cyrus, with his ash-colored hair and stylish goatee he habitually groomed with his front teeth, appeared one more magic puff away from leaving reality's highway and waving, queen-like, at passing planets.

"Cyrus?" Dale asked again.

No response.

The action within Cyrus's orbital cavities increased, to where the man's upper face resembled a half-baked but still functioning accordion.

"Cyrus is out," Dale announced in a sedated voice, relieving his zonked friend of the social burden of answering. In the state Cyrus was currently experiencing, *anything* might have come out of him if he'd talked. Stoned fucker might have started reciting Shakespeare in perfect Portuguese.

"One," Blake said as he tossed a card into the table's center. Blake Reeves rubbed his black-stubbled chin which, coupled with his naturally dark complexion, made the dentist resemble an axe-murderer. He inspected his cards with a grim consternation as if they were prophetic tea leaves. Of them all, Blah-Blah Blake was the least conversational. And the scariest-looking around the card table.

"One?" Dale asked.

"One."

"You want one?"

"One."

"So you're saying you want only one?"

"One."

"All right. I'm giving you one. One card. Just to clarify. That's one, right?"

Blake nodded. Once.

"There are three muses," Johnny started, his eyes looking as splendid as freshly blown glass. "Some even say there are as many as nine, depending on what you read or believe."

"Here," Dale said, placing Johnny's comment on hold and dealing Blake his card. He tried to keep drunk conversations to a personal limit of one at a time.

"Folks sometimes call them the *Pierides*."

"Pie o' what?" Cory asked in a blend of disbelief and contempt, massaging his hairy neck with the same wet fingers he fed himself with.

"There were nine of them," Johnny went on, squinting thoughtfully as he took an enlightening drag off a joint, holding it European style. The joint's tip flared and died.

"Not one?" Cory asked.

"Depends on who you ask," Johnny squeaked.

"Oh yeah, my wife and I were talkin' about this same thing the other night," Cory said casually, flashing a *holy shit* look at Dale.

"I like pies," Cyrus muttered from somewhere to the left of Jupiter.

"Nine daughters," stated Johnny, "all from the loins of a guy called Pierus. Of Pella. But I don't … subscribe to that particular myth."

"And it's a good thing, too," Cory remarked sternly and studied his cards. "Fuckers lose *eyes* over that shit."

"How the hell do you know about that? About Muses?" Dale asked Johnny.

"Read about them."

"You read about them."

"Yeah."

"For fun."

"Yeah."

"Like, in your spare time?"

"Yeah."

"Goddamn," Dale exclaimed in a whisper and dealt himself two cards.

"All right," Cory exclaimed, inspecting his current hand. "All right, you bastards. Especially *you*, Blake. Let's play some fuckin' cards. Right here. Let's throw down, goddamnit. Let's fuckin' *roll.*"

"Thing is, them nine daughters *supposedly...*" Johnny emphasized with a lazy look around the table, "challenged the Muses to, like, a challenge."

"They what who now?" Dale asked in confusion.

"I like women with hang," Cyrus muttered, fumbling for a nacho and getting double-takes from both Cory and Dale.

"I thought the Muses were the pie bitches?" Cory asked, turning away from Cyrus and wanting clarification.

"Depends on who you ask," Johnny replied.

"Well, I'm asking you."

"I just said who the Muses were."

"No, you didn't."

"You weren't listening."

"Listen," Cory smirked. "I know I'm high. And drunk. Whatever the word is that describes both of those together, well, I'm it. And just a little bit shit-faced *but...* I sure as hell was listening to you go on about Muses and daughters of some guy called Penis—"

"Pierus," Johnny corrected while taking another drag.

"Like when she bends over for something," Cyrus released into the mix, "and everything's hangin'? Y'know? Just... swayin'."

All talk about Muses and Pierus and such got placed on standby as Cyrus stole the floor. "Like... like in a tropical breeze, y'know, one that carries the scent of sweet illegal rum."

"Stoned," Johnny remarked without concern.

"Yup," Cory agreed.

"Uh-huh," Dale added.

"I like a girl with hang," Blake said with a discerning nod. "My wife's got hang."

Dale felt his stomach rumble then, followed by an unsettling push toward the escape hatch of his colon.

"Whaddaya got there, black Blake?" Cory asked, choosing to get back to the game at hand.

"And I like fish," Cyrus said thoughtfully.

"Anyway," Johnny carried on, "these nine daughters, see, they wanted to be Muses. Musing was a pretty lucrative trade back then. Every parent wanted their daughters to be muses, right? They drove all the nice cars. And there were nine of these daughters to the muses' regular three, so the girls were pretty sure they could kung fu their asses. So, anyway, they challenged the regular Muses to a *dance* off, right? To see who would be, like, the head bitches of musing. Who got to sit on the shoulders of hundreds, no, thousands… of taxpayers."

Cory regarded his friend with stone-drunk bafflement.

"True story," Johnny said, pointing his joint. "It was televised."

"All across Greece?" Blake asked.

"Yup."

"Think I saw that show."

"They lost, too," Johnny said. "And the whole works of them got transformed into urban hippos. And to this day, hippos are the most vicious bitches downtown."

Cory leaned back and checked his hand as if holding a pocket watch. "Dunno where you come up with your shit."

"Speaking of shit," Dale stood and tossed down his cards, feeling the internal pressure build. "I'm out. Feel a caramel spritz coming on."

"I like twist tops," Johnny said, his face partially hidden in haze.

Cory rolled red eyes at Dale. "Don't leave me."

"Have to. At least five minutes."

"You and me are the only sane ones left."

Dale chuckled and headed for the can, a preventative hand placed across his bum.

"Hey, light a candle when you're done in there," Johnny yelled.

Dale closed the door just as Cory frowned at the others sitting around the table. "You bastards are *so* fucking high right now."

5

"You think BC bud is better than east coast bud?" Johnny asked thoughtfully after the last hand, a hand where *Cyrus* had somehow won. That magical feat informed Cory that he had just departed Shit-faced Avenue and entered the realm of Mind Fucked.

"Ooooh yeah," Cyrus chortled, teeth clamped.

"Hands down," Blake added.

"Anything's better than the government's medicinal shit," Cory muttered while shuffling.

Johnny stuck one then a second finger into his ear. He rooted around and grimly inspected the findings, before using the same two digits to dip and shovel a nacho into his bearded face.

Blake stood.

"Where you goin'?" Cory asked as he dealt cards.

"To open the door," Blake reported, indicating Dale in the bathroom. "This place is gonna be rancid after he's done in there."

"Good idea," Cory said. "That man deserves public

recognition for what he does in there."

Cyrus and Johnny surfaced from a mutual haze to mutter agreement. Blake disengaged himself from the table and stumbled.

"Watch yourself, man," Johnny said.

Blake indicated he would do just that and went to the front door. He straightened upon reaching the door and turned the knob. Night air gushed into the cabin.

Cory shivered violently. "Jesus, don't let too much air in here. Last thing I need to see are party darts on you guys."

"You won't see any on me," Johnny said, inspecting his cards. "My chest hair pads everything out nicely."

Cory convulsed again. "I didn't need that. At all."

He rose from the table and stumbled toward the woodstove. The fire needed another log. Cory lifted a forearm-sized chunk from a nearby pile, cracked the stove's front lid, and idly glanced in the direction of the front door.

Blake stood there, holding a pose and gazing up at the night sky, the evening's worth of smoke surrounding him like dreamy gauze.

Then a black streak blurred into him, yanking him from the picture and leaving a door slapping against the cabin. Just like that, Blake was gone, his dirty white-socked feet winking out of sight. An empty space framed by a rectangle remained.

Cory saw the whole scene and didn't bat an eye. He calmly replayed the event in the hazy theater of his mind. He replayed it a second time, then a third just to be sure. He understood he was ridonkulously smashed, and knew that

Blake could have simply stepped outside for a breath of fresh air. Cory then considered the joint he left smoldering in an ashtray back at the table before the cabin door stole his attention once again.

"Hey," Cory asked the others around the table. "You guys see that?"

The men sitting around the table looked back in stoned innocence while the fire before Cory demanded to be fed.

A flash of a second later, the wet sound of things being ripped free of the earth transformed their expressions to disbelief.

"The hell is—" Cory started.

A growl emanated from beyond the cabin's interdimensional doorway. The men's attention shifted at the sound, all except Johnny's, who regarded his joint with suspicion. Cyrus blinked repeatedly, obviously sensing wrongness, and if his lids had been blinds, they would've been spinning at the top. He remained sitting, holding his cards like they were bulletproof bed sheets.

Cory headed for the door.

And soon stopped as the noise that emanated from beyond the open doorway made his heart hammer and his bladder tighten. Images of unwanted flowers—perhaps dandelions—being uprooted from a person's front lawn by the fist-full sprang into Cory's head, but whoever was doing the yanking was doing it right beside a microphone. His heart ready to rupture, he took three steps toward the commotion, unarmed, yet ready to lend any necessary aid to his friend.

A wolf appeared in the doorway, a *big* wolf, hunched over, the size of a freezer across the shoulders. Long, viscous lines stretched from its chin and puddled the front porch just as the raw septic smell of shit and blood flooded the cabin's interior.

"Christ," Cory croaked, stopping at the sight.

Jaws opened and the monster dropped a slab of meat onto the floor.

Meat that bled and wore clothing. The words dissolved in Cory's throat, a half-fueled whimper.

The wolf lunged.

*

Inside the bathroom, Dale Hutchinson heard the crash-boom-bah and froze as if someone had superglued his hairy ass to the toilet seat. Outside the bathroom voices erupted into piglet squeals of terror, the most shocking belonging to Cyrus, who screamed *Oh Jesus!* just before a meaty thud hushed his voice. With an unused wad of toilet paper in hand, Dale tried to rise but the screams paralyzed him. Furniture crashed and splintered as if a centralized tornado had decided to renovate the inside of the cabin. Cloth shredded. Wood snapped. Metal groaned and clanged. The line of light marking the base of the bathroom door flickered and winked out entirely. One of Dale's friends started sobbing, wailing, repeating *oh no, oh no*, until the voice was a wet gurgle, as if chugging an unending beer and unable to keep up with the flow. A bony snap straightened Dale's back, staring eyes about to burst and arms braced against the bathroom's enclosed walls.

Things quickly died down, enough for Dale to catch the distinct crack of vertebrae, then the vicious ripping of carpet off the cabin floor. *That* sound disturbed Dale the most.

The cabin didn't *have* carpeting.

His jaws ached and he realized his mouth had been opened at its widest, as if at the end of a very long scream. He closed his trap and focused on the bathroom door, ignoring the fir planks and the mangy robe hanging from a hook.

A slow squawk got his attention as a chair was shoved aside.

Oh Jesus.

Oh Jesus Christ our Savior, Dale thought, eyes pinging inside his skull as if he'd caught every one of his toes under a ravenous lawnmower and watched the shreds being spat out the side.

Something *whuffed*.

Floorboards squeaked.

It was *still* inside the cabin. Dale clamped two hands over his mouth as his nose fired a double-barreled blast of snot over his fingers. He sat like that, the odd bubble bursting in his nostrils, crouched and strained to hear more.

Nothing could be heard, however.

A litany of curses streamed through Dale's mind like an overloaded teleprompter, an uninterrupted line banged out by his supercharged heart. His lungs begged for more oxygen. His muscles thrummed with tension, poised to slingshot him out the bathroom door if, in the next few crucial seconds, something yanked it open. He leaned forward, meaning to hold on to the doorknob, and realized his jeans and boxer briefs remained puddled around his ankles. Dale yanked everything up without cleaning himself, eying the door and distrusting the silence beyond.

Another floorboard squeaked. A heavy *whump* made Dale crouch and flatten his palms against the walls. He waited, guessing that the last noise might have been close to the front door. The barest of moans straightened Dale's spine and he ceased breathing. Blood thumped in his ears while, out there, he heard teeth crunching, smacking, that turned his protesting knees to soft butter. Against better judgement, Dale took a step to the door and pressed an ear against the smooth surface, his hand poised to grab the shining knob if needed.

He listened.

The moaning had stopped but he heard, *sensed* a monstrous presence, inside the cabin. An evil manifestation of flesh and bone and teeth, probably a lot of teeth, stalking the interior, and that thought brought an eye-bulging Dale to a gulp and a click as he realized his friends were all dead, killed while playing cards like any bunch of guys would when away from civilization. No more than what? Two or three minutes since he left for a meditative moment aboard the porcelain dunk tank. And now they were all gone. Most certainly all gone.

With his ear pressed against the wood, Dale winced in misery.

The doorknob was no more than a finger's width from

his hand and he felt a supernatural current buzzing through its metal, daring him to grab and twist and behold what was what. As self-destructively tempting as it seemed, Dale set his jaw and forced himself to wait, just wait, while every other cell in his body wanted nothing better than to flee for the hills and not look back.

Nothing moved outside. The disturbing snare of his heart filled his ears, which had to be one of the most unsettling noises ever in Dale's panicked mind.

Then he remembered his shotgun. In his room. Hung lengthwise on a rack, right under a hunting rifle. Right across the hallway. Not even five feet. Five *inches* didn't even seem like a safe bet with that thing out there. But the gun was there. Waiting. If he could get to it, he could speed-load a fistful of shells into the magazine and then… he'd face the nightmare. Or at least avenge his friends not so long gone from this earth.

Five feet to the room, followed by a hop and roll across the bed, and then a race to load the boomstick.

Hooked fingers loomed closer to the doorknob. Dale took a series of deep breaths that failed to calm him.

A low rumbling matched the mad drumroll of Dale's heart, one that prompted him to flatten his head against the wood. His eyes squeezed shut and when he opened them, he cracked open the door and peeked outside.

And gasped.

Thick smoke flooded the interior, hiding its secrets in a dreamy, sepia haze. Fire flicked at the edge of the short hallway, where Dale knew a three-seater sofa lay against the wall. Smoke screened the center of the room but still he saw.

And moaned.

Limbs—forearms and legs—were strewn about in thick slicks that glistened, garnished with meat and tubing best left inside a person's body. Pools thickened. A moory fog rolled across the floor, revealing what appeared to be a hairy coconut half, just for a second, before being cloaked once again. So shocking was the scene that Dale inhaled with reflexive fright, sucking down two lungfuls of near-corrosive vapor belonging to a ruptured septic tank. The stink choked him.

That chest-hitching, barely lessened by clamping both hands across his mouth, summoned a monster.

From the gloom a huge dog emerged, as if materializing within an unseen pentagram. *A dog*, part of Dale's mind shrieked in terror. *That's no goddamn dog!*

The beast's sizeable maw leered. Its teeth looked capable enough of shredding the world in half.

Dale scurried in retreat and slammed the bathroom door.

*

Bailey stood in glossy pools, breathing deeply of blood and smoke and fire as a pang of delight nearly burst his heart. He'd missed one. In the heady aroma of bodily juices both foul and pure, even his heightened sense of smell could be skewed at times. He crept toward the door where the man hid, catching an underlying yet tangy scent of fear. Each step left a paw print in the blood. Bailey had ripped apart the four men with all the savage gusto of a child on Christmas morning, and blood spray-painted the floor and walls as if shot through an overcharged lawn sprinkler. In the short melee, he'd slammed the table into the small woodstove, toppling it and spilling fire from its lid. A single flaming chunk of wood landed on a nearby sofa, quickly lighting the fabric.

Bailey stopped with his nose a foot away from his target, catching a familiar scent. He glanced over his shoulder.

There, lurking beyond the open doorway, was a second wolf, growling in warning.

Bailey's answering rumble issued from a throat slick with blood. He faced the beast while flames waved merrily from the sofa, marching upon other nearby combustibles.

Morris growled again but he wouldn't enter the burning cabin, wouldn't dare enter the cage.

That was fine with Bailey.

He'd killed plenty of little shits like the Pictou warden. Little shits who'd rather sniff holes and lick balls than establish dominance. Bailey strode forward and Morris backed away, allowing the ancient creature to step outside into the night.

The two werewolves expressed their intentions with racks of teeth.

Morris projected an aura of outrage over the savage killings within the cabin.

A crazed cold front of anticipation oozed from Bailey.

And on some subconscious signal they leaped for each other's throats at the same time. Gravelly snarls cut the air as the two opposing masses crashed together. Heads spiraled around snapping jaws, defending throats. Morris backed the larger werewolf against a wall, but Bailey's greater mass eventually pushed back, twisting the smaller *were* to the side. They rolled, swatting each other with fully extended claws.

Morris slashed open the killer's left side to the bone.

Bailey ripped an ear from his prey's head in a puff.

Morris sank teeth into the *were's* shoulder and shredded muscle.

Bailey jerked away in a dark arc of clumpy matter. He rolled onto his back, raking Morris's legs and causing the smaller werewolf to jump. They clashed again, wrestled with teeth and talons, rolling into the front of the cabin as the flames grew bolder, urging them on, illuminating the struggle and casting long shadows upon the front lawn.

Morris attempted to duck under Bailey's toothy maw, but the larger beast slapped him down, splitting the warden's fur and flesh to the skull. Morris lunged again and got a horrific bar code down the side of his face, claws nearly slashing his other ear free.

The warden withdrew without so much as a yelp.

A part of Bailey respected that. Another part feared it. The warden circled and Bailey matched him, both supernatural foes keeping their throats low to the ground. Slits gleamed bone by firelight. Black eyes glittered with malefic intent. Ink dripped from wounds and wrote jagged lines through grass.

Bailey decided to give the younger warden an opening. He faltered, pretending to stumble because of his damaged leg.

Morris lunged.

In a blink, Bailey twisted onto his back while bringing up his powerful hind legs. Claws hooked into the meat of Morris's lower chest and Bailey *pulled*, launching the werewolf into the space behind him.

Through the front window of the burning cabin.

Bailey regained his stance and panted evil delight as an agonized howl pierced the night. He quickly blocked the doorway and waited for the frenzied werewolf to bolt outside—upon which Bailey would take advantage of his burning adversary and rip out his throat.

Or, if the fire had already enveloped the *were*, simply corral Morris until the flames finally killed him.

Another cry of pain and misery and a blazing Morris exploded from the front window, his pelt trailing streamers of smoke and flame. Bailey quickly backed away from the four-legged fireball, not expecting such spectacular results. A frenzied Morris shot past the *were* killer and rammed a shoulder into a tree trunk with a heavy thud. The impact altered the trajectory of his panicked rush and Morris scampered off in a new direction, wailing as he disappeared into the night.

Bailey intended to follow, keen on seeing the *were* cook until only ash remained.

A loud *schlacking* stopped him cold, a distinct priming of metal on metal.

The werewolf turned to the cabin, the violent fire scorching his face and wounds. A man stood at the corner of the burning structure. The monster barely had time to comprehend the shape of the shotgun as Dale Hutchinson blew apart the wolf's head in one blast, dropping the monster in a twitching heap.

Gasping and shivering, Dale cautiously approached the convulsing creature. He didn't waste any time, remembering how pieces of his friends lay scattered about the cabin floor.

He fired again. And again.

What Dale didn't shoot off in that first twelve-gauge salvo, he targeted and removed with vengeful righteousness. Skull fragments jumped as he emptied the shotgun's magazine into the beast. When he finished, the Pictou man dropped to his knees and witnessed what he'd done. What he'd killed. A second later he broke down and wept before the bloody monstrosity on his property.

All the while, the flames from the cabin grew.

6

The cabin's smoldering husk could be seen on the other side of Claymore Lake, an eerie, after-midnight beacon that drew the curious and the nosy and the death seekers. The sky above the fiery structure flashed, indicating a crew of firefighters were on scene. Corporal Roy Richter glanced at his cruiser's dashboard and noted the time. Just after twelve. The cruiser's headlights whitened the road ahead, illuminating trees and bushes hedging the gravel shoulders. A few potholes appeared in the rain-washed surface, and Richter avoided these with an afterthought.

Buttfuck nowhere, he mulled. An amazing thought in itself since his detachment was posted in the *middle* of buttfuck nowhere. Not that he minded being situated in the sticks, as he certainly didn't want the headaches that came with peacekeeping Halifax. The worst he saw out here were mostly domestic abuse cases, which were bad enough, but at least no one was shooting at each other. Or him. At least not up to this point.

Cars, pickups and ubiquitous SUVs lined both sides of

the road leading up to the destroyed cabin. Richter had been called out of bed an hour earlier by Constable Bob Hines. Bob wasn't one to call him after hours unless some pretty thick shit had gone through the fan. Matter of fact, Richter couldn't remember ever being called to a scene while off duty, not in his last nine years of living in the nearby community of Antigonish. Not even when the students of the local university were at their tribal rowdiest. Some might consider that history a grim portent of things to come—that they were due for a shit storm. Richter supposed they were, to some degree. The question was when… and how big.

Spinning firetruck lights flashed through the trees and Richter suspected the chief probably wasn't none too happy about having to rush out to the lake either. The pump truck could barely manage the old country roads. A rescue truck came into view and with it, the gathered crowds of late-night busybodies. One officer held the lot of them at bay and as Richter approached, the civilians pulled back in a retreating tide of white faces. Richter didn't understand why they gathered like crows. Didn't see the fascination. If they saw the things he tried to forget…

A hand rose and Richter stopped the car beside his junior officer. He lowered his window and smelled the last few puffs of smoke along with a heavy lathering of foam.

"Bob's up ahead," one Officer Ryan reported.

Nodding, Richter eased his window up and drove toward the bright collection of firetrucks, police cruisers, and cars parked haphazardly over a driveway and the front lawn. He parked his cruiser and cracked the door, taking a breath before pulling himself out into the night. He inhaled spent moisture along with the reek of smoke. The unsavory blend flooded the back of his throat and sinus cavity. The smell tugged free his own experience with fire, when his father's old station wagon had gone up in an electrical fire one night. As the vehicle was parked close to the house, he and his father heaved buckets of water onto the flames in an attempt to slow the blaze until the fire department arrived. By the time the firefighters got there, Richter and his father were sputtering from smoke inhalation.

Three cars filled the cabin's driveway but appeared untouched. Firefighters clad in heavy Nomex gear went through the motions of hunting for hot spots around the gutted wooden structure. Richter nodded at the faces he recognized before his attention centered on the charred ruins. Spotlights revealed a drowned porch and interior. Thermal exposure had scorched the one intact window while another had completely shattered. Firefighters splashed through puddles as they ventured in and out of the cabin. A Mountie was on one knee, placing numbered cards upon the front lawn.

"Corporal Richter."

He turned to Constable Hines. His junior's normally ruddy face was absent of color.

"Bob. What happened?"

"Homicide," Bob reported. "At first glance, anyway. We have the shooter. A Dale Hutchinson. This was supposed to be a weekend with the boys."

'Party got out of hand?"

"Something like that."

"How many?"

"Five in all. Four now deceased."

"Where's Mr. Hutchinson now?"

"In my cruiser."

"And?"

Bob took a breath and glanced around at the firefighters. "I think we'll have to do some digging on this one. Get blood samples just to be sure. But this is what he told me. All five of them were sitting around a table playing cards. Enjoying themselves. They were kicking off a weekend of deer hunting. At one point Mr. Hutchinson got up to use the facilities. He didn't see what happened outside the bathroom, because he was too scared to open the door. He did hear a commotion outside followed by the growling of a large wolf."

Hines continued with his report, and Richter shook his head at the more graphic parts.

When the officer finished, Richter sighed. "So the wolf killed them all?"

"Tore them to pieces. There are cooked remains inside and out."

"There's no conclusive evidence of wolves being in the province."

"But there are wolf and coyote hybrids," Bob countered.

Richter chewed on that. "All right."

"The burning wolf," Bob continued, "disappeared into the bush, but the other wolf was right on Mr. Hutchinson's front lawn here. Mr. Hutchinson turned the corner and shot the wolf repeatedly, effectively taking the head off the animal."

Lips tightened, Richter turned to the blanket-covered lump decorating the front lawn.

"Now for the weird part," Bob quietly announced.

"It gets weirder?"

"Unfortunately, yes. And gruesome."

"Wonderful. Lead on."

Bob led his superior officer to a blanket. He crouched at the edge and pinched a corner.

Richter nodded that he was ready.

Officer Hines lifted the blanket off a headless torso of a naked, well-muscled man, the flesh tone eerily pale under the artificial lighting. Boots splashed and water hissed in the background.

"This is the wolf?" Richter asked without a trace of emotion.

"This is it."

"Jesus H...."

"Mr. Hutchinson has stated for the record that he and the others had been consuming a large amount of marijuana and beer."

"They were high?"

"Yes sir," Bob confirmed, covering up the corpse. "That is correct."

"High enough to mistake a man for a wolf?"

Bob didn't answer that.

"Anything extra in those joints?"

"Mr. Hutchinson says 'no.'"

"Yeah. Right. That's one for the labs to decide. Who knows what's in these loads these days. Might've been Shatter." Richter rubbed the side of his face. "First question, Bob. Why is that corpse naked?"

"Good one, sir. I have no idea. Maybe the lab reports will show something."

Richter looked to the points marked on the lawn, each one denoting a little tent of white plastic. "And what are these?"

Bob met his superior's eyes. "Body parts."

Richter's stony façade trembled and dropped. There were about a dozen of the little tents all over the lawn. "Jesus H."

"It gets weirder," Bob said and approached the nearest pile of human remains. Once more he squatted and gestured for his commanding officer to join him. Richter did so, ignoring the cracking of his knees.

Bob pulled the plastic cover back to reveal a pale shin still connected to a black-socked foot. Meat and bone gleamed.

Richter made a face. "Oh my."

"Right here," Bob said and got in close with a finger, tracing the jagged edges of the detached limb.

Richter saw and a cold rush of unease fluttered through his frame.

The limb hadn't been shot or cut off. With the ragged indentations around the skin, Richter recognized the bite pattern as easily as seeing his own in a hamburger.

Except this pattern didn't belong to a person.

7

With a case of beer underneath his left arm and a pair of grocery bags at the end of his right, Douglas Kirk approached the parking lot of his apartment complex and huffed from the light exertion. It was October and, after months of guiding Ross Kelly through his initial transformation and then educating him on the finer points of life as a *were* and a warden, Kirk believed he'd earned a little R&R. A little *me* time. The case of beer was actually the second dozen he'd carried to his apartment from the nearby liquor store, and he was debating purchasing a third. Or maybe something a little harder, to really take the edge off.

That thought appealed to him.

He entered the apartment complex and headed for the stairwell, having no desire to take the elevator or risk a chance encounter with the other tenants. It wasn't worth the awkward angst, and going up six flights was good for a light burn in his legs. Kirk took the stairs a pair at a time, still carrying the dozen beer and cloth grocery bags. He smelled the two descending people before he passed them. Kirk kept his head down and didn't make eye contact. Didn't greet. He wasn't sociable, and his neighbors thankfully left him alone. The other tenants were wary about the recluse on the sixth floor, and he'd long since picked up on the vibe and welcomed it.

His ensemble of old jeans, thick black fisherman sweater, and an olive-green army surplus jacket didn't attract much attention on the streets of Halifax. He didn't dress to impress. Same could be said for his shaving habits, having allowed his beard to grow to epic biker lengths. He did buzz his light brown hair on top regularly, as a shorn head somehow offset the tangled wildness of his chin moss.

He pulled open the sixth-floor door with the hand holding his groceries. Two minutes later, he was inside his apartment, turning and sliding the locks behind him. Somber daylight shone through the living room's picture window, partially blocked by a half-drawn curtain. Kirk moved through his home's shadows, depositing the beer on a countertop, right next to the other for an impressive collection. The groceries followed and he made quick work of stowing them away. Eight beers crowded into the lower shelf of his fridge and Kirk smiled at them all, his little arsenal of bubbly happiness. Hamburgers were on the menu tonight. He'd thought about ordering out for pizza but overruled it in favor of a cheeseburger. He wanted a cheeseburger badly and hoped the rare taste of fried meat with just a squirt of barbecue sauce would do the trick. Help him take the edge off. That wicked edge that made his jaws ache and most food tasteless.

That thought made him crack open the first beer of the evening.

A beat-up copy of *Salem's Lot* rested on the coffee table and Kirk meant to be a good thirty pages into it before the beer rushed his senses. It was a departure from the classics he usually read, but early King was a classic unto itself.

Kirk plodded deeper into the living room with his beer in hand. He groaned as his ass sank into a comfortable couch. He tussled his hair, scratching at the places that demanded it. The King book captured his attention and he glanced toward the half-open curtains, gauging the light. It would be enough to read by.

He drained half the bottle in one determined bout, breaking contact with a gasp.

"Good stuff," he huffed and solemnly regarded the label. *Alexander Keith's*. No finer existed, although he did enjoy some of the imported Korean and Japanese brands.

Kirk studied the couch and lay down, socked feet hanging over the armrest, beer placed on the coffee table. The white field that was his ceiling held his attention, and he took the moment to relax and empty his mind. A lot of shit had gone down over the last few months. All of it concerned watching over Ross Kelly's initiation to the *were* world. Kirk's emotions were divided over that, since he was the one who brought the Newfoundlander into the fold. He wondered if Ross would ever hate him for what he'd done, bringing him over to the "weird" side, as the Newfoundlander had come to call it.

At the time, Kirk thought infecting Ross was the only way to save his life. He couldn't allow the alternative, didn't want to consider the alternative. Kirk hoped he'd done the best thing with Ross. The slow drag of years would eventually reveal all.

Cheeseburgers. Kirk decided he'd go for as rare as possible. The thought of blood made his mouth squirt. Kirk didn't appreciate that so he chugged the remainder of his beer, pouring the suds down as if it could douse a fire.

His cell phone vibrated, making circles on the far end of the coffee table. Kirk watched the thing buzz out a donut, stop as if exhausted, and then spin again, its single red eye glowing on and off. It reminded him all too much of a Klaxon. Kirk didn't move, deciding to wait out the storm. He didn't want to talk to anyone. No interest in talking to an elder.

He answered the phone on the eighth ring, hoping the caller had already hung up.

"Yeah?"

"It's Morris."

No such luck.

"Afternoon, Moses."

The void-like pause on the other end suggested the Pictou warden was none too happy with the greeting.

"Kirk," Morris pushed on, "I need you. Up here."

"What?"

"You. Heard."

Kirk stared at the numbness of the white ceiling. "You okay?"

"No."

That prompted Kirk to sit up and swing his long legs off the couch, listening to the flip phone as if it were a stubborn combination lock.

"What's wrong?"

"Just. Get here."

"You sound like shit."

"Yeah." Morris giggled, the sound as nasty and raw as a deep-cutting bone saw.

Unknown to Kirk, his breathing quickened. "Something happened?"

"Get here. Tonight."

Kirk's eyes fell upon his empty beer and the paperback.

"I'll… wait," Morris said and hung up.

The Durango had seen better moons, but its engine growled when Kirk put the pedal to the floor. He rarely drove the fifteen-year-old pickup, opting to walk as most of the amenities were well within range of his apartment complex. The Durango, however, was reserved for out of town jaunts. The odometer showed over three hundred and fifty-two thousand and change in traveled kilometers. New rust rashes appeared with every passing season, but the engine still worked and the ride wasn't bad at all. Kirk didn't mind the rust. He figured if he let it go, sooner or later, they'd all become a new color.

Plus, no one would ever carjack the pickup. And if someone did, well, Kirk would only head out and buy something else. He might look like a bum, but money wasn't an issue for him.

Nor was time.

Morris's place was a two-hour drive away, and since it was only early afternoon when Kirk got the call, he wasted little time in getting moving. He didn't really want to go out into the sticks, but in his mind, Morris and he shared a past in surviving Borland and Newfoundland. He didn't really owe the warden anything, but that haunting, hurting tone to Morris's voice and the horrors of the island warranted a courtesy call at the very least.

Besides, it wasn't every day a warden called another for a meeting.

Something was in the wind.

Kirk drove north and arrived at the warden's hidden cabin just as the sun slipped behind darkening treetops. He stopped on the front lawn and, with hands still on the wheel, took note of a motorcycle not ten feet away from the tree line. That puzzled Kirk. Morris was more Harley-Davidson than a foreign ride. Having inspected the motorcycle, Kirk studied the cabin ahead. No lights in the descending dark. No sign of life. The picture window to the right of the door had been smashed out. The front door lay ajar. A black line marked the opening and stayed his attention.

Kirk left the keys in the Durango, doubting anyone in the sticks was sick enough to steal it. He got out of the pickup and glanced left and right, scanning the shadows for danger. Nothing in sight, sound, or smell.

Not even Morris.

Kirk paused, one hand resting on the hood of his ride, and cocked his head. Waves of verboten lapped against his senses, and the open door drew his attention. Morris was nowhere in sight and that alone placed the Halifax warden a little more on edge.

But after Newfoundland, Kirk had also become a little more cautious.

"Morris?"

Nothing.

"You in there?" Kirk asked in a normal tone. "You better do something about that road of yours. You have more than a few canyons in that thing. I left a fuckin' trail of spare parts all the way up here."

Still no answer.

Taking a breath, Kirk studied the tree line as he walked to the front door. His paranoia was spiking. Morris should've met him out front. Instead, Kirk picked up the faint smell of charred meat, like something that had dropped between a crusty grill and shriveled up to a charcoal nugget. That barely detected smell made Kirk even more uneasy.

He stopped in his tracks, not wanting to enter the cabin. Morris was inside, he suspected, but something very bad had happened to him. Something Kirk didn't want to see. The Durango waited just behind him, but he wasn't about to drive away either. He craned his neck, attempting to peer inside the cabin's windows, and stopped when he sighted the upper torso of a man in the living room, his features draped entirely in shadow.

Kirk held his breath. "Morris?"

The door wavered, enough to squeak, but there was no breeze. The figure in the chair might've moved, but Kirk wasn't entirely certain. He went to the entrance and cringed when his weight bore down on the steps, the sound carrying.

"That you in there?"

The warden pushed the door open. It swung inward on its hinges with a fibrous groan, and weakly rebounded.

"Kirk," the shade spoke. "Fuck you. Creeping around. Out there. Like a goddamn pansy."

Relief melted the ice buildup in Kirk's chest. "Jesus Christ. I thought you died or something. The fuck you sitting in the dark for?"

Morris didn't answer right away and as Kirk stepped inside, he saw the reason why. Morris sat in an easy chair, a thick towel covering his naughty bits and a case of beer placed on a nearby end table. A cell phone rested next to the beer. Morris was otherwise naked, and his flesh, from scalp to toe, resembled a mottled red raisin. A glaze of juices glossed his scorched flesh, as if the first few layers of skin had melted away into a pasty grease. The smell Kirk had picked up on outside the cabin suddenly became clear.

The Halifax warden's mouth hung open in shock.

"Close. The door," Morris muttered, his melted lips mangling the words. He managed a car wreck of a smile then, or at least Kirk believed it was a smile, revealing a frightening grill of blackened teeth.

"And… feed me."

For the next hour, Kirk did just that.

He plundered the fridge and channeled everything he found

into Morris's lipless mouth. Cold roast beef, salami, carrots, yogurt (which struck Kirk as being utterly out of place), leftover nachos, apples, oranges, bread, and anything else that didn't require cooking. Kirk poured water down the Pictou warden's throat as well, wetting that deep-fried maw until it snapped for more. *Food.* Morris needed a lot of it, and would probably consume everything in the cabin in order to fully regenerate.

"You eat yogurt," Kirk said with mild disbelief, spooning it into Morris and trying hard not to dwell on the creamy mess around the guy's mouth.

Morris glared back with black slits that sparkled in the failing light.

When he could eat no more, Morris lifted a hand that might've been doused in cooking oil before being torched. "I'm good."

"You're good?" Kirk asked, poised with more cold cuts.

Morris nodded weakly.

"Can you talk any?"

That brought on a chuckle, wrenching a grimace from the stricken warden.

"Just… watch the place," Morris eventually whispered.

"Watch the place."

"Yeah."

"For what?"

Morris's eyes cracked open a little wider, enough for Kirk to fear the lids might stick and pull themselves off.

"*Were.*"

Kirk straightened and looked to the windows. "There's a wolf around here?"

"Yeah," Morris answered. "Tell you. All about it."

"Had a hunt?"

"Yeah."

"Deer?"

"No. Me."

That silenced Kirk.

Morris attempted a smile. His lips split and oozed bright blood.

"Yeah," he chuckled through roasted lungs. "*Me.*"

Kirk wasn't amused.

"Watch. The place," Morris said. "Be careful."

His strength gone, the warden relaxed, his melted skull slumping against the headrest.

A moment later, he was snoring.

That medieval rumble rooted Kirk in place for a few seconds before he glanced around the interior and spotted a quilt. This he grabbed and spread out over Morris's sleeping form, taking the time to tuck the ends over his shoulders. Once that was done, Kirk stepped back and inspected the rest of the cabin before going to the front door. Night had fallen and a swath of stars touched by milky sails of celestial white eased into existence. Kirk gazed at the brightening cosmos and spotted the Big Dipper.

The motorcycle parked on the front lawn hadn't moved. Kirk studied the metallic outline softly gleaming under the night sky and smelled the air. Nothing wild, unless the werewolf had taken to wearing its suit, as some of them referred to their human guises. Kirk did not.

Watch the place, Morris had charged him. *Be careful.*

That didn't bode well with the Halifax warden. He walked out the front door and returned to his truck, where he kept a leather sheath under the driver's seat. Kirk took his time strapping the sheath and the silver blade it contained across the small of his back. The gathering dark allowed him to arm himself, and Kirk sensed no danger hidden within the surrounding forest. All the same, he didn't relax his guard as he adjusted his knife, closed the door to his truck, and returned to the cabin.

One last look around the perimeter revealed nothing. Kirk locked the cabin door and settled into a corner, where the east wall joined the south. From where he stood, he had a full view of the road, his truck, and whoever owned the motorcycle.

After a concerned glance at Morris's barbecued ass, Kirk waited.

The hours crept by, and nothing emerged from the forest. The landscape beyond the window didn't change. No one approached the cabin or the vehicles. Kirk's right hand strayed to the comforting knob of his silver Bowie knife.

And in time, Morris's snoring intensified.

At first, Kirk frowned at the crackling drum solo issuing from the Pictou warden, but after the first ten minutes of the glacier breakup, he could only shake his head in wonder.

There were other sounds as well, heard in between breaths as deep as canyons. The subtle shifting and pop of flesh as it repaired itself. The greasy bacon and eggs crackle of the regenerative process in full gear. Morris's face rippled in the dark every now and again, as if an invisible brush feathered and smoothed out the horrific damage of his burns.

Kirk studied the process in between glances out the window.

He was very grateful for the dark.

8

That Friday, at ten minutes to four in the morning, paramedics delivered the body bag to the medical examiner building at the very end of Percy Street, near a wooden copse and hillside that had already been earmarked for development later in the year. They deposited the corpse on a steel bed and unzipped the bag. A toe was tagged and paperwork was filled out, signed off, and handed over. Once the paramedics left, a pair of staff members wearing scrubs collected the body and steered along cinder-block walls. The wheels squeaked all the way to the morgue. Once there, the body was transferred to a rectangular platter and covered with a drab green sheet.

A mechanical lift raised the body to its final stop, and the attendants slid the morgue's newest resident into a freezer unit.

They closed the door, locked it, and then settled into their routine duties.

Behind the departing attendants, within its stainless steel box, the body of Bailey—Balsa Milutin of Montenegro—lay still. Unmoving.

But on inspection, if one were closely studying the jagged fragments of the gunshot wound, where the blast ripped Bailey's head from his neck, one might notice the once blood-dewy tatters of skin stretching forth like fingers grasping for a handhold, or flattened sea worms swaying in a deep and remorseless undercurrent.

Slowly stretching.

Elongating.

Thickening.

9

"Kirk."

Kirk's ears perked. A gray dawn filtered in through lowered blinds of Morris's cabin, slashing the interior in straight razors of shadow and light. The lines rose to just about Morris's quilt-covered knees.

"Moses."

Morris didn't say anything to that, but Kirk sensed the annoyance at being called by his first name.

"Nothing happened last night?" Morris asked, his voice no longer sounding like scorched skin on sandpaper.

Kirk didn't answer right away. "Nothing."

Morris sighed. "That's too bad, then."

"You wanna tell me what's going on?"

"Yeah. Sure. Jesus, I haveta piss first."

With that, Morris shrugged off the quilt with a groan. He rose from his chair, bare assed and none too shy about it. Kirk glanced away with a frown as Morris zombie-shuffled toward the bathroom, his movements herky-jerky, spastic. The new skin covering him was raw, pinkish, as if he'd just emerged from a vigorous Turkish bath.

Kirk looked out the window.

Morris made it to the toilet and offered a short concert of bathroom notes. Kirk cringed at the sporadic bugle blasts and the hiss of an emptying bladder. There were a couple of wet thumps and fleshy squeaks as feet scuffed across floor. Morris returned a few minutes later. A black T-shirt covered his upper body while a wrapped towel concealed his lower half.

"No pants?" Kirk asked.

"Couldn't be bothered. Besides, my boys got fricasseed something bad. They need all the air they can get."

"Didn't need to hear that."

"Yeah, well, next time don't ask."

Morris walked to the kitchen and opened the fridge. "There were beers in here."

"I know."

"Why the hell didn't you give me a beer then? Instead of water?"

"The beer would only dehydrate you more."

Morris's face puckered up in annoyance and Kirk realized with a start of clarity that the usually hairy beast of a man was completely bald all over this morning. Ignoring the Halifax warden, Morris dug into his own beer supply and shuffled back to his chair with two cans in his hand.

"One of them for me?" Kirk asked.

"Get your own."

"Thanks, Moses. You snore like shit, by the way."

"And my shit snores on the way out. Funny, ain't it."

Morris hissed as he eased himself into his chair. Once he situated himself, he cracked a beer open. He drank heavily, gulping down huge amounts. A mighty belch ripped through the cabin's interior.

"Goddamn. That was good. That was good."

"Sounded like it," Kirk said.

Morris sat and absorbed the beer in his belly, breathing hard and gazing at the ceiling. His T-shirt read *Bad Dog*.

"Thanks for coming," Morris eventually said and crushed the empty can.

"You're welcome."

"Nothing happened last night?"

"Nothing."

"Shit."

Kirk let that hang in the air before pursuing it. "You gonna tell me what's going on, now?"

Morris met the other warden's eyes and didn't say a word for seconds. "Yeah. Yeah, I guess so."

Kirk gestured, *Well?*

"I think…" Morris swallowed noisily and sniffed, "someone tried to kill me a night ago. A *were* no less. Guy called Bailey."

That brought Kirk to attention.

"And," Morris continued, "if that guy didn't come back around here last night, well, I think he wasn't able to. You're going to have to find him. Check on him."

"Not until you start talking."

One beer later, Morris did just that. He told Kirk about the weird vibes he got from the *were* called Bailey, how he talked shit one minute and then zeroed in on Morris, like a hunter sizing up the best spot to sink a bullet. He even told him about Borland's little whispers from beyond the grave, warning him that *They'll be after ya. One day.* Well, in Morris's mind Bailey was after him. The warden was certain of it. He described how Bailey stayed close to the cabin leading up to the change, which weirded out Morris enough to change himself and retreat into the forest. Shortly after a hurried transformation, he heard Bailey crash through his picture window.

"Goddamn bastard went right through it," Morris croaked. "And then he sniffed around the cabin. He was hunting, I tell you. He was hunting. For my ass. And when he couldn't find it, he turned around and headed back into the bush. Know why?"

Kirk shook his head.

"Because he knew I was waiting for him. Looking to ambush him in the woods. And I was. I knew places to go, where to mask my trail and scent. He knew it, too. Smart fucker, y'see. Instead of following me into the bush where I had the advantage, he turned around and went the other way."

"And you followed?" Kirk asked.

"Oh fuck yeah I followed. What else could I do? Had to. And he *knew* I would. Lunatic like that running around the woods? No hesitation. Stalked him two or three kilometers to the southeast, to a place called Claymore Lake. Big weekend spot. The Halifax crowd drives up there on the weekends. And guess what? He picked out a cabin like this one and ripped the sorry bastards into pieces. I mean, he gutted them, chowed down on lips and assholes. I don't know how many exactly."

Kirk placed a hand to his forehead as if checking for a temperature. "Why?"

"Because he knew I was out there," Morris said without emotion. "He knew I was close and he needed something to draw me out. Those people he killed? They were bait. All bait. And I bit. I bit big time. I knew he'd nailed at least two or three guys, maybe more. I knew he'd broken the law. And when I showed up to the party, he was ready and waiting."

Morris relaxed, the memory summoning an expression of distaste. "He was waiting. The cabin was on fire, lighting up that whole part of the lake. We found each other easy enough and went straight for the throat. He was strong, too. Way stronger than he looked. And fast. And... and smart. At one point I thought I had him and went for the throat, but he fucking twisted on his back and slingshot me into the cabin. Yeah, that's right, the cabin that was on fire. And Dougie? All the stories are true. You do *not* want your ass on fire. I went up like fireworks doused in gasoline. Everything was burning—my body, head, everything. Couldn't see anything. Couldn't breathe. Sure as shit couldn't *think*. I was a flame, a living, racing jet of flame. That cabin was on a lake. A lake. Water was maybe twenty, thirty feet away. Guess which direction I went? Wait, I'll tell you. I think I slammed into something and totally fucked up my sense of direction, which was pretty much a guess anyway, and charged *away* from the water. Straight into the woods, leaving a trail of smoke and crashing into every fuckin' tree between there and creation. Felt like I was bashing my way through an army of defensive linesmen. And as I was running away, I heard… I *think* I heard…"

Kirk waited, holding his breath.

"Gunshots."

"Gunshots?" Kirk repeated.

"Yeah. Pop-pop-pop. I *think*. I'm not one hundred percent sure. I was *this* close," Morris pinched his finger and thumb together, "to being a roadhouse steak at the time. And every fucking tree in the forest was ringing my dinner bell. Then the miracle. I hit water. Pure luck. I splashed into a creek and that's where I doused the fire. Literally wasn't out of the woods though, and every part of me was smoldering. Didn't think about Bailey. If he could've, he would've finished me off. I had nothing left. But he wasn't around as far as I could detect, and my eyes and smell weren't workin' so good, so I crawled back here. Got back by dawn. Slunk into the house, planted myself in the chair here and promptly passed out. When I came to, I called you."

"Thanks."

"Don't mention it."

Kirk squeezed his eyes shut, absorbing the glut of information, attempting to sift through the details.

"He didn't come back here," Morris continued, "which means he couldn't. Which means I might've heard gunshots, which means who the hell knows what that crazy fucker might've gotten himself into. That's where you come in. You need to head over to Claymore Lake and see what went down after I left."

"Why would he want you dead?"

"Why do flying squirrels try to fuck birds? I don't know."

But Morris quieted and chewed on the inside corner of his mouth, deep thoughts taking him for a ride. "You remember what Borland said to us? Just before we killed him?"

That shut Kirk up fast. He remembered. Of course he did. "Yeah."

"I do, too. And I've been thinking about that in the wee hours, when I've been conscious that is, and not simmering over a low heat."

"And?"

"You remember the conversation we had, back in Newfoundland? After we called the elders and reported in? Remember how weird they got? Especially when…"

Kirk nodded pensively.

"Well, this is what I think, subject to change if you have a better idea. I think that… when we ate Borland—"

"You ate Borland," Kirk interrupted. "I ate the breeds."

"Still a *were*."

"Just getting things straight."

"So what are you sayin'?"

Kirk shrugged. "You tell me. You're the cannibal."

That put a scowl on Morris's healing face. "The fuck you mean by that?"

"I just said it."

"Hey, I did what I had to do."

"Oh, you did," Kirk acknowledged. "You chowed down on Borland's dead ass."

"*You* chowed down on a bunch of them dogs."

"That's different."

"Are you fucking kiddin' me?" Morris leered in shock. "See, it's not different. Not in the least. You're healing just as fast as I am these days. Your leg. Your ears. I don't remember what else that last dog did to you but it wasn't fuckin' pretty. Yet here you are. Walkin', talkin' and with skin smoother than a baby's ass."

Kirk had nothing to say to that. It was all true. "The dogs had the juice in them," he finally admitted. "The gift, the curse, whatever you wanna call it. And I ate them. So whatever was in the dogs is now in me. We had this conversation back on the island."

"Yeah, we did. We supped at the same table."

"And didn't you eat one of the dogs, too?" Kirk asked.

Morris quieted. "Only one."

"Yeah, that's what I remembered." Kirk let it go. "So that's it, then. We're healing faster than normal. And better."

"Apparently. You got any aches or scars from the silver?"

Kirk lifted the front of his fisherman's sweater and clawed at the T-shirt underneath to show off his lean chest. There was nothing showing of the grisly wound he'd sustained in his fight with Borland.

Morris matched him by stretching out the neck of his T-shirt and revealing his shoulder where a silver knife had impaled him. The skin was smooth. Seamless.

"So we're healing faster," Kirk established. "We already knew that."

"And better," Morris added.

"And better. No scars or silver aches."

The Pictou warden shook his head.

"Because we ate the *weres*."

"Yeah. Guilty as charged."

"And because of that…" Kirk began.

"The elders are watching us. Worse, they're sending bastards to kill us."

"We don't know that," Kirk waved that thought away. "Bailey could've been just crazy."

"Like Borland?"

"All right," Kirk said. "So what if they are sending *weres* after you? For what? I still don't understand why. We *healed* faster. That's all. Different meat, is all. Different effect. Is that reason to take out a warden? Doesn't make sense."

"To take out wardens," Morris corrected darkly. "Both of us. I think once Bailey was done with me, he was going after you."

That halted Kirk's thinking. "Doesn't make sense."

"Maybe they're worried about us going crazy. Like Borland."

"Borland was just old. We're… not. It's all just too weird. Insane."

"No, it isn't," Morris agreed. "But one thing's crystal. Bailey was out to bag me. Exact reason is a little fudgy, other than what we ate on the island, but maybe we'll think it out. I'm thinking it's our one-time diet and the results. If that ain't strange enough for you, then I don't know what is. Borland did something to those dogs, that's a given, and maybe that something is in us. Permanently. Or worse."

Kirk couldn't wrap his head around the reasoning.

Morris cleared his throat. "You better get on over to Claymore Lake. See what you can find out."

"How do I get there?"

Morris supplied directions. "And get back here when you can. Just in case that bastard's still alive. I don't think he is, but better safer than sorry."

"You'll be okay?"

A scowl cut the warden's face. "Yes, goddammit, I'll be okay. Getting better by the second. My asshole's a ring of fire from all the sunshine I'm holdin' in."

"All right," Kirk fished his keys from his pocket. "I'm gone."

"And Kirk?"

The Halifax warden stopped with his hand on the doorknob. Morris fixed him with a dark, unwavering glare. "One more thing. Something we didn't talk about since the island, but since you're here. Since I'm here. Maybe another thing to think about why Bailey did what he did…"

"What?"

"Have you…" Morris stopped, visibly struggling with how to word his thoughts. "Have you been getting cravings?"

Kirk slowly released the doorknob and regarded the sitting warden with growing unease. "Like what?"

"Like… more."

Kirk suddenly felt very cold.

"More… substance. Y'know?"

The cabin seemed small to Kirk then, the walls constricting. His guts clenched and froze as if he'd just downed a shovel's worth of ice.

"I, ah," Morris sniffed and swallowed thickly. "I get these urges, y'know? I mean, we all hunger for meat, people being the best cuts, but you know how that is. Can't have steak every night so we make do with other cuts. It's takeout compared to prime rib. But… ever since Borland, whatever I eat just isn't doing the trick. I want… I want more."

"Jesus Christ, Morris," Kirk hissed, knowing exactly what he meant, what was coming.

The Pictou Warden stayed firm, however, and didn't change course. "Yeah. More of that. More of what I had on the island. You know what I mean, right? Ever since Borland. And every day since then, the, uh, craving is only getting…"

"No," Kirk said in a low tone. "I don't have any of that."

Morris closed his mouth and studied his companion. "You sure?"

Kirk left the cabin.

10

Gravel crunched under the pickup's tires as Kirk drove along the dirt road. Flower arrangements tastefully adorned with purple and pink ribbons lined the shoulders. The attack only took place a night ago but people moved quickly to respect the dead. The sun splashed gold across the lake's edge, the water glimpsed through tall posts of birch that reminded Kirk of prison bars. A cage.

Life's a cage, he thought darkly. *This caged life.*

He clung to that thought, using it like a flimsy shield to divert his mind from darker, more insidious paths.

The outpouring of sympathetic flowers blurred by and Kirk took his foot off the gas, realizing he was speeding. He crossed his wrists as he turned the wheel and eased onto the brake. Up ahead, the blackened husk of a ravaged lakeside cabin stood in the strengthening morning light, the one blemish in an otherwise picturesque October dawn. Yellow strips of police tape spanned the driveway and sections of the front lawn beyond, like a spider's web left in ruins by something much too big to catch.

Kirk put the old truck in park and ran a finger across his brow in a contemplative line, absorbing the destruction at the end of the driveway. The roof of the cabin had fallen in and, looking at the skeletal beams pointing at the sky, Kirk was struck by the impression that something mighty had descended from above and pinched the roof away, causing it to crumble. Morris whispered at the absolute fringes of his mind, an eerie but electric line of syllables Kirk mentally shoved away.

Only to have his own traitorous conscience gnaw away at his thoughts.

What if Morris was right? What if the werewolf called Bailey *was* trying to kill him? Kirk winced at the idea. Why would Bailey attempt to kill him? Because he was crazy? Like Borland? But if he *wasn't* crazy, then why was he trying to kill Morris? And if successful in killing Morris, would Bailey have then hunted down Kirk?

That train of thought arrived at an even more disturbing destination.

Who sent Bailey?

A sensation of nausea erupted in the base of his stomach, just above his jeans, and Kirk frowned at the unwanted feeling. Just what he needed—to suspect the elders. But if the elders hadn't sent Bailey, then who? Or was Bailey merely operating alone?

A tapping on the window startled him.

An older, bearded man stared into the truck. Concern clouded his face. Kirk composed himself and fumbled for the window crank. As the glass descended, the old guy's face lightened.

"Mornin'," he greeted in a voice that bespoke a three-pack-a-day habit.

"How you doin'?"

"Good. Good mornin'."

"Better for some, I imagine," Kirk said, nodding toward the cabin's remains.

"Yeah, I suppose it is. You a friend of the deceased?"

Kirk had to think for a second. "No. Just out for a drive. Saw the cabin from the road. Stopped to take it all in."

"Just takin' a look?"

"Yeah."

"You're late then. All the action happened the other night. I have a place just down the road here. Gunshots got me moving for the phone. I moved out here to get away from this kinda shit in Halifax. Never figured I'd move *closer* to it."

"That bad, huh?"

"Terrible, terrible night," the old guy said and stared sadly at the scorched structure. "Three men died in that blaze. All burned up. A fourth was torn apart and a fifth was shot. Had his damn head blown off. Damn, damn shame. Drugs and booze behind it all, least that's what I heard."

Kirk studied the old man's profile. "Really? Drugs and booze?"

"Oh yeah. Overheard some of the paramedics leaving the scene. The one guy who lived was strung out on a mix of *ganja* and beer. Or so I heard, like I said. I'm not so sure. I've seen a lot of violent drunks, but not one violent hophead. Strange."

"A guy was torn apart, you say?" Kirk asked.

"Yeah," the neighbor said with face of horror. "Didn't see it, only the little markers the cops set up to show all those places. Where the limbs and other parts fell."

"Holy shit."

"Yeah. Something, 'eh? Done by a wolf or a breed of coyote and wolf. There were tracks all over the place. Strange thing, though."

"Another strange thing?"

"This one has strange all over it," the old guy said with an incredulous air. "The owner of the place was a man by the name of Hutchinson. He was taken away by the police for questioning. As he was being walked out—walked out, mind you—he was going on about how he shot the animal right there on his front lawn."

A hand pointed in the general location but nothing marked the spot.

"Anyway, the weird thing was… Hutchinson swore that he blew the head off the animal. Like, emptied the magazine into the thing until there was nothing left. A shotgun decapitation."

A ghostly breath chilled Kirk and his mouth went dry.

"Killed the thing dead, and left fragments of head all over the place. But when the cops got there, it wasn't a wolf or coyote or whatever. It was a naked man."

Kirk tried hard not to show any emotion, but blinked all the same.

"What?" the warden whispered, knowing he *had* to have heard wrong.

"Oh yeah," the old guy said with the conviction of a person who'd witnessed it all. "Shot an animal, he said, and it changed into a dead man. Makes me wonder just what they're loading into them Mary-Ju-Wanna sticks these days."

Kirk's head swiveled toward the cabin's front, his eyes narrowing, magnifying the wrecked details of the destroyed weekend getaway. His body temperature dropped a couple of degrees. More words zipped past him, spoken by the kindly old codger orbiting on his left, but Kirk had zoned out of the message.

"Excuse me," the Halifax warden finally said. "You mentioned… you mentioned something about a wolf having its head shot off?"

"Oh yeah. Well, it was really a g—"

"The whole head?"

The neighborly gent studied Kirk as if he were a victim of a car wreck. "You okay, buddy?"

Kirk couldn't muster a smile. "Stomach cramps. Listen, the head. Of the wolf. You're sure it was gone? I mean, destroyed?"

The old man whisked his fingertips underneath his chin and across his throat in the universal meaning. "Nothing above the shoulders. Hutchinson unloaded the whole magazine of a twelve gauge into that poor bastard's pudding. The whole melon was gone. Totally gone. I didn't see but someone said there was nothing left but shards. Like a clay pot dropped from three or four floors up. And afterwards? There was a whole army of cops and plainclothes types like them you see on the forensic TV shows, 'eh? At one point I thought they might break out the vacuum cleaners, just to see what they might turn up in the grass. One woman was using tweezers on yon tree over there. They bagged what they could, I imagine, and hauled it off to Halifax."

Kirk didn't bother looking. "Halifax."

The man smiled. "Yeah. Guess they'll inspect the body down there. Try and figure out the cause of death."

"Thanks," the warden replied, senses whirling. He fumbled for the keys and started up the truck, allowing one last, thanking nod at the accommodating neighbor.

Spinning dirt, Kirk racked the pickup into reverse and got the hell away from the cabin.

As trees fluted by, the singular thought of *Oh shit* ran circles in his mind. He was no longer feeling sick. That sensation had been replaced. Someone had done the impossible—a fairy-tale nightmare deeply rooted in legend and fear, the expressly *forbidden.*

Someone had decapitated a werewolf.

A werewolf could only be killed by silver, fire, or having its throat ripped out by the jaws of another werewolf. The magic that enabled them all to transform—for better or for worse—possessed an even darker side, a sinister side, unleashed only upon the first transformation. Or when the *were* had its head separated from its body.

A body which would eventually *regrow* the missing bauble.

Kirk's foot pushed down on the accelerator, urging the machine to fly.

He had to get back to Morris.

They had to contact the elders.

11

The truck made it back to Morris's cabin, but Kirk believed the rugged dirt road had claimed every vital part needed for the vehicle to ever start again. He stopped on the front lawn, right at the cabin door, and nearly snapped the gearstick in half upon placing the pickup in park. Kirk leaped from the machine to the steps and crashed into the front door. He barged into the Pictou warden's dwelling and halted just beyond the threshold.

Morris remained in his easy chair and cocked an eyebrow at the intrusion. He had donned a pair of cut-off jeans and sandals and administered several medicinal beers, the empties collecting at the chair's base. A half-emptied case was well within reach of his right arm. His skin appeared to be in even better condition than before, and black fuzz had sprouted from his scalp.

"We have to contact the elders," Kirk blurted. "Bailey had his head blown off."

"Wha…" Morris trailed off in disbelief. "But that means… what?"

"You know what."

"But that's only…" Morris faltered in the distressed glare Kirk fixed him with. "That's only a fuckin' *legend.*"

"It's enough for me," Kirk said and pulled out his phone. "You good with this?"

Morris shrank back in his chair, the *Bad Dog* decal of his shirt partially obscured by wrinkles. "No. But, yeah. Do it."

Kirk speed-dialed the elders' number and slapped the unit to his ear. "Yeah, it's Kirk in Halifax. Call me when you can. It's urgent. Real urgent. A real fuckin' emergency."

He hung up and immediately plucked a beer from Morris's case without asking. Morris didn't stop him.

"Holy shit…" the Pictou warden whispered.

Kirk answered by popping the beer tab and chugging half the can's contents.

"You think it's possible?" Morris asked with uncharacteristic fear.

"That Bailey will go on a fuckin' rampage once he regrows his head? Only happened once, right?"

"Supposedly."

"In 1202."

"The year of the Fourth Crusade. The—the sacking of that city."

"Zabor."

"Zadar," Morris corrected.

Kirk drained the other half of the beer and tossed a crumpled can into the case. He quickly extracted another and Morris joined him.

"This shit doesn't work fast enough," Kirk complained.

"I'm through half a dozen," Morris said. "Now I'm suddenly sober."

"Should call again."

"You called already."

"Why haven't they called back, then?" Kirk shouted. He glanced out the window.

"Fuckin' slow down and breathe," Morris ordered. "They'll call. They always call. It's what they do."

Kirk went to his favorite corner in the cabin and watched the road.

"What happened out there?" Morris finally asked.

Kirk told him.

"Christ," Morris exhaled. "This is… bad. Like dirty bomb bad."

"I know," Kirk agreed. He studied his beer, knowing he shouldn't be drinking at such a time.

The phone rang, silencing both wardens. They exchanged pensive looks before Kirk answered.

"Yes?" the elder asked, cold and calculated with the barest touch of annoyance.

"This is Kirk. I'm in Pictou with Morris. We might have a problem."

"What's the problem?"

"A *were* called Bailey came out this way a couple of nights ago. Morris got a weird vibe from the bastard and it turned out he wasn't wrong. He says the *were* tried to kill him and it almost did. Almost cooked him in a fire. Bailey nearly killed him, except Bailey got shot by a man. Got his head blown off. I mean *off*, like there was nothing left."

The other end of the connection remained quiet, the air grim and contemplative, ominous in its silence.

"Hello?"

A pause. "I'm listening."

"What should we do?"

"Is Morris with you now?"

Kirk cast a look in the warden's direction. "Yes."

"Where do you think they'll take the body?"

"I'm not sure. Halifax, probably, but where I don't know."

The line buzzed with silence, stretching out for uncomfortable seconds, hooked to the farthest side of an unknown void. "Take Morris. Return to Halifax. Return to your address. We'll send reinforcements."

Reinforcements? Kirk's eyes narrowed. "What?"

"They'll meet you within a day. From there, you must locate the abomination before it awakens. Before the next full moon. You don't have much time. Find it and kill it before it realizes its true potential. Before it changes. Before the human herds realize what it is, what it represents. Kill it before the next full moon. Do you understand?"

"Are you saying the stories are *true?*"

"All legends and myths are steeped in truth to some degree. Unfortunately for us, this is the absolute worst kind. This has happened before, as you've no doubt heard. The carnage wrought during that period is one of the founding reasons we strive for secrecy, and why we established and maintain the system of wardens. In any case, you will do as I've said."

"Yeah… understood."

"We'll be in touch."

Click.

Kirk's heart slapped against its cage and a coldness enveloped him, as if he'd been body slammed into a deep freezer. He regarded the small plastic receiver in horror.

"What'd he say?" Morris asked.

"It's true," Kirk whispered, remembering the stories of headless werewolves rising after death, possessing a rage unmatched, an unholy power, and a gluttonous craving for blood. The slaughter carried out by just *one* of those monsters wrought in ancient times was something told to frighten young pups. "It's all true."

Morris swallowed, clearly disturbed. "So what do we do?"

Kirk faced him. "We find it. And kill it. Before it changes."

"And if we can't?"

"The elder hung up before I could ask."

*

In a darkened cubicle of a room, where the only light emanated dimly from within an elegant glass lamp, a hand lowered a cell phone—a flip phone—to a nearby table. Murky hazel eyes stared off into space, processing the information reported by the warden, and pondered the consequences.

Bailey had failed.

But in the assassin's failure there was another opportunity to remove the pack of unwanted ends. An extremely dangerous opportunity, and certainly one which would take a toll on the human herds. Not that it overly concerned the elder. The people of the day were every bit the villagers of centuries past, and while the potential for destruction was great, he believed that his breed's continued secrecy would be maintained. Any person suspecting otherwise would be characterized as insane, anyway, despite any proof of existence possibly gleaned from the war to follow.

The elder explored the possibilities open to him and arrived at one solution: to do exactly as he'd promised the Halifax warden. He'd provide the one called Douglas Kirk with the means to hunt down Bailey.

Halifax, he thought and remembered a visit there in the early 1800s, well before the documented explosion there. He hoped the city would survive this with minimal damage.

The lamp burned brightly, the light shimmering behind spotless glass.

He picked up his flip phone once more, paused, and punched in a number.

12

"Reinforcements," Morris muttered under his breath. He rubbed the dark velour sprouting from his scalp. It was as thin as a tattoo, but the *were* seemed to draw comfort that his locks were returning. Kirk never thought he'd be driving back to Halifax with a bald Sasquatch riding shotgun, but here he was, hairless Big Foot on his right.

"The fuck we need reinforcements for?" Morris asked. "We got, what, nine days to the next full moon?"

"Yeah," Kirk said, paying attention to the highway as he drove the truck south. Traffic flow thickened as they neared the city. Evening was also getting on, and a low ceiling of cloud cover foreshadowed dark times. At least that was how Kirk interpreted it, and he was still feeling more than a little spooked over the whole affair.

"Nine days," Morris said. "Fucking easy. This ain't the Dark Ages no more. We just go to the cops and say we know the guy who had his head blown away. Say we can identify him. Go into the morgue or freezer or ice cooler—wherever the hell they keep the pizza fixings—and when they show us

Bailey's corpse, we stick him right there."

"We stick him right there."

"Yeah."

"With our knives?" Kirk shook his head and checked his blind spot before overtaking a four-door sedan.

"What?" Morris asked. "What's wrong with that plan?"

"It's goddamn idiotic."

"Whaddaya mean?"

"Whaddaya think I mean? I think goddamn idiotic says it all. Can't get much clearer than that. Think, y'fucking testicle, think. You go into a cop shop and announce 'I can identify who that headless guy is' and what do you think they're going to do?"

Kirk had Morris's attention. The biker—as suggested by the black special forces ensemble complete with a leather duster that the Pictou warden currently wore—turned to Kirk with dark intent.

"What?" he asked with a huff of his shoulders.

"They're going to ask who *you* are and do a background check on you, then they're gonna find out that Moses Morris doesn't exist. Or maybe that he's eighty-something years old. Which will open up another line of questioning, since you're looking so damn fine and spry these days. Eventually, they'll get to the conclusion that Morris doesn't really exist, that you're a fucking mysterious, livin'-off-the-grid bastard, and then that'll open up *more* questioning, and before you know it, and I can guarantee this part, you'll be in lockdown three cells over from whatever box they're keeping Bailey in. *That's* what'll happen. Next thing you know they'll be wondering why the hell a bald guy is sprouting hair like he's taken a shot of secret growth tonic up the ass."

A simmering Morris concentrated on the four lanes of the highway.

"And I haven't even gotten to the part about trying to stab a corpse with cops present, because they *would* be present."

No reply to that. Victory was Kirk's.

"Nine days," he continued in a softer tone. He hated the taste of the words. "Nine fuckin' days. Part of me just wants to bug out right now and drive for the west coast, because I got a rotten feeling about this one. This one is going to be bad. Like, epic bad."

"So what should we do?" Morris asked. Kirk knew then that Morris was every bit as uneasy as he was.

"Get back to my place and wait for the cavalry."

Morris held his forehead. "Don't like the sound of that. We should be out there doin' something."

"It's better than watching you sweet-talk your way past some cops, which any other time I'd buy popcorn for, but not this one."

"You think I can't do it?"

"*Exactly* what I think."

Morris didn't like that either. "Well, why don't you try it, then?"

"Because I'm not a dumbass."

Morris regarded the Halifax warden with a dangerous look, dangerous enough to send warning tingles all over Kirk's person.

"Look, we get back to my place, hole up, and wait for reinforcements. Hammer out a solid plan."

The sound of passing cars filled the gap in the discussion.

"How many will come, I wonder?" Morris asked quietly.

"Good question. I don't know."

"Nine fuckin' days."

"Nine," Kirk repeated. "But I think it'll all go to hell sooner."

They pulled into Kirk's parking spot and shut the truck down. The air greeted them with frosty kisses to the cheeks, prompting both of the wardens to draw their coats a little closer. In short time, they arrived at Kirk's apartment.

"Place smells like shit and beer," Morris said upon entering, screwing up his near-hairless face in a pucker of lemon.

"I'll crack a window."

"You should," Morris grumbled and walked into the living room without removing his boots. "Christ. Thought I was bad."

"Yeah, well," Kirk stood with his hands on his hips and glanced around. "I'm not big on housekeeping, but it's not a sty either."

"My place is better."

"You live in the sticks."

"What's location got to do with smelling like ass crack?"

Kirk set his jaw. "You want a beer?"

"Yeah."

Kirk went to the fridge and picked out a couple of bottles. When he returned to the living room, Morris had already plopped down on the sofa and inspected the copy of *Salem's Lot*.

"Make yourself at home," Kirk said sardonically and handed him a beer.

"Thanks."

Kirk dropped into the nearby sofa chair. They cracked open the drinks and tossed the caps onto the coffee table. They drank without a toast. A muffled door slam broke the silence somewhere down the corridor, while the rush of traffic outside sounded like the flights of low-flying meteors.

"You live like this?" Morris's legs were spread wide in a classic trucker's spread.

"Yeah."

"I couldn't. I'd go crazy. Be ripping someone's head off."

"That's about the only thing you hear," Kirk said, gesturing to the door. "Not much else. They built this place solid."

"They bother you?"

"Who? Neighbors?"

"Yeah."

Kirk shook his head. "No one. I don't interact with anyone. Keep a low profile, like any of us. Been here all of twelve years now. No troubles so far."

"So far," Morris grunted and drank another mouthful.

"They stay away from me, probably think I'm a dope dealer or something. Doesn't matter. Whatever serves the purpose."

"Y'know, I've been thinking," Morris started. "About Bailey. More I think about it, the more I'm convinced he was there to kill me. That bastard was going to kill me."

"That's scary."

"Yeah. It is. But you know what's scarier?"

Kirk didn't want to know.

Morris carried on. "Who sent him."

"Jesus," Kirk said. "Listen, you keep that to yourself. A pack of wardens are on their way here. Now. And you do *not* want to be spewing some conspiracy theory all over them. Word travels and each one of them will be reporting back to the elders, you understand that? Each one has the same number as we do. And you're nothing to them. You're just an east coast warden they're being ordered to back up. That's all. Some of them probably won't even like you."

A sullen Morris drank more of his beer.

"So you keep quiet about someone sending Bailey," Kirk continued. "As far as we know, he went crazy. Borland went crazy. Something in the water, who knows?"

"I don't believe that anymore."

"Believe what?"

"That Borland went crazy."

Kirk exhaled and considered his bottle. He didn't either.

"How many do you think they'll send?" Morris eventually asked.

Kirk shrugged. "No idea. Four. Maybe five. There's no one in PEI. Two in New Brunswick. Two in Maine. They'll be here the fastest. By car or bus."

"You think they'll send over your Ross Kelly recruit?"

"No," Kirk answered after a moment. "The elders weren't too happy with me changing Ross over. He's only got a few months in. They won't send him."

"Yeah. Suppose so."

"So. We wait."

Morris grunted in the affirmative and propped his feet up on the coffee table, boots out. Kirk joined him. Together, they kept to the soft lighting of the living room, rested, and when the need arose, went to the fridge for more beer.

The soft swishing of traffic reminded them of the world beyond the apartment, and sleep eventually found the two men.

13

It was Sunday evening at the medical examiner's main office, and the night was already damn boring. Worse still, it was only the first hour of a scheduled ten-hour shift. Private security officer Deb Cohn stood before the front desk, situated in a modern-designed facility, half-listening to her coworkers' inane yammering regarding the afternoon's televised hockey games. She adjusted her belt, shifted her firearm's holster, and gazed toward the darkened parking lot, clearly visible through a wall of glass. Deb sighed, not caring what the lads thought, and heard a distant noise from deep within the center.

A sound that puzzled the hell out of her. She stood at attention and listened.

"You hear that?" she asked, looking down the inner corridor of glass. A multitude of fluorescent lights reflected in the surface, as if trapped between microscope slides. The men behind the desk stopped talking about face-offs and icing pucks.

"No," Al said, following her gaze. "What was it?"

"A thump."

"Didn't hear anything."

"Well I heard something."

"Nothing here," Noah smirked, and kept his thumbs hooked off his belt while his double chin threatened to burst from his neck. "Ghosts, maybe. Not even three years old and already got ghosts. Everywhere. Fuckin' ghosts. Makes me sick. More taxpayer money down the shitter."

"This place doesn't have ghosts," Al grated and wiggled a finger into an ear canal, perhaps hoping to improve matters on that side. "Now, the morgue over at Halifax General? That place has 'em. Heard guys talk about all sorts of weird shit over there."

"I'm going to take a walk," Deb said and left the front desk to stalk the corridor.

"Don't wanna hear the story about the floating baby?"

"No."

Al shrugged a *suit yourself* but then frowned. "You okay to go alone?"

Deb didn't dignify that with an answer.

"You got off lucky that time," Noah said under his breath as she winked out of sight. "I asked her once if it bothered her to be working the night shift, guarding a bunch of dead folks."

"Ohhhh," Al winced, knowing where this was going.

"Yeah, she told me to fuck off. Just like that. And when I chuckled, oh my, she didn't like that. Won't tell you what she told me to do to myself, but it's anatomically impossible."

"Is it anatomically or physically?"

"I don't know. Either one works for me."

"Yeah, I suppose," Al remarked, folding his hands behind his head. "Yep, that's Deb. She doesn't say too much to me. I think she likes me for some reason. Must be my seniority."

"Sure as hell ain't your ass."

"You don't be thinking about my ass."

"Well, *my* ass is telling me it's time for a deposit."

"You best listen then, before it starts grumbling."

"Hold the fort," Noah said and walked off to the left of a living room-style waiting area for visitors.

In answer, Al grabbed his crotch.

*

Perhaps thirty meters from the front desk, Deb could still hear her coworkers' mutterings. She stopped without a shoe squeak, in a straight hallway that was sterile in its cleanliness and robust with its beige cinder blocks. Two lanes of gurneys could chug along its wide breadth if needed.

She listened, her face a dim, green reflection in the shiny floor.

Footsteps. Back at the front desk.

In full hunting mode, she leaned to her left, to one gray door, and grasped its lever. Locked. Its twin lay only two steps down the corridor on the right. She stepped lightly toward the door and confirmed it was also locked. Behind her, her two males—as she occasionally referred to Al and Noah—had stopped yakking at each other, which suited her fine. Deb didn't mind in the least working the graveyard shift at the center. She liked the quiet. A person could hear a fresh corpse squeeze off a butthole ringtone if the right sequence of doors was left open.

The next door led to the garage bay. She crept along, grateful for the soft rubber soles of her work shoes. They weren't exactly ninja level, but they did grant her a phantom-like degree of silence if she kept her key ring from jingling. She stopped and gripped the door's lever, placed her ear a hair's breadth from the gray surface.

Nothing. Spotless green tiles gleamed underneath the light.

Seconds passed, melting the knot of anticipation in Deb's chest. She tried the lever, confirming it was still secured, and released it. She heard something and it wasn't old wood settling from a warm spell, pipes rattling, some dead guy farting, or any other reasonable explanation. This particular sound had potential. Real potential. To be something freaky.

And truthfully, Deb *wanted* it to be freaky. She'd practically danced around her Windmill Lane apartment when she got the call to report to work five months ago. A war child of eighties and nineties horror thrillers, Debra Cohn wanted to have a real-life, honest-to-God encounter with the dead. Or at least the spiritual residue of the dead. The security aspect of watching the building was secondary. Each and every evening when she started her shift (always the night shift), Deb hoped and prayed that she be witness to the unexplainable. A flicker of the afterlife. A gust of graveyard coldness. A goddamn giggle from down the hall, even. Or the motherlode of them all, an honest to Christ crashing from the freezer unit. *Anything* for her to record on her smartphone, which she carried gunslinger-style in her hip pocket. Folks would pay top dollar for shit like that.

But besides the monetary value of an authentic supernatural experience (and not the fucking paranormal, Lord how she despised the word), she honestly craved seeing a ghost. She wanted a full elephant-sized load of adrenaline to flood her system, and fucking straighten her curly, raven-haired locks. One would think a morgue would be the place to sneak peeks of the recently deceased. Much to her disappointment, however, Deb had not. No ghost, no specter, no haunting. Not even a fucking reanimated corpse, though she still remained optimistic on encountering one of those.

Five months in, however, and *squat*.

Except for the occasional flatulent corpse, and no one was going to pay money for a sound bite anywhere between a mouse squeak and a rock god of thunder.

Another *thump* whipped her head around, shattering her moment of disappointed musings and raising goose bumps along the length of her arms and back. She quickly zoomed in on the location and ninja-walked at double time down the hall. Hope spread across Deb's face as she realized where she was headed. Her heart revved, aching for action.

Holy shit.

The noise came from the cooler unit.

Maybe this was the night. Maybe the stars had aligned and she was about to catch a glimpse of the macabre. Her hand went to her right hip and gripped the stainless steel Smith and Wesson holstered there. The sound led her into the autopsy suite, where she flicked the nearest light switch. Chemical cleaners and a trace of formaldehyde lingered upon the air, noticeable but far from overpowering. The three workstations were empty; the sterile arrangement of dissection tables, weighing scales, steel scrub sinks, and cabinets were all undisturbed. At any point, three bodies could be worked on at once, though the center maintained only two full-time medical examiners. Plastic refuse boxes and red containers stood out amongst the colorless metal. Not a bone saw was in sight, although a tray set near one of the sinks did hold an assortment of forceps, knives, and chisels. A wall clock displayed the time at just after two in the morning.

The cooler unit's gray door remained closed. A bare skeleton hung from a stainless steel framework to the right, standing on guard.

"You hear anything?" Al whispered just behind, startling Deb with a sharp intake of air. She took a moment to compose herself and glared at her coworker.

"You mean I got you?" Al asked.

"You just let me know next time," Deb warned, her hand on her weapon. "I was ready to draw."

"I saw that."

"What're you doing here?"

"Heard something, so I came."

"Where's Noah?"

"In the can. Doing what he does. The man's regular, I'll

give him that. Told him I was going to check on you."

Deb nodded at the cooler door. "It came from over there."

Al moved ahead of her and pulled out an electronic swipe card. He pressed the plastic against the nearby pad, generating a sharp click. Deb cringed at the noise, knowing that anything inside the cooler no doubt knew they were outside.

"You ready?" Al said, his hands on the door's lever.

Deb slipped her S&W out of its holster and nodded grimly. Al pushed the door open and an overhead fluorescent light flickered to life, illuminating the cold steel cave where up to forty guests could be stored if needed. The cooler hummed as ceiling vents blew a cold, underlying wave of formaldehyde, lemon juice, and an underlying smell of decomposing flesh into their faces. A wall consisting of coffin-sized freezer units was to their immediate left, while just past that was a parking area for a pair of automated cadaver lifts.

The smell of chilled flesh caused Deb to pucker her lips as she took the lead and slipped into the room, ignoring the sharp drop in temperature. She immediately checked behind the door before proceeding deeper into the cooler. Al lowered a rubber doorstop, secured the opening, and followed her inside. Deb straightened and signaled that the main floor was clear. Stout refrigeration doors remained secured, the individual units stacked three rows high and ten long. The exact location of the noise had stumped her. She shot a questioning look in Al's direction and got a shrug in return.

Thanks. *Male.*

No sooner did she project that last thought when the faintest scratching perked her ears and straightened her backbone. An unrelenting, inquisitive digging, as if the source of the noise was somehow puzzled at its predicament. Al stood with mouth open and eyes lit, clearly disbelieving what was happening, and ready to sprint for the parking lot.

One look from Deb quashed that notion. Al would not run on her watch. She'd shoot him in the back if he did.

She chopped a hand at a second tier unit on the right.

Deb held her weapon low as the scratching grew in intensity, growing frantic as the two guards neared the chrome-faced tomb.

"Someone's alive in there," Al insisted, astonished.

"No one's alive in there," Deb answered, still in control and eyeing the cabinet's number. "This is the fresh one brought in Friday evening. Damn thing didn't have a head."

The scratching stopped.

Both Al and Debra exchanged pensive looks. The noise had ceased when she'd spoken. Deb slowly became aware of a presence listening for more, and that notion prickled the flesh of both security guards.

Sweet Jesus, a voice whispered in Deb's mind with icy stark realization. She was about to encounter her first weird happening at the morgue and she had her gun out instead of her camera. Not that she was about to swap the weapon for the device. Fuck that noise.

Lower teeth grazing her upper lip, she nodded for Al to open the unit's door.

"I'm not going to open that," he whispered, moisture beading on his face despite the chill.

"You open that now."

"I am *not* opening that thing."

"What could be in there?"

"I don't mind telling you, Deb, I'm a little freaked out here."

A blunt smack of flesh on metal caused them both to flinch, the sound brought on by their voices. A wide-eyed Al jerked back a step. He flicked a wrist and extended a steel combat baton that professional security forces used for riot suppression. He glanced fearfully at Deb.

"I'm going to call Noah," he mumbled.

"You are not leaving me alone here."

"I'm going to call Noah."

"You do and I'll fucking go goddamn dayshift."

Another meaty blow from the cabinet's interior and Deb thought for an instant the door panel actually quivered, like a vibration in calm water.

"There's nothing in there," she said from behind her aimed pistol.

Thump.

"Noah!" Al shouted. He pressed his back against the other side of the unit's door. He faced Deb, chanced a frightened look over her shoulder and into the hall, and regarded the troubled cabinet. "Noah!"

Thump.

"Christ," Deb muttered, and reached out for the lever. One twist was all it took. There was a muffled clatter from within the cabinet, a rattling of thick drumsticks as if the entombed mass was repositioning itself, but nothing near as intense as the focused strikes on the metal door.

"*Noah!*"

The scratching resumed. Feverish. Seemingly excited by the voices, as if a big dog was attempting to dig its way through the steel and chrome. The sound strengthened, like a supercharged engine surging in neutral, waiting to be thrown into gear. A meaty *thump* punctuated the stream of near-constant static, the metal bulging from the impact.

"I'm gonna open it," Deb declared over the unnerving racket.

"*Noah, get down here for Christ's sake!*" Al cut loose, eyes brighter than headlights. He had one hand on the unit's door frame as if testing it for heat, his very posture resembling a man on the window ledge of a skyscraper.

Deb clasped the lever. Al actually moaned before clamping his mouth shut.

THUMPTHUMPTHUMPTHUMP. The metal shivered with each successive blow, but the hinges remained resolute. The unexpected burst surprised Deb and she drew back, gun aimed at the lid.

But there was nothing in there, Deb's mind rallied her nerves. *The guy had no* fucking *head.*

Al squirmed in place, his frame pressed against the calmer refrigeration units. He knew if he bolted for the door, something exceptionally frightening would escape its tomb and grab him by the ankles.

"*NOOOOOOOAAAAAAAH!*"

Noah materialized in the open doorway with gun in hand, just as Deb cranked the lever down. The loud release brought everything to a halt. The artillery shell pounding within the unit stopped as if momentarily stunned. Deb whipped the door open and flung it wide, the metal rebounding off the far side and missing a retreating Al by a hand. Deb slammed herself flat against her side of the chamber, her S&W held two-handed and angled at the black hole. Al readied his baton and swallowed.

Faint ribbons of steam emerged from the darkness within. Nothing moved.

"The hell's all that racket?" Noah gasped, winded from his dash from the washroom.

"Fuck if I know," Al blurted, eyes on the opened cabinet.

And for long seconds, the silence held.

Her heart exploding in her chest, Deb flashed a cautionary look at her coworkers before edging toward the freezer unit's gaping hole. She was on the verge of something special. She could feel it. Teetering on the very cusp of something exceptionally supernatural.

The black opening beckoned, all steam evaporated, and the strong smell of musk and blood and other unidentifiable fluids permeated the room, gushing from the cavity as if under some malefic pressure.

Deb inched forward as a white hand slunk into existence, emerging from the unit's depths like a five-legged spider. The fingers dropped over the cabinet's edge and hung there for a moment, seemingly exhausted, before pressing their tips into the bordering chrome. Blood beaded and pattered to the floor.

A trembling Deb leveled her S&W at the appendage and swallowed several times, trying to jumpstart her voice. But that well had gone dry.

The hand before her relaxed, suddenly lifeless.

"Holy shit," Al muttered from the other side. Noah stepped closer, widening his arc of vision, seeing the hand, then the wrist, then the wiry forearm beyond.

"That's a…" Noah whispered, seeing what filled the individual unit. He tightened his two-handed grip on his weapon. "That's a muh—a *man* in there."

Shock bleaching her face, Deb considered the opened container and eventually leaned forward in spastic movements, as if her brain wanted to see but her heart refused to go any further. But then she saw what Noah saw, what Al was being drawn into seeing.

There, lying on its body tray, was a man. *Black hair.* Only the top of his head was visible, but Deb instinctively knew it was a man. He lay motionless on his right side, with forehead sunk against the nearby wall, as if his effort to escape had left him spent.

"Sir?" Deb asked softly.

The head lifted, awakening. It glanced to the ceiling before homing in on the voice. The head looked up, reacting further to light and sound.

Deb's voice failed her, horror paralyzing her whole.

Black, red-rimmed eyes regarded her with angry curiosity. The man's shoulders heaved with a great, frustrated intake of breath, but what truly rooted Debra Cohn to the steel floor were the revenant's features. The nose was a grotesque squish of colorful jelly and white cartilage. The forehead was split open to the bone like a series of fat, bleeding gills.

Beating his face, she realized in horror. *He'd been beating his face and head against the wall.*

The man's mashed lips twisted into a snarl, flashing shards of ruined teeth.

Deb remembered her S&W.

The dead man's hand flashed out and grabbed hers, crushing bones against gunmetal. Deb shrieked, jerked back, the force extracting the animated corpse free of its tomb like a newborn calf, except the blood-dappled figure sloughing onto the floor, still clutching a screaming Debra Cohn, snapped and writhed with hellish life.

And if one stood at the far end of the L-shaped corridor and watched, one would hear and see this: A fluorescent light shatters and glass fragments salt the floor. An unhinged, half-lit tube swings across tiles and cinder blocks. Shadows flitter and merge, some angry, some terror-stricken. Shrieks erupt, sounding like trapped rabbits. Those same voices are twisted into wheezes and gurgles of shock and pain. A gun discharges, five times before a man squeals, *Oh God*. Bones break as if shattered over a knee. A man's voice reaches a piercing high note before silenced.

Sounds of ripping. Of bones breaking and splintering. A rustle of metal and glass ends in a startling crunch.

In a very short time all becomes quiet, except for a

guttural gasping, as if a person has grossly overexerted himself. A moaning breaks the silence, in torture somehow, and bones crack once again.

There's a mighty grunt and a wet torso smacks against the far end of the corridor before crumbling to a heap at the base. Darkness oozes from the unmoving lump, creating a rich, ever-widening puddle. If there was anyone behind the front desk, all that person would need to do is lean over the countertop to behold that gruesome spectacle on the floor.

Footsteps. Bare soles smacking against cold tiles. The cadence is ungainly, clumsy. Perhaps drunken, even.

A shadow grows, staggering as it comes closer. It stops just behind a corner, but the shade looms over the body. A naked man steps into view. His chest heaves. Black sap oozes from holes in his half-lit torso.

He stops directly over the heap on the floor.

Takes a deep, shuddering breath.

Groaning in misery, his naked frame trembles. He reaches down and pulls up an arm still connected to the body at his feet.

A moment's hesitation, as if studying the limb.

Then he bites.

And after a short time, he screams.

14

The pounding upon the door jerked Kirk from his dreamless sleep. He sat up in confusion, groggy and frowning at Morris, who had stretched out on his couch with boots elevated over one end. A blanket covered his head and shoulders. They'd both slept the day away, getting what rest they could. A second hard knock brought Kirk unsteadily to his feet, as if he'd downed much more than three beers.

"Get the fuckin' door," Morris muttered under the blanket.

"Where're your manners?" Kirk mumbled right back, en route.

"*Please* get the fuckin' door."

That brought a scowl to Kirk's features. Some people's children. He got to the entryway and squinted into the peephole. A rush of relief replaced the sour note of Morris. Kirk flipped the locks and opened the door.

"Hey," he greeted.

"You Doug Kirk?" asked a bald black man the size of a bear. He was tall and noble-looking in an intimidating way, wearing a winter trench coat that might've been bought at a secondhand shop. A square-cut beard hung from a head that might've been a medicine ball at one time. It was the only hair on the entire skull.

"Yeah. Who're you?"

A low brow hooded a set of murderous eyes. "You gonna let me in?"

The question hung upon the air for a couple of seconds before Kirk stepped back and let the big man inside.

"I'm Baxter," the new arrival said, inspecting the interior before settling on the living room. "From the next yard over."

New Brunswick.

"I don't know you."

"I don't know you either."

"Fair enough."

"Who is it?" Morris asked, uncovering himself and rubbing the fresh stubble on his head.

"First of the electric horsemen," Baxter announced with an unimpressed air. "Hello, Moses."

Much to Kirk's surprise, Morris didn't respond with an expletive-loaded remark or two. He sat up while Baxter approached him.

"Wait a second at the door," Baxter charged Kirk with a stern finger. "My driver's comin'."

"Not fuckin' Zeke," Morris moaned as if he'd injected pure poison into his jugular.

Baxter leveled a stone-cold gaze upon him. "Surprised at you, Morris. And not just because you finally shaved your wild man ass. You wanna be respected but you sure as hell don't mind putting down others behind their backs. And, by the way, I was wrong from before. About you shaving. You're still fuckin' ugly."

Morris looked to the picture window's drawn curtains.

"Got you nappin', I see," Baxter said, hands spreading his ankle-length coat and finding his hips. "I'll give you a minute to get up to speed. Ezekiel here yet, Doug?"

"Uh," Kirk massaged the back of his neck. "No."

"He will be. Then we can all sit down for story time."

Morris fumed but kept his mouth shut. Baxter walked to the picture window and peeked outside before placing his back against the curtains.

A second knocking at the door distracted Kirk. He opened the door and a second man, a few fingers shorter than Kirk, gave a *hey, howya doin'* nod and wink before walking into the apartment. Though only around five-nine or eight, he was at least that across the shoulders, and his pale head had been buzzed to the scalp.

Ezekiel Allen held out a dark suitcase to Kirk.

"What?"

"Where can I put this?" Ezekiel asked in a raspy voice.

Kirk considered the request. "Anywhere. As long it's not underfoot."

"I'm Ezekiel."

"Kirk."

The bulldoggish warden bared crooked teeth in what might have been a smile or a grimace, and chucked the bag right beside a coat closet, slamming the inside wall.

"Yeah…" Kirk muttered as the second visitor invaded his home.

"There's others comin'," Ezekiel said to him.

"Others?"

"We drove into Halifax together," Baxter explained, his large arms folded as he nodded at Ezekiel. "People got moving as they got the call. Everyone meets here."

"Yeah," Ezekiel said and plopped into the sofa chair with all the subtlety of a wrecking ball. He lifted his hiker boots to the coffee table.

"How many is everyone?" Kirk asked, not appreciating the *were's* quickness to get comfortable.

"Don't know," Baxter answered, "but we will before the night's done. There are a few late-night landings in Halifax, though I'd say the others are driving or taking the bus. I'd say anyone who got a call will be here by tomorrow afternoon."

"Do we have that long?" Morris asked from the couch.

Baxter didn't look in the man's direction. "Word is this Bailey character had his head shot off. That right?"

"Yeah, that's right."

"Well then, that's a major wound. Major. And I'm understating that. A head shot is goddamn critical. Going to take time to replace an entire head. At least a week."

Morris exchanged looks with Kirk.

"Something you want to share?" Baxter asked, picking up on the vibe.

From where he sat, the pug-like Ezekiel looked from one speaker to the other, his jolly snarl inquisitive.

"No," Kirk said. "Nothing. I'm… I'm just a little on edge is all. We've all heard the stories."

Ezekiel let out a smoky chuckle.

"Why're you so goddamn happy?" Morris growled.

Ezekiel didn't answer him. Instead, he fixed Morris with a marble-eyed gaze that seemed oddly crazy.

"Ezekiel is looking forward to this hunt," Baxter spoke for him. "It's not every day something of this…magnitude… comes along."

"It's history," Ezekiel whispered through those crooked teeth.

An unimpressed Morris didn't flinch from the stocky *were's* bizarre stare down. "Just remember that. History. And what the last one did."

"The last one," Baxter began, "was killed by four *weres*. After the beast killed hundreds of human cattle—civilians and warriors. This is the new millennium. Doesn't take weeks before we hear of the slaughter via the hearsay of some peasant traveler. We've got superior communication now. Airlines to get boots on the ground in record time. The downside is law and emergency response teams are just as fast and have protocols to follow. Now, Bailey had his head shot off. To the police, that's probably a homicide. Homicide victims will be taken to the nearest medical examiner for an autopsy. That medical examiner is located in Halifax. Already got the address off the internet."

"So what are you saying?" Kirk asked.

Baxter unsheathed his silver Bowie knife—the same weapon issued to all wardens—and grimaced at the gleam before putting the weapon away. "I'm thinking since it's Sunday and after midnight, I propose we go straight to the medical examiner and politely ask the security team there to let us in. We kill them, disable any cameras, and then search the building—'specially the freezers. We find this snoring beauty and get medieval on the bastard. Rip out the throat. Stab that fucker through the heart. Cut it out, even. Hell, dismember and sprinkle the pieces around the far parts of the kingdom. We end this quick and get out of there before dawn."

An overeager Ezekiel nodded in support of the plan.

"Well," Morris said, "either I'm shitfaced or half-asleep, but that all sounds doable to me."

"We shouldn't kill those guards," Kirk said.

That muted the enthusiasm in the room. Ezekiel's smile faltered and Morris was clearly exasperated.

"You have a problem with that?" Baxter asked.

"Yeah, I do."

"You a fuckin' vegan or something?"

"Those people have families," Kirk said.

A happy Ezekiel spread his hands in a gesture of, *So?*

"Isn't that enough?"

"No," Baxter said. "That isn't enough. What's a few rent-a-cops to a city populace? One or two or ten guards dying so we can save hundreds of lives? A city, even? Which may very well happen if this thing crosses over. That's more than a fair price to pay."

"All right, how about this?" Kirk pointed at the warden. "If we kill those guards, suddenly the whole province goes on high alert. Every cop will be hunting for us, and they'll cross lines and borders to find us. Nothing will be spared. Even after the fact we're long gone. And, truthfully, you two are the ones long gone. Morris and I are still here. Now, if we don't kill the guards then it's just a bunch of sick kids doing weird shit to dead people. A lot less attention and fewer motivated police."

Ezekiel's smile dimmed once more. Even Morris gave the matter greater thought, eventually nodding in favor of Kirk's wisdom.

"Fuck it," Baxter blurted. "Fine. They'll wake up with headaches. I still say we go now. It only took four of our guys to put the first one down. And that was after it had already changed and was running about on some medieval hillside. This one's already been bagged. We pack up and kill that sleeper while he's still on a slab."

Ezekiel leaped to his feet, keen to the suggestion. Morris wavered, but Kirk knew he'd go for it in the end.

"I'm in," Ezekiel said.

"Never doubted you," Baxter said. He looked to Morris.

"Yeah," the Pictou warden said. "All right. Let's do it."

They looked to Kirk and he scowled, knowing they were going anyway, with or without him.

"What do you drive?" Baxter asked.

"A truck," Kirk answered.

"Then you can sit in your truck. Keep it running while we take care of things."

"Why don't we take your car?"

"We drove my car all the way here in a very short time.

We use your ride in town."

"We should wait for the others."

"This is how it is," Baxter said evenly. "It's the weekend. Any morgue will have its new occupants on a plate and stuck into a freezer until Monday morning. A steel freezer. Our buddy Bailey's got nowhere to go, already in tight confinement and ready to be put down. All we got to do is yank open the door and stab it with our shiny knives. Repeatedly. With extreme prejudice. That's all. We don't need a team."

"We're *told* to wait for the others," Kirk insisted, pointing a finger at the floor. "From the elders, remember?"

Ezekiel shook his head in sunny disbelief.

Morris didn't appear too happy with the counterpoint either. "Fuck it. I think you're right, Bax. If Bailey is in a freezer I'd say it's only gonna take three of us. Probably not even that."

A frustrated Kirk hung his head.

"Let's go then," Baxter announced and held out a hand to the Halifax warden. "Keys, please?"

"You overeager bastards," the warden seethed as he regarded them all. "I'm driving."

15

The truck pulled into the medical examiner's parking lot and stopped parallel to the main doors. The vehicle's reflection blazed in the lobby's glass wall, so Kirk turned off his headlights. A thick fence of elm trees lay to the right of the three-level structure. The odd city light glittered peacefully through that wooded veil, and Kirk suddenly wished he could just vanish in that distant urban maze. With a sigh he regarded the building. The front lobby was dark, except for a weak glow from the front desk and a hallway beyond. Kirk scanned the area but couldn't see any guards. His relief was brief, quickly replaced by concern.

"No guards," Morris said dryly. "Lucky us. Your conscience is saved."

Kirk didn't bother with a reply.

"You coming in now?"

"No."

Morris shrugged and opened the door. "Suit yourself. Keep the motor running."

The shapes of Baxter and Ezekiel jumped from the

pickup's bed, their heels clattering on the pavement. Ezekiel slapped the hood and pointed gun fingers at Kirk as he passed, still wearing that shit-eating smirk that had to hurt. Kirk glanced around the empty parking lot as the three wardens regrouped at the main door. Two other cars were parked nearby, facing the building.

He rolled down the window. "Hey."

All three wardens looked back to the truck.

"Can't see any guards at all. Outside or in the lobby."

No one answered him.

Kirk sighed. "Be careful."

Ezekiel's smile widened. The *weres* ignored the warden in the truck and studied the glass door. Morris inspected the wide handle before rattling the door in its frame.

"Locked," he reported.

The lobby and reception area beyond the clear glass door was deserted.

"Break it," he said to Ezekiel.

"There might be alarms," Morris pointed out.

Baxter considered that possibility. He peered inside the office building and reluctantly rapped a knuckle off the glass.

Nothing appeared.

He knocked a second time with more urgency.

"Where are the guards?" Morris asked impatiently.

"Maybe a late-night poker game?" Baxter offered.

Morris ignored him. "You smell that?"

The two wardens took deep whiffs.

"Blood," Baxter said.

"Yeah," Morris agreed, reaching underneath his coat and

gripping the handle of his knife.

"I'm breaking it," Baxter said.

"That'll bring the cops."

"We're on the outskirts of town here," Baxter pointed out. "I give the cops a good fifteen to twenty minutes before they respond."

Morris gestured, *Be my guest.*

Baxter drew his own length of silver, a great silver Bowie knife that dazzled in the scant lobby light. The glass was strong and it took three solid blows before the warden smashed a hole through, just above the door handle. He then stepped away and Ezekiel replaced him. The stocky warden jammed a fist through the opening, his crooked teeth bared as he manipulated the lock. A loud *snap* rewarded his efforts.

"No alarm," Morris said as Ezekiel pushed the door open with a hydraulic hiss.

"No guards either," Baxter observed.

All conversation died as a rich waft of blood and meat accosted the three wardens. The smell was so strong, so unexpected, that Ezekiel's smile actually dimmed at the corners.

"Blood," Baxter said, his knife tapping at his thigh. The others bared their own weapons.

"Cooling," Morris added, taking a breath.

"A lot of it."

The three wardens proceeded, fanning out in a line as they entered the lobby. Baxter drifted to the front desk and looked behind it while Ezekiel headed for the washroom.

"Hey," Morris said softly, stopping both men. The

Pictou warden nodded toward the single L-shaped corridor. A wide shard of shadow coated the juncture in sharp lines. There still wasn't any difficulty in discerning the huge blood blot on the wall and at the base of the hall's crook, or the black streak leading out of sight. The jagged stripe painted the center of the floor tiles and disappeared around a corner.

"Smell that?" Morris asked, his senses alive and thrumming.

"I smell it," Baxter answered.

Ezekiel nodded. "It got out."

Baxter studied the empty corridor. "Couldn't have gotten out. Couldn't have fucking healed so fast. It's a *head* for Christ's sake."

Morris didn't reply, which was an answer in itself. He walked down the corridor with his knife out, wary of the corner where the glass ended and cinder blocks began. Ezekiel followed, strolling not three paces behind the lead warden. Baxter brought up the rear, his attention divided between the gruesome blood spatters and the glossy partitions forming the hall.

The rooms behind the glass were an assortment of classrooms, laboratories, and even meeting halls with overhead projectors. Morris inspected the dark splotch at the wall's base as he neared it. Black and thick and dried, it looked like several full blood bags had been pitched at the wall. He stopped at the corner and stuck his head out for a peek.

"Sweet Jesus," he whispered.

Baxter stopped directly behind Morris's back and looked over his shoulder.

Ahead lay a twenty-five-meter walk, give or take a meter, of beige cinder blocks. Gray doors marked both walls at regular intervals, and fluorescent lights hung overhead. Some of the tubes had been smashed, drizzling the tiles in glass, while one dark set hung off kilter from its metal casing. The remaining functioning lights streaked the passageway in broad tiger stripes of shadow and light.

But that was all secondary.

The real attention-grabber was the blood streak right down the middle of the corridor as if a person had been dragging a fat mop. From the initial spatter behind the wardens, all the way to the shadowed far end. In that patch of darkness was an open door, a gaping black cave that might have been the facility's walk-in freezer. Blood spattered the walls in thick lines of code. Detached limbs rested against the bases. Glass fragments sparkled within the maroon pools like fizzy bubbles. Slabs of skin and fingers further drizzled the tiles like morbid cake sprinkles. Morris counted three arms and what might have been a knee, with no thigh and only half of an exposed shin.

The three wardens stared, motionless, at the carnage spread out before them.

"It got out," Ezekiel whispered. He was no longer smiling.

"And fucked up whoever was handy," Morris whispered, catching a curious scent of fear emanating from one of the wardens. He gripped his knife tighter and approached the distant freezer door bathed in a curtain of shadow. The others trekked behind him, through sticky smears, each step squeaking like sneakers on a basketball court.

Morris kept his attention on the nearing doorway, his face half-hitched into a grimace. Other smells assaulted him as he walked through the massacre—unknown chemical compounds, perhaps cleaners, as well as what might have been formaldehyde. And the unmistakable reek of stomach matter, ripped straight from the source. A tantalizing scent of something familiar mixed with the butchery on the floors and walls, teasing Morris with its mystery.

A sharp expulsion of breath issuing from the corridor's end halted the advancing wardens. They stopped midway to the freezer door, knives drawn, tensed, and waited.

They didn't wait for long.

A figure from some haunted nightmare stepped into view, partially draped in shadow as if abhorring the light. The thing stood just a little shorter than Morris himself, but that wasn't the disturbing thing. The reborn was without clothing, the meager light revealing only patches of his stained person, a deep maroon hue, as if he'd just emerged from a violent bath.

The *were*-thing lingered near a wall and eyed the three wardens curiously, a slight frown on otherwise smooth features. Morris gawked. The face, the eyes, nose, and mouth resembled the one called Bailey, he realized, but there were some features not quite right. Minor details and flourishes, as if the sculptor had rushed the finer points. The wild light in the *were's* eyes belonged to Bailey, however, there was no mistake there, but brighter. Much more feral.

The *were*-thing stepped into a gunslinger's pose,

presenting itself face-on to the three law bringers.

Morris lifted his knife. The pair behind him palpably tensed.

That subtle change in posture brought a growl from Bailey. His hands came up, fingers extended into hooks. He stepped toward the three newcomers with a thick splash of red, and flashed his teeth.

Some of those teeth had been shattered into shards.

"Bailey," the Pictou warden greeted as he lifted his knife like a holy relic.

The reborn *were* charged, blurring forward, possessing a speed entirely unexpected. Morris slashed for the creature's neck but Bailey slapped the weapon away, pinging if off a wall. The naked *were* gathered Morris up with two fists and, using him as an unwilling shield, crashed into all three wardens.

Morris got stomped on like a welcome mat.

Bailey slapped Baxter across the face, faster than the warden could react, and slammed the New Brunswick warden into the cement blocks, bouncing him off the unyielding material.

Ezekiel lunged, his weapon instantly caught and broken. Bailey whipped him into one wall, reset himself, and slapped the stunned warden into another.

Baxter attempted to rise and had his head cracked left then right, the blows staggering him. Skin split. Blood sprayed.

Morris attempted to rise and got a one-handed shove from behind, driving his face into a cement block. His nose and teeth shattered.

A livid Ezekiel, furious at being manhandled, got to one knee and sprang forward, landing on Bailey's back. He clamped a hand over the *were*-thing's mouth, but Bailey yanked it away and threw himself backwards, mashing the smaller warden against a wall. The reborn *were* turned and grabbed the smaller man's throat, sinking his fingers in to the knuckles. Ezekiel's rage winked out with the abrupt pinching of his air pipes. Bailey pulled, the resulting explosion as spectacular as it was gory.

A pale Ezekiel crumpled, grasping at the rich tide spurting through his fingers.

Morris got to his feet and roared. Bailey spun, grabbed him by his coat's front and flung him into the lights above. Metal clanged. Glass blew apart in slivers and rendered the battlefield even darker. Morris fell in a heap. Bailey stomped on an arm, a hand, and kicked the warden's head hard enough to snap vertebrae.

Baxter recovered and pinned the monster to the wall, stabbing his silver deep into the creature's back. Bailey hissed, screamed, and grabbed the warden. He whipped Baxter headfirst into the cement, where the warden's skull shattered like a knob of sunbaked clay.

Triumphant, Bailey threw his arms wide and screamed again, the sound ear-splitting inside the narrow confines.

His legs still working, Ezekiel kicked and crawled along the white floor tiles like a tadpole half crushed. He'd been badly hurt. Badly. The worst he could remember, but he was alive. Already he could feel the arterial flow slowing, his body repairing the damage. He would live to fight another day.

All he needed was to get *away*.

A hand clamped around his ankle.

Ezekiel no longer had the vocal cords to scream.

*

On impulse, Kirk glanced through the driver's window and caught a whiff of that metallic bouquet he knew in an instant. Fresh blood. And not the foulness that had drifted to his parked truck like septic gas. He fumbled for the latch, intent on leaving the vehicle when, from the depths of the medical examiner's building, came a man—a naked man—striding toward the main door. Kirk blinked as disbelief seized his innards and gave them a yank. The figure slapped the door open with bare palms. The door rebounded and crashed into his face as he was halfway through. He stopped, surprised at the contact, and shoved it back. Metal yipped as the hinges gave away and the barrier crashed into the glass wall. The *were*—as this clearly was no human—yelled gibberish at the thing's brazenness until determining it to no longer be a threat.

The *were* proceeded to walk across the parking lot.

In his wake, the door toppled to the concrete.

The naked *were*-thing marched into the night air. Then he stopped and turned toward Kirk's truck.

Fuck this, Kirk thought and started the engine. The *were*-thing half crouched at the sound. Kirk shoved the truck into drive, lit the creature up with headlights, and accelerated right at the beast.

The *were*-creature ran, shot off like an Olympic sprinter

with a couple of afterburners mounted on his ass, and disappeared into the trees. Kirk watched the figure wink out of sight and, for a fleeting second, contemplated giving chase. He gripped the door and pulled it open.

Then stopped.

Three wardens armed with silver had gone into the building. They had not walked out. Kirk hesitated, dreading what that meant. If he did go after the *were*-creature, he'd probably fare no better than Morris and the others.

Which brought Kirk to his next concern.

He shoved the truck into drive and positioned the vehicle next to the ruined entrance. He parked it and hopped out, scanning the forest to see if the creature had decided to return. Kirk ran inside and slowed, breathing in the thick, unchecked violence lacing the air. He coughed, held a hand to his nose, and raced down a hall to a corner.

The sight ahead stopped him in his tracks.

Morris floundered in a pool of gore. He twitched and drunkenly rolled around, pitifully attempting to will his limbs to function. But his body was anchored to one spot by his head. Morris was the only one moving among the three splayed wardens. When the Pictou law bringer saw Kirk, his eyes widened and he grunted a high note of relief.

Then he collapsed, nose down in blood.

Baxter and Ezekiel didn't move. Both appeared as if they'd been stomped on by the heel of God. Baxter, in particular, resembled an egg that had fallen from a very high place.

"Oh sweet Lord," Kirk whispered, horrified at the

carnage. He stumbled forward, slipping in places, heedless of the spawny slush drenching the soles of his sneakers. He hurried along the hall, dismayed at the battle's aftermath, and located an orange bin tucked near the freezer door at the corridor's end. Other half-devoured corpses lay strewn about, but the contents of the bin were untouched. Kirk reached down and grabbed handfuls of gray sheets. He spread out two and covered up Morris.

The warden mewed, a soft string of unintelligible syllables.

"I got you," Kirk muttered, hoping to calm him. "I got you. Bailey got away. He's gone. Into the forest."

Morris released a childlike note of despair.

"Gonna get you out of here," Kirk whispered, hauling the warden up and hoisting him over a shoulder. Morris grunted and went limp. Kirk thought that was for the best.

"Okay then." He got moving.

In a little under ten minutes, Kirk had deposited the three wardens into the truck bed, their fluids trickling over the tailgate and onto the pavement. He stopped when he loaded Baxter into the truck, taking great gulps of air. Kirk wasn't tired, wasn't gassed in the least, but the sight and smell of all the blood...

God help him, he wanted...he wanted to...

Kirk rubbed his face as if that might alleviate the aching in his jaws, the rumbling of his stomach. One of Ezekiel's boots was uncovered, so the Halifax warden quickly covered it up to remove the growing temptation. He needed to get out of there, away from all that blood. He staggered to the driver's side and stopped, bent over at the waist.

Well, *shit*.

He almost forgot.

Kirk returned to the corridor and retrieved all three knives where they'd fallen. On impulse, he grabbed another fistful of sheets. The sheets he used to soak up the excess blood in his truck.

Knowing he should've been gone from the place twenty minutes ago, Kirk slammed the tailgate shut and tried not to look upon Morris, lying on his back with his eyes staring at the heavens. Of the three, Morris appeared the only one semiconscious. Kirk wasn't certain if that was a good thing or not. Ezekiel was missing a huge chunk of meat from his throat, and Baxter—Baxter was the worst.

The New Brunswick man had had his face pulverized, squished to an unrecognizable strawberry pulp, while the back of his head remained intact. Kirk quickly covered that ruined face, covered the others with equal urgency.

He climbed aboard the truck, started the engine, and stared at the city beyond, shocked at how the episode at the medical examiner's building had gone down, but also struggling to keep a more sinister urge under control.

Regaining his senses, Kirk put the truck into gear and drove away.

16

Pre-dawn traffic was nonexistent, so Kirk drove quickly, speeding along empty streets and navigating his way back to his apartment building complex. He glimpsed a police cruiser speed through a nearby intersection, but they continued on without pause. Kirk started breathing again. The last thing he needed was the local authorities stopping him. Not with the bleeding mess he'd collected in the back of his pickup.

City lights flashed by and finally, after what seemed like an hour, Kirk pulled into his building's parking lot and regarded the dark heights. He circled once, scanning the lower levels as well as the high ones, ensuring there were no early smokers standing on their decks for a puff. Deciding the coast was clear, he pulled into his parking space, jumped out and went straight to the truck bed.

Covered in sheets, the three unmoving shapes resembled bloody cabbage rolls. Kirk really didn't want to bring them up to the apartment, but he was at a loss, so he pulled the tailgate down. One positive development was that the drive had quelled his earlier cravings, and for that, Kirk was grateful. He grabbed the nearest pair of ankles and hauled out Baxter's limp form. Of the three, Kirk feared for him the most.

He swung Baxter's considerable weight onto a shoulder, knowing he'd probably have to trash his coat, and turned around.

"Jesus," Kirk blurted, coming face-to-face with not one, not two, but five individuals. And one of them…

Kirk's guts froze again and he doubted they would ever unfreeze.

One of them was *her*, dressed in a blue mid-length winter coat.

"You stupid fuck," Carma Jones said to his face, her pallid features a snarl of disbelief and anger. "You stupid, stupid…"

"You live here?" asked a hard-looking guy on her right flank who looked like he'd fought in every war in the last century.

The question unlocked Kirk's tongue. "Yeah."

"Nowhere else to take them?" he asked as Carma pushed by Kirk and studied the other wardens in the back of the truck.

"No," Kirk said, stepping out of her way.

Carma motioned at the two men behind her. "Get these two inside." A second woman stood back, scanning the surrounding area for witnesses.

"You left your door locked," Carma directed at Kirk, who again lost all ability of speech.

The guy resembling a war veteran studied the Halifax warden's face. "You in shock?"

Kirk nodded.

"Come on, then," the war veteran said. "Hope you got a key on you."

Surprised at their appearance and grateful for the help, Kirk led the group into the building. The elevator wasn't a large one, so four of them packed themselves inside, carrying the wounded. Kirk found himself unintentionally standing close to Carma. He sighed at his awkward luck, crammed into an elevator with her, two strangers, and three dying *weres*, though he believed the bodies were no longer bleeding. The elevator doors closed and as they rose, he stared straight ahead, very much aware of Carma's presence, very much smelling her hair, and trying very hard to think clearly.

The two wardens behind him were relatively tall and pensive-looking. One wore a lumberjack beard that might have been frayed by a killing jolt of electricity, while the other was an Asian who kept his eyes on the escalating numbers over the door.

"You brought friends," Kirk muttered.

"I brought reinforcements," Carma said flatly, also watching the numbers as they lit up. "Last I heard, you guys were supposed to sit on your asses and wait until everyone gathered."

Kirk exhaled mightily and shook his head. "It was Baxter's idea."

"Baxter?" Carma turned and studied Kirk's profile.

"Baxter Ryan? That's him?"

She indicated the bundle slung over his shoulder.

"Yeah. What's left of him."

"He ordered you all to go?"

"Sort of. Peer pressure."

"Peer pressure. Jesus Christ, Kirk."

The elevator screeched to a stop. Kirk exited first and led the three along a quiet hallway to his door. He struggled with the lock and, once opened, bade them all enter.

"Dump them in here," he said and went into his spare bedroom. He gently placed Baxter on the thick quilts of his bed while the tall lumberjack dropped Ezekiel next to the unconscious warden. Carma's men plopped Morris onto the extra white mattress at the foot of the bed.

"Get out here," Carma said, standing before the living room couch. When Kirk appeared, she locked onto his eyes with a level of disapproval that made him squirm with guilt.

"You got a story to tell," she said to him as the Asian stepped to his right. The lumberjack leaned against a wall.

"You look tired," Kirk said.

"I jumped into my car as soon as I got the call. Drove until my eyes crossed and then got a bus. And I'm not the only one, so, yeah. I'm tired. Everyone's tired."

"Got your badge?"

"Don't ask stupid questions," Carma warned. "And wait a second. For the others to get here."

So Kirk shut up and fidgeted in place, until he rested his hands on his hips. As annoying as she was, Kirk thought she looked good. Carma wasn't one for sappy reunions—not that they'd parted on the best of terms. She spurned his advances, left him dejected and thinking about her every day since. For twelve years. Even as he thought it, he realized the absurdity of being so hooked on a single person. Embarrassment fired inside of him like a rusty furnace kicking into action. Kirk struggled to keep his face neutral, knowing if he displayed anything else other than stoic professionalism, Carma would probably, literally, rip him a new asshole.

In short time, the others arrived and filed into the apartment's living room. The lumberjack closed and locked the main door. The war veteran and the other female eyed Kirk with a dark curiosity. They all looked tired, as if they'd dropped everything and raced to Halifax.

"All right," Carma began, and Kirk wasn't sure if she'd blinked once since entering his home. "You can start with the story. Leave nothing out."

Taking a breath, Kirk told them everything. To his surprise, no one interrupted him. No one pressed for details. He kept the report short, and when he'd finished he badly wanted a beer.

"You idiot," Carma said in a low voice. "What part of 'wait for reinforcements' did you not understand?"

"It wasn't my call," Kirk stated, watching her from underneath his lowered brow. "It was Baxter's. He convinced the others to go. Like I said, we figured Bailey would be in one of the morgue's steel freezers."

"You didn't have to take them," Carma said.

"They would've taken Baxter's car. Or gotten a cab. They

were determined to kill it before it… awakened."

Carma shook her head, short blonde locks bouncing. "And now Baxter's dead."

"He's not dead."

"You take a look at his face? The guy's nose is stuck in his sinus cavity, along with his forehead. A lot of bone has been pushed through that brain of his."

Kirk's shoulders slumped. Yeah, he'd thought the same thing.

"Who's the other one?" the war veteran asked.

"Ezekiel something," Kirk answered.

"Ezekiel Allen," the other female said in a scratchy singer's voice. "They're both from New Brunswick."

"He might pull through," Kirk said. "Only had his throat ripped out."

"He should," the second female said, standing with her hands loose by her sides, ready for a confrontation. "Don't think he'll be talking, though. I'd say the thing got more than just a fistful of meat when it ripped out his throat. Ezekiel's lucky it didn't use its teeth, else we'd have two dead wardens on our hands."

That frank assessment quieted the room.

Carma regarded the assembly and motioned them to follow her into the bedroom. She stopped beside the wreckage of Baxter Ryan. The big man lay on his back, his feet dangling over the bed's edge. Carma unwrapped the blood-soaked sheets and dropped them on Baxter's knees. The warden's chest didn't appear to be moving and his face was a devastated implosion of white shards and swollen flesh.

Just gazing upon the warden's unrecognizable features was difficult for Kirk. The others looked down on the figure and didn't say a word, but their thoughts were all the same: When Baxter came to, would he be Baxter, or would he be another Bailey?

"You see him?" Carma asked the assembled wardens. "I've been given authority by the elders to pass judgement on cases such as Baxter. His head is caved in. Do you agree?"

Nods and grunts. Kirk's own feelings tightened into a barbed knot of unease.

"Do you agree?" Carma asked him directly.

"He's in hard shape."

"Hard shape? If he were a human, he'd be dead. But he's not dead, because he's a *were*. That's the only thing keeping him in this world. Look at him. He's been flattened. I'd say his frontal lobe resembles a crushed loaf of bread. When he comes back, there's no chance in hell he'll be the same Baxter. He'll be something else. He'll be another Bailey."

"You don't know that," Kirk said softly.

"I know it," Carma said and extracted a huge knife from behind her back. The weapon's appearance robbed Kirk of any further argument. The sparse light made the silver appear all the more dangerous. "Anyone disagree with this act of mercy?"

No one answered or moved.

Kirk regarded Baxter on the bed and his voice caught in his throat. "I think we should wait. Just to be sure."

"Anyone else think the same way?"

They didn't.

Carma's stern expression didn't change as she stabbed Baxter through the throat. She sawed, releasing a weak red stream that quickly seeped into the quilt.

Kirk winced.

Carma stopped halfway. "Baxter's case isn't the first time a *were's* been hurt to a point where a mercy killing's been called for. It's just the most recent, and knowing Baxter, I know he'd *want* to be put down, considering the alternative. Are you in agreement, Kirk?"

Kirk wasn't. "Yeah."

Carma wasn't buying his lie, but she didn't pursue it. She addressed the others. "Remember Baxter Ryan. I've known the man for over forty years, and I know what he would have done if our roles were reversed."

Hearing that, a twang of hurt resounded through Kirk.

"Baxter wouldn't hesitate to do the same," Carma continued, meeting each of their faces, "and I promise you, if you're reduced to that, I'll do the same to you—as I expect you to do the same for me. Or anyone. Understood?"

A solemn round of nods. Kirk was the last to answer, and he barely dipped his chin.

Without a trace of emotion, Carma regarded Baxter's dead form. She pulled her knife out, wiped it on the stained sheets, and returned it to her hidden sheath.

"All right then," she said to Kirk. "What do you have to eat in this place?"

Jesus Christ, the Halifax warden thought. *The woman was cold.*

"Not much," he muttered.

"Well, what?"

"Mostly canned stuff. Bread. Might be a roast in the freezer."

"Let's see."

"Ah," Kirk stopped her as she rounded the bed's corner. "What about Baxter's body?"

"He's fine where he is."

"He can't stay here."

Carma frowned. "I've got orders. From the elders. I'll make a call and get someone here to pick him up. They'll take care of it."

Kirk held out a hand. "At least move Ezekiel into the other room."

"Do it, Sam," she said as she walked to the kitchen. The others followed her out, except for Sam—the war veteran.

Kirk left the room and stopped in the hall. Carma was already inspecting the contents of his fridge, unimpressed with the collection of processed sausages, cheeses, bread and milk. Not to mention a few cold bottles of beer.

"You eat like a mutt," she muttered.

"Thanks," Kirk replied, not appreciating the jab.

"This everything?"

"No, there's a freezer in the laundry room." Kirk pointed. Carma went into the room, switched on the light and threw open the freezer's lid. It was a small affair, no more than fourteen cubic feet, and a lonely lump of what looked like a frozen meteor rested on the bottom, keeping a couple of boxes of small pizzas stacked upright.

"This is pathetic. Morris and Ezekiel alone are going to

need a ton of calories to repair themselves."

Standing in the doorway, Kirk shrugged and agreed with her. It was pathetic, now that it was pointed out to him. *Weres* in general burned through a lot of food. Regenerating *weres* even more so.

The food didn't impress Carma in the least. She closed the lid and reached into her coat's inner pocket.

"Can't believe you didn't stock this place." She pulled out a wad of bills and straightened out an impressive collection of reddish-pink and browns, with a smattering of green just for color.

"Here," she said, holding out half of the cash to Kirk. "Two things. First, Janice and Ken are going to strip out your linen closet and clean up the bed of your truck. You got cleaners, right?"

Kirk nodded as he took the money.

"Once that's done, get your ass to a supermarket somewhere and buy up everything they got in ways of meat. You know what we like. Ian, you go with him. Keep in mind we have a freezer to fill. I'll leave this here."

She slapped the remainder of the cash on a nearby counter. "We'll refill this tank as necessary."

All that money in plain sight didn't even raise an eyebrow amongst the assembled crew.

Carma fixed her attention upon Kirk as she pulled out a cell phone. "Well?"

She placed the device to her ear.

"Move your ass."

17

Perhaps forty minutes later, Kirk followed Ian Bryce—the lumberjack—through the empty aisles of a twenty-four-hour supermarket. Overhead lighting flashed off the freshly waxed white floor tiles, the cleaner a sickly cherry scent in Kirk's nose. Bryce wasn't the kind of guy Kirk kept company with, and not because he was a *were*. Bryce struck Kirk as every bit the soldier that Carma had become. He said little on the ten-minute drive to the warehouse supermarket and merely pointed at the row of shopping carts as he entered the building, leaving that task to Kirk. The task of an underling.

Kirk shook his head, really having no time for the unconcealed exhibition of rank.

Bryce grabbed items as he saw them and tossed them into the cart. A fifty-pound sack of potatoes, bags of carrots, and other assorted vegetables. Condiments, breads, and even some choice canned goods. He passed the frozen foods section and stopped to inspect the selection of turkey and chicken.

"Turkey's on special," Kirk muttered and was ignored.

But Bryce did load up on eight of the birds, however, so Kirk mentally patted himself on the back.

"Not much room left," he observed after the final bird had fallen into the cart.

"So get another cart," Bryce said and moved to the chicken.

"You gonna take this one?"

Bryce dumped three birds into the fray, considerably adding to the total, and regarded his companion with a scowl. "What do you think?"

"Hey man, I'm just asking."

"Yeah, I'll take the cart," an impatient Bryce remarked.

Kirk didn't like the waves of negative energy coming off the guy. He glanced around to ensure they were relatively alone. "You got a problem with me?"

Bryce pulled the cart over and straightened his back, a few fingers taller than his shorter companion and broader across the shoulders. The guy could've played football and terrorized defensive lines. Wavy hair covered his face and head, but some flesh could be seen, permanently tanned.

"What do you think?"

"There wasn't anything I could've done," Kirk said.

"There's always something you could've done," Bryce said, fixing Kirk with a steely gaze. "Always. You had orders. You all had orders. Baxter was wrong but you followed the pack anyway."

"Seemed like a good plan at the time," Kirk muttered.

"Yeah, well, here's a good plan. Get another fucking cart and we can finish grocery shopping."

Lips puckered and cheeks burning, Kirk returned to the long rows of carts and yanked one free. Bryce was right, to a point—he could've done something. But what that was exactly escaped him. Kirk wondered how he would've fared against the gung-ho trio of Baxter, Ezekiel, and Moses Morris. In the end, he buried the thought, caged the anger, knowing he'd need that and all his energy for later. He wheeled his way back and located Bryce before the beef section. The warden proceeded to dump chunk after plastic-wrapped chunk of beef into the new cart, and when he finished, he pulled it away from Kirk, leaving him the first one to push.

A light bulb flickered to life in Kirk's head. "Can't believe you're out shopping for Carma, can you?"

In answer, Bryce unloaded an armful of pork chops into his cart, but Kirk sensed he'd hit the mark. Bryce might have been annoyed with him, but he was pissed at having to pick up food.

Kirk was careful to hide his amusement.

"Where's the booze section?" Bryce asked after the two of them had filled the second cart to the rim.

"No booze here. That's what the liquor corporations are for."

"Not even any beer?"

"No. Where are you from anyway?"

"Montreal."

"You can get booze in a grocery store there?"

"Sure can. Hell, even Newfoundland and Labrador has beer in corner stores."

"Yeah, I know," and Kirk did, remembering his time in the easterly province.

"No wine either?"

"No wine."

Scowling, Bryce shook his heavily bearded head and looked ready to growl. "Fuckin' backwards."

"We can pick some up in the morning," Kirk offered.

Bryce didn't answer. The Montrealer led Kirk to the nearest checkout counter. He stood tall, dressed in a denim tuxedo. Bryce was about Baxter's height, and he puffed out his substantial chest while the young guy at the register stoically checked the items.

A snack rack containing bags of beef jerky hung to the left of the register and Bryce eyed them, calculating how many he could buy with the money in hand. Kirk watched him deliberate with solemn concentration as the checkout clerk continued to scan items.

"Go ahead," Kirk finally said.

Bryce made side-eyes at him, sending the message that he didn't need *his* permission to buy a few packs of beef jerky. He grabbed four packages off the rack and tossed them amongst the chicken, still eyeing Kirk with condescension, daring him to comment.

Kirk, however, didn't give a damn. He moved past the bigger man and started bagging the food.

His thoughts drifted to Carma.

18

In the back alley of a late-night donut shop, Haley Walker peered eagerly at the large, green dumpster. There she stood for a few moments, breathing in the cold air, staring in disappointment at the thick padlock barring her progress. She hefted the lock, studied it, and let it be with gentle acceptance. The manager of the donut shop had finally gotten sick of the mess made by the throngs of homeless folks who'd show up after-hours, so he put a halt to the midnight feedings. The dumpster was a treasure chest of goodies—donuts, cookies, muffins—everything from the day that had failed to sell and what the nightshift didn't care to take home. Two nights ago, however, Haley had dropped by and discovered a young couple, barely out of their teens, inside the dumpster and pawing through the garbage bags with rabid delight. Plastic and refuse and unwanted baked goods littered the floor, and bent over it all was a pair of dumbfounded fuckheads looking like cornered raccoons. Animals who quickly realized Haley was much older (in her late fifties), much smaller (a "fuck-all" five-foot height) and, most importantly, all alone.

They'd driven her away with threats and curses, loud enough that Haley departed because she didn't need the hassle. They seemed wild, those kids. Strung out on Crack or Meth or any number of street drugs. Perhaps even a combination. She silently cursed them back, not for their threats or their addictions, but for their blatant ignorance of others who frequented the place for edible refuse. Folks who took care not to make a mess in the dumpster.

A mess pissed off the owners and brought about padlocks. Padlocks ruined it for *everybody*.

The early morning air had a dampness about it that bespoke of an autumn ready to spit snow. Haley wore a pair of men's gloves, a thick scarf that nearly mummified her face, and a puffy winter coat that, though tattered in places, was still quite warm. She'd already had a late-night meal at the soup truck, which was her second bowl of the day, and figured, what the hell. Leftover donuts sounded pretty damn good.

But the dumpster was locked.

Well, she thought, backing away from the property and minding the shadows, there were other places to visit. Other secrets the city had to offer a homeless woman like herself. One only had to walk there and be prepared to do a little foraging.

And she wasn't really homeless. Not truly. She had a home, squatting in a tumbledown two-story Victorian over on Whitewood Street, just off of Quinnpool. She'd lived there for the past three years, waiting for the city to do something about the aging house and the attic that cooed damn near all hours of the night. Haley didn't go into the attic. That much accumulated pigeon shit couldn't be good for a person.

Thoughts of where to strike next ran through her head. She wondered where she could hunt for something a little tastier, maybe even a little sweeter, than soup. The sun would rise in a few hours so she had time to walk home before it got light. The light distressed her. Revealed her plight to others, for better or, on occasions, for worse. Haley splashed through a puddle, cursed softly, and felt the dampness soak through her worn sneakers. She stopped and turned, an environmentally friendly reusable bag dangling from her right hand, and studied the water.

Great.

She hated walking in soaked socks. Just hated it.

And she'd already decided upon the pizza place over on Discovery Road. A little place only a few people knew of besides herself. The garbage bin out back was hit or miss at times, but just last week Haley had taken a look inside the topless container and discovered a large pizza pie with all the toppings. A discarded deluxe pie just staring back at her. The edges had been singed to a crisp and deemed unsellable, so the cooks chucked it. Perfectly edible yet trashed because no one wanted to pay full price for charred pizza. Haley wasn't surprised. Over the years of scrounging the streets, very little surprised her at what people threw away. Food, drinks, clothing, electronics, everything. She remembered one summer how whole boxes of bananas had been thrown into a garbage bin. The skin was black and unfit to look at but the fruit underneath (though her friend Andy had argued that, *botanically*, a banana was a berry) was ripe and perhaps the sweetest she'd ever tasted. That had been a real prize, to find whole fruit without teeth marks. That find had made her a local celebrity amongst the other homeless folks, as she told everyone at the shelter about it and where to go. It was how she liked to roll. She'd take what she wanted, share if she could, and give a little when she located a motherlode. She even traded goods and services with the guys under the bridge and around the docks. Everything was of value to someone, Haley knew—it was only a matter of finding that someone.

Pizza place it was then, she decided. It was worth it. She waddled along the back alleys and avenues, shoulders slack and head somewhat lowered, enjoying the really early hours and the emptiness they provided. There were few people on the prowl at such a time. Few people to glare at her or hold their nose at her—which was something Haley couldn't rightly understand, as she bathed at the homeless shelter once a week and washed her clothing there, too, whenever she was able. If she'd habitually stepped in dog shit she might understand, but for some reason, folks were repelled by her scent.

Regardless, pizza popped back into her head. She hoped she got lucky, thinking that hope was a good thing.

Enjoying the damp dark and the freedom it provided, Haley threaded her way a little farther downtown, hiking toward Barrington, finding Discovery, and looping around the long way to get to the back alley of the pizza place. The streets, clean and utterly deserted, gleamed under yellow cones of light. A car roared somewhere down the street, but Haley paid it no mind as she slipped deeper into the city's many crevices, where the alleys weren't so clean, and a person minded the dark.

Soggy newspapers and discarded cardboard cases lined the sides of the alley, and the ripe smell of sewage forced Haley to screw up her nose despite her scarf. She moved along the nearby walls, maintaining silence and spotting the garbage bin's bulk just ahead, a large angular mass that blocked the distant streetlight on the other side. She stopped beside the back door of the pizzeria, saw no light behind the barred windows, and waited, just to be sure. Once, a couple of cooks had hung on despite it being almost morning—a near encounter that almost ended badly for Haley.

All was presently quiet, so she proceeded to the bin. Her chin rested on the metal edge and she peered inside, sticking her nose in places she'd gone before. There, in the corner just to her left, was a generic white box dumped right atop a batch of old pizza dough. The dough could stay, but the box interested her greatly. She got her arm over the edge and reached for it only to come up short a good four inches.

Shit, she thought and looked around. A milk crate rested near the back door of the pizzeria. That would definitely stretch her reach, Haley knew, so she gathered it up and knocked over an empty bottle just behind it. The glass rattled brightly along the concrete floor, pulling her mouth into a frown, so she got a foot down to halt the roll. Empty beer bottle, she saw. That went into a pocket. There was good money in collecting empties.

She lifted the crate and placed it with care against the side of the bin, testing its bottom with a solid two-handed push. It would hold her. She climbed aboard and, now waist high, got a better look at the bin's goods. Pizza box sighted, she leaned over and stretched out a hand.

A car passed by the alley's mouth on the far side. Haley glanced over her shoulder on impulse and saw a large figure rising from the bin's other side.

"Oh," Haley said, startled by the sudden appearance and swearing to herself for not checking better.

"Oh is right," the shadow grumbled and inspected itself. "Well, shit. Fucking pissed myself. God*damnit*."

Haley froze on the crate. Beer bottle. She should have realized it. A drunk. A drunk passed out on the other side of the dumpster. Drunks were unpredictable. Some folks she knew had been sent to the hospital after encounters with drunk people. Some others had been showered with kindness.

"The fuck you staring at?" the shadow barked, the outline tensing.

Haley's legs quivered.

"Huh? The fuck you doing back here? Hey, you just—"

The man patted himself down, the noise like soft firecrackers. Haley placed one foot on the ground and then the other, already forgetting about the pizza box.

"The fuck's my wallet?" the man slurred and spun around, accidentally crashing his right arm into the bin. He grunted at the connection and bent at the waist.

Haley ran, ran with all the speed her bundled frame could muster.

She almost made it.

The drunk quickly recovered, detecting her attempted escape. Knowing that a guiltless person wouldn't have run at all, he took after her and caught her almost twenty strides from the dumpster.

"Hey!"

Hands grabbed Haley by the shoulders and slammed her against the wall. She crumpled with a gasp. Her bottom touched concrete just as a knee crashed into her face, bouncing her head off a brick wall.

"The fuck you going, huh? The fuck you going?" the dark face demanded, the head now only a mouth. A hand grabbed her chin, yanked it up where a hand slapped her twice. The impact summoned flickering explosions before Haley's eyes. She gasped again.

"You steal my wallet? You little bitch?"

Her head was plied one way and then the other before being shoved against the wall. The drunk slapped her again before invading her pockets, turning them out.

"Where is it?" he demanded and pulled her to her feet with enough force to dislocate her shoulders. "Where is it?"

He slammed her against the bricks.

"I don't have it," Haley squawked and got slapped hard across the face a second before he punched her square in the gut. The old back-alley one-two. Haley collapsed, holding her middle while croaking for breath.

"Like fuck you don't have it. You got it. Damn good thing I woke up when I did. Christ almighty. Bad enough I fucking pass out in the street, but to have you steal my wallet? The fuck's the world coming to? This town used to be safe."

He smacked her across the forehead, powerful enough to daze her. "You smell like week-old BO, honey. Thought I smelled bad."

Without pausing, he ripped at the front of her coat, but his fingers slipped. Growling, he lifted her chin and yanked the zipper down. A second later, hands roughly explored her breasts, hefting and squeezing them through her old but warm sweatshirt.

"Not here, either," he muttered, his tone softening, becoming curious. "Geez, you got a set."

More rough fondling, hard enough to restart Haley's breathing. "No."

"Oh fuck yeah, you do."

She grabbed his wrists but he pushed her away and slapped her. *Hard.* Her nose let loose upon contact. A pained whimper left her before he waved a finger in front of her face.

"Don't fucking flatter yourself, bitch. I'd just as soon fuck a tea bag. I just want my wallet."

"I don't have it."

He pulled on her arms, dragging Haley to her feet. He whirled her around and pushed her against the wall. His hands groped her again and she whimpered at the rude and painful exploration.

"Nothing. Where the hell did you hide it? Where'd you hide it?"

Haley squeezed her eyes shut, knowing what was coming. He shoved her into the cold bricks again and kneed her right buttock, the pain sparkling.

"All right," he wheezed, a different tone to his voice. "All right. Time for a full body search. I'm gonna find that wallet, honey. You bet your balls I'm gonna—"

The sound of feet slapping the ground turned both Haley and her attacker's heads to the left. An outline streaked into the drunk groper, lifting him and carrying him a good five or six strides. The vengeful silhouette heaved Haley's attacker at the pizza dumpster, where he crashed against the iron hide like a sack of bones bouncing off a stern dinner gong.

That was the fight. Over and done in no more than two seconds.

Haley covered her bleeding nose and mouth and coughed pure undiluted relief into her hands. She slunk toward the alley mouth, back the way she'd come, swearing to never venture into this part of town ever again.

She glanced over her shoulder to check on her rescuer, turning around as if bewildered. In the scant light, Haley gasped at the blackness covering his otherwise bare back.

"You're bleeding," she gasped, stopping in her tracks and wondering where the drunk had a knife, let alone the time to stab. That thought struck her as near senseless. If her attacker had a knife, he would have used it on her.

Sonofabitch.

The man who'd saved her whirled at the sound of her voice, and Haley got the second surprise of the pre-dawn hours. The guy who'd saved her neck didn't have a stitch of clothing on him.

"Are you high?" she demanded, leaning against the wall. "You've got nothing on."

Muscular shoulders heaving, the man said nothing. He watched her, like a dog stalking a rabbit, but abruptly walked away. Haley watched him. If he was homeless, the guy was hurting. He stumbled past the unmoving shape of the drunk and let him be. The alley mouth on the far end beckoned and the naked man headed in that direction. He winked out at times but then emerged, framed between two buildings and illuminated by streetlights.

She exhaled in relief and looked to the ground.

Her giblets had been righteously saved.

A screech of tires combined with a fleshy *clap* frightened her. She whipped around in time to see a car skidding to a stop. Someone screamed from inside the vehicle, the voice angry and a little freaked out, just seconds before the driver backed up and sped off into the night.

Haley looked to the alley mouth, the retreating car's roar in her ears.

What just happened? She waited, faltered on what to do for just a second, then burst into motion. A naked guy had saved her, high or not. She hurried to the other side, ignoring the still prone shape of her drunk attacker, and emerged underneath glaring streetlights. There, pushing himself to his hands and knees and showing a back that had been shredded to tatters of skin and bloody musculature, was the guy who'd saved her.

Perhaps it was the way he rose to his feet and looked around like a dazed boxer being warned by a referee. Perhaps it was because, despite his lack of clothing, the freak had saved Haley's bacon. Or perhaps it was because it was a damp fall night, and there was a person hurt and in need after a hit-and-run.

Whatever the reason, Haley Walker approached the injured stranger in the street. She took her warm coat off and, despite the blood streaming down his waist and over bare buttocks, bundled him up as best as she could.

He didn't resist.

19

With the shopping completed, the two wardens returned to the apartment building and lugged nearly a thousand dollars' worth of food up to Kirk's place. The time was just after six in the morning, and the sky remained dark with cloudy indecision. Bryce dumped most of the meat into the freezer, but not before selecting four roasts and slapping them on the kitchen counter. Kirk stowed the remaining food away in cupboards while trying hard not to take notice of Carma or make eye contact with her. The pack leader sat in the living room with the others leaning in, going over plans for the approaching hunt. A city map lay spread out over the coffee table, covering his paperback. Kirk frowned, hoping Carma didn't toss it away. A stream of thoughts, situations, lines and how they played out went through his mind, then, and he willed himself to stay cool, stay aloof, and let her come to him.

Only problem was… he knew she wouldn't come to him.

"Kirk, get in here," Carma said from the living room.

With a sigh, he finished stashing away the vegetables,

knowing that there was more grub in his apartment now than he'd kept on hand all last year. Wiping his nose and warning himself to be alert, he walked into the living room and faced the pack. Some names he picked up while he was working, and while he knew a little of Bryce and his particular personality, he knew nothing about the others.

"Where's this medical examiner's building?"

"On the southwest side of town." Kirk pointed to the location on the map.

"And Bailey ran where when he escaped?"

"Into the city," he replied, indicating a mesh of street names and lines.

"Won't be long then," said the other woman in the group, a slender, muscular brunette called Janice. She sat on the sofa, her legs crossed, dark eyes narrowed and emanating waves of hard ass.

Carma ignored her. "And we'll be searching right up to the end. In a suit, we can't sniff him out, and he's going to be in a suit until he changes. We can't change and comb the city for obvious reasons, so we'll stay in our own suits during the hunt."

Suits. Kirk rolled his eyes. He never got used to thinking of his own human flesh as a suit.

"Until we find him," said the Asian guy named Ken Cyler. Ken had tossed his winter coat off and stood with his arms crossed, sweater sleeves pushed up to his elbows. His heavily corded forearms resembled intertwined steel cables. His hair was buzzed short on the sides and spiked on top, displaying an angular face.

"Even then, you stay back and follow Bailey to his den. Don't spook him and don't engage him. No one fucking goes one-on-one with this thing. Hear that? Call here if and when you make contact. Two people will be here at all times and if you call, they'll relay the message to the rest, so keep your phones charged and make sure they're switched on. Wait for the rest of the pack to arrive on scene. When that happens, I'll assess the situation and we'll take Bailey as a unit. The elders prefer to have his body back but they've also informed me it's not a priority. As long as we can dispose of it correctly. So. Any questions?"

No one spoke up.

"All right, I'll be sending some of you out immediately. You'll be on your own. Call back here with updates every half hour and leave a message if you can't get through at the time. Stay on the line if you got him. Understood?"

Heads nodded.

Carma studied their faces in turn, even locking eyes with Kirk for a second. The brief contact lit up his spine.

"As of now, we have eight days before the next full moon. Eight. I don't think we'll have to wait that long, one way or the other. If history repeats itself, he'll be tearing into people while in his suit, which will bring the authorities into the picture. Our biggest concern will be that. I shouldn't have to say this, but I will…do not engage the police. If they shoot you and there's no way out, go down. Stay down, and escape the ambulance when it's en route to the hospital."

"What about Tasers?" Ken asked.

"Treat them as guns and go down."

"What if they shoot us in the head?" asked Sam Mausler, the war veteran. Stubbly and as tough as stropped leather, his gray eyes were sharp enough to pick up on individual auras.

"They won't shoot you in the head unless you give them reason to," Carma answered mechanically. "So don't give them reason to. You good?"

Tight-lipped and contemplative, Mausler nodded.

"Don't give anyone a reason to unload into your face. That's what brought us here, and if the police get wind of something beyond a naked crackhead running through the streets, they might opt for heavier firepower and escalate the situation to a level we don't want to deal with. We want this finished before the moon hits. Before Bailey changes. He'll be a pup all over again, with a capacity for violence on a scale that we're all aware of. And in a city of this size, that's a disaster waiting to happen. A time bomb."

Kirk blinked at the word. A time bomb. In downtown Halifax. A horror show just ticking away.

Carma looked to the Halifax warden. "Kirk, this is your town, but I want you here with me for the next few hours. There's one more warden coming in. We can start searching in teams now. In shifts. There are seven of us total here. That's almost double what the elders had in the field the last time this happened. Janice, Sam, Ian, and Ken, you guys are up. Head back to the medical examiners building and see if you can catch a scent and a trail. Go as far as you can before you lose it. Then split. Remember your streets and landmarks. Janice, you're north. Sam, south. Ken's west and

Ian's east. Get out there and start sniffing. I don't care if you're tired. For the next six hours, you're out there until I call you back. You good?"

The assortment of *weres* nodded. Kirk tried to relax, realizing he'd be around his apartment.

"One last thing," Carma said. "I've been thinking about the way this thing attacked Baxter, Ezekiel, and Morris. It smashed Baxter's head against a wall and tore out Ezekiel's throat. It broke Morris's neck. That tells me the thing might not remember exactly how to kill a *were*, but based on those attacks, I think it instinctively knows where to strike, even though it might not fully realize why. So be careful out there. It's not completely mindless."

No one moved, the pack leader's words instilling yet another layer of danger to the hunt.

"All right," Carma said. "Go pee if you have to. I suggest keeping your ears to the ground. Chase any police cars or ambulances with their lights flashing. It might not be our boy, but it might be our boy. Take Kirk's truck over to the site. Don't take any cabs and don't leave the truck in a place where someone might get curious about it. Keys."

She snapped her hand out to Kirk, who dug the set out of a pocket. When Carma had them, she passed them along to Ian.

The pack leader grew quiet then, eyes downcast, her features stern. "Happy hunting," she finally said.

The four wardens picked up their coats and went for the door. Kirk watched them depart, watching each of them leave.

"That's it?" he asked the pack leader.

Carma met his question with a blank face. "We stay here. Mind the treehouse and the wounded. Cook up some of the roasts and have food ready for when they get back. You know they burn through it fast. If they can eat, feed the wounded. You got a local news channel?"

Kirk looked at his small LCD flat screen. He didn't watch much on it, preferring to read when he wanted to relax. "Yeah."

"Then switch on that television. Bailey's out there and sooner or later, he'll hurt someone. When he does, there might very well be a news flash. That shit travels fast over today's tech. If Bailey strikes and the cops are called in, we can maybe intervene before there's a major loss of life. At the very least, we can pick up Bailey's scent from nearby. Better than chasing down every cop car with the lights flashing. Or ambulance, for that matter."

"Okay."

"And Kirk?"

"Yeah?"

"We're on guard duty, understand? So you get that lost puppy look off your goddamn face."

The words slapped him hard, harder than a bared palm to the cheek. He nodded.

"All right," Carma sighed. "Fire up that oven and let's get cooking."

"Don't want to eat raw?" Kirk asked, still stinging.

"Don't be a smartass," Carma warned. "Nobody likes a smartass."

It seemed strange to Kirk that in such a dire situation, with the city on the brink of mass killings, he'd be in the kitchen cutting up vegetables and splashing juice over simmering roasts. Carma fired up every burner, using every pot, pan, and the only roaster that came with the apartment. She then placed her phone on the kitchen counter, well within reach, tossed her coat onto a couch, and rolled up her sleeves.

Kirk was in charge of the cutting board and making things fit, while Carma puttered about, checking in on the recovering Morris and Ezekiel. Kirk allowed himself one peek at her as she passed through the apartment. Slim, barely a lick of body fat on her, and wearing a loose denim shirt and black jeans that hinted at an athletic frame. Not a trace of makeup, and skin tanned naturally by the sun. She radiated confidence, exuded military discipline. Kirk knew she could kick his ass twice over if she got angry enough.

The elders had sent their best. There was no question of who was in charge.

And because of that, he stayed close to the kitchen.

He checked on the roast, pulling the oven door down and peeking in at the chunk of meat. The heat baked his face, but the aroma.

Sweet.

But not the sweetest.

Kirk stood there, bent over, and remembered Morris's fumbling question about eating *weres*. His mouth moistened at the dark memory, one he'd tried to repress ever since Newfoundland. A forbidden hankering that initially gripped him while on the island, but had only increased over the months. A yearning for just what Morris had described, lurking within Kirk's mind and at every meal—the food ingested never satisfying his palate, always demanding a tad *more* and being denied every time. The trouble was, the craving never stopped. It only increased over time, until about a month ago, when he had to deal with it. While reading a book on his couch, a voracious hunger arose within his gullet like a winter squall, prompting him to gorge himself on everything in the apartment. He'd eaten everything he had—raw—but nothing appeased that voracious appetite. So he'd fled to a late-night grocery store, bought a forty-five-dollar prime rib roast, and devoured it raw in his kitchen. And the hardest thing to deal with, the absolute torture, was resisting the impulse to tear into the food while at the checkout counter. The drive home had been no picnic either.

And the sad thing was, after he had finally devoured the meat, the craving was still there. Only partially sated.

Kirk remembered how he'd bent over his kitchen countertop, chewing away like a rabid beaver and swallowing in chunks, eying up the next bite.

The oven heat brought him back, his face cooking. Kirk closed the lid, straightened, and placed a steadying hand on the nearby counter.

The first call came thirty minutes later and Carma answered, digesting the reports with stoic authority.

"Police are on-site," she said to Kirk, who stood wiping

his hands. "They guesstimated where Bailey might've hit the city. Now they're on foot."

"You think they'll find him?"

"We have to find him. And we have to find him before the next full moon. Else this city's gonna get a new asshole ripped."

"Yeah," Kirk agreed solemnly.

The two were interrupted by a third voice drifting from the bedroom. "Hey."

Carma immediately left the kitchen and Kirk fiddled with utensils before dropping them and following. Morris had woken up in bloodstained sheets and had shoved them down to his waist. Ezekiel lay beside him. The Pictou warden lifted his head weakly and grimaced at the two *weres*.

"Well, shit," Morris said without a smile. "Look who it is."

"Moses," Kirk greeted.

Morris frowned, hating his first name.

"Back from the dead," Carma said from the foot of the bed, ignoring the frown on the Pictou warden's face.

"Smelled dinner."

"Breakfast," Kirk corrected.

Carma went in close to Morris. "How you feel?"

"Achy. But getting better."

"You're recovering pretty damn fast," Carma noted.

Morris and Kirk shared a look then, one that the pack leader missed.

"Your neck was broken. And you were…" Carma inspected where his skin had broken and bled. "These are all healed."

Morris grunted. "Take it easy."

But Carma didn't appear to have heard. "I mean, healed. Not even a scar. Just crusted blood. Turn your head."

"I don't want to. Hurts."

"Turn your fucking head. You already moved it, so do it."

His frown deepening, Morris did so, left and right.

"How's that feel?" she asked.

"Okay."

"Like before?"

"Before what?"

"Don't fuck around," Carma warned him. "Before you got your goddamn neck snapped, that's before what."

Morris made a face like he was swallowing a shit sandwich. "Yeah. Like that. I'm good."

"Did you eat anything after you were attacked? To help yourself heal?" Carma asked, but then answered her own question. "But you were unconscious then. And banged up pretty bad."

Morris glanced at Ezekiel's still form and took a breath. "He stinks."

"You don't smell so good yourself," Carma said. She drew back and studied him. "You look fine."

"Feel fine."

But the puzzlement on Carma's face did not go away.

"It's a miracle," Morris whispered, feigning awe.

"It's something, but it ain't no miracle."

"What's cooking?" he asked.

"Beef roasts," Kirk reported. "Your favorite."

"Thanks."

"Bring him something," Carma said.

"Like what?"

"Goddammit Kirk, I don't know. Bring the poor bastard something to eat, okay?"

"Yeah, yeah," he grumbled and went off to find exactly that. He got a tray down from one of the cupboards, opened the oven and pulled the cooking meat close. He even got out a pack of hotdogs from the fridge. In five minutes he returned to the bedroom with a small hill of food.

Carma leaned against a wall while Morris sat up in bed. Ezekiel remained passed out, the mess of his neck slowly mending itself.

"Hotdogs," Carma said flatly. "You brought him hotdogs."

"Yeah, so?" Kirk asked. "The roast is pink."

"Pink is fine," Morris rumbled.

Kirk dropped the tray before him.

"Chicken lips and assholes," Carma smirked, flashing the first semblance of a smile since she arrived at the apartment. "All pushed into a pig's foreskin. Yum."

Morris ate one in two bites.

"Chew that," the pack leader said, folding her arms. "You'll get indigestion."

Morris ignored her.

"So," she said, turning her attention on Kirk. "While you were gone, Morris told me everything that happened inside. Bailey got out and killed the security force. Morris and company went in, busting open the door and allowing Bailey to escape into the wild. I would have agreed with Baxter's original plan, but I still wish you guys had held off until we got here."

Morris chewed away. Kirk kept his mouth shut.

"What's puzzling the hell out of me now is your rate of recovery."

Morris stopped, glowered, shrugged, and resumed eating.

"That all you have to say?"

"Nothin' else to say, honey."

Carma's features darkened. "You know something, Moses? I can smell shit. And shit is going on here. One look at you and then Ezekiel only proves it, not that I need the blatant comparison between brands A and B. I saw you when Kirk brought you in. You were stomped on. A lump of jelly. Now look at you. Look at Ezekiel. Who do you think you're talking to, here? Tell you what. You eat. Rest up. When you're ready, I'll listen."

The phone rang and Carma exited the bedroom to answer it. When she was gone, Kirk directed his baleful attention upon Morris.

Who went right on eating.

20

"You comfortable?"

The early morning sun speared through ripped old blankets that Haley had nailed over the windows. Dust particles rode the light. She stood at a safe distance from the man in her living room. The guy was a brute, but he possessed as much sense as an automaton. He still wore her coat across the shoulders, but it had been some protection against the cold. He had followed her back home through the waking streets and back alleys without so much as a grunt, like an exhausted dog without a collar. He was hard-looking, perhaps in his early thirties, but with wild, haunted eyes and a staring expression that bordered on traumatic.

Not once did he moan or show any signs of discomfort while they hiked back to her place. Haley was a little nervous as she led him along, making sure she kept her eyes averted from his freely swinging junk. After a while, she had tried asking a few questions, but only got the wide-eyed gawk that made her wonder if he'd hurt his head in the hit-and-run. That or perhaps he had mental issues. Haley couldn't decide.

She had brought him to the emergency entrance of the nearest hospital, but he didn't want to go in. Oddly, the lights seemed to agitate him. So Haley had done the next best thing.

She'd brought him home.

As she opened her front door, the startling rush of a hundred pigeons evacuating her attic all at once caused her to stare skyward. The birds streaked through the early Halifax morning in a mass of frantic migration.

Not that she'd miss the little shitters.

It was presently mid-morning, and Haley tried to make the strange man feel at home. He sat in the frayed easy chair, looking at her and the surroundings, his bare feet flat against smooth floorboards swept clean. An old blanket lay across his legs, covering up his nakedness and keeping him warm.

"Do you hear me at all?" Haley asked.

He studied her with a Neanderthal's curiosity.

"Can you remember anything that happened a couple hours ago?"

No response.

"A car hit you. After you fought off a drunk who was attacking me."

The guy blinked, smacked his lips and swallowed, but didn't say a word.

Haley scratched at her gray hair. "A name, maybe?"

She'd asked that one before and got the same blank look. "Just my luck, I guess. The first man I bring home in years and you're brain dead."

That comment left her in a foul mood. She frowned and

folded her arms. "Sorry. That was uncalled for. I'm a survivor myself, and here I am badmouthing you. You take your time. I don't have much to eat here, but I do have water. A couple of buckets full. I take it from the public washrooms or fountains. Hasn't killed me yet."

She smiled at him and, to her surprise, one corner of the guy's face hitched in return. Then it was gone.

"I don't have any clothes that'll fit you, so you just stay here and I'll head down to the shelter. They have bins full of clothing. Used, but you can't really tell. I'd say you're a size thirty-three in the waist? Extra-large? Yeah? Well, a little bigger won't hurt you. Shoe size about what? Eleven? Twelve? I'll try elevens. See if they have anything. Stay there now."

Holding up a halting hand, she backed away from her guest, and he tracked her leaving with his eyes. She wasn't nervous around him. The poor soul had saved her. That counted for something. And if he was going to try anything, he could've done it long ago. The least she could do was get him in out of the cold and get some decent clothes on him.

A closet held an assortment of towels she'd found in a garbage heap. The cheap thin kind, but they would absorb some amount of blood. She took out a particularly large sweatshirt that she sometimes wore on cold nights as a final outer layer. It might fit him. She returned to the living room with an armload, the sounds of morning traffic permeating the house's old walls.

Her guest perked up when she entered.

"Let me see that back of yours," she said, coming in close

and going around the chair. He leaned back instead, so Haley placed a hand on his broad shoulder and gently pushed him forward. His head twisted left and right, questioning her intentions, and when she attempted to lift the back of the coat, his eyes narrowed.

"Listen," she said, staring into those black orbs and sensing the tension. "I better check. You got wicked road rash. I mean really bad. You should've let me take you to the hospital at least. If any of that gets infected, well, you know what that'll mean."

Whether it was the soft warning in her voice or the words, he relaxed. Haley pulled the coat up.

And up.

Her breath caught in her throat.

Spiny knobs and shoulder blades flexed and rippled under the new skin of her guest's back. Not a blemish. Haley smoothed the area that had once resembled a peeled tomato with a backbone. The flesh and muscle were warm and strong.

"My Lord," Haley whispered, and his ears visibly moved. "And here I was worried about the coat." A joke, and a bad one. She hoisted up the coat to his upper shoulders and searched for wounds, any wounds from the early morning, and found nothing. There were bloodstains inside the coat but nothing else.

Haley released the material, allowing it to drop.

"Well, that's not right," she whispered. She faced the man and studied his earnest features. He studied her in return. "You should be—should be delirious with pain. I saw your back. You looked like you'd been skinned with a cheese grater."

She retreated to a beanbag chair, one she'd lugged all the way from the trash of Marty's Home Fixin's, and plopped down in it. She tapped her temples and concentrated on the events in the alley.

The man wearing her coat watched her, and for long moments she sat and thought about what she'd seen that morning. She'd been attacked, and her pulse rate had certainly been rushing, but she'd seen his back, even *grimaced* at his back.

And now look at it.

Haley massaged her temples. The first two years of the last nine had been a horror show, wherein her memory only permitted selected peeks when she was asleep. Those two dark years so long ago had started when her husband and daughter died in a highway car crash outside of Dartmouth. A drunk driver had rammed into Chris's car from behind, spinning him like a clumsy top, a full three-sixty degrees, and right into the opposing traffic lane.

Where a huge diesel transport hit their vehicle dead center, mashing them like potatoes.

Or so the police informed her that afternoon. She could summon the memory too fast, too well. The smell returned to her first, always the smell, of spaghetti sauce cooking in a pot, and garlic bread in the oven, wafted by her frozen form in the doorway as the police officers' solemn faces informed her at once something very bad had happened. The worst kind of bad. Haley had been a single child herself, both of her parents gone to Cancer. She had no relatives known to her and no one to turn to, so it really wasn't a big surprise that, upon learning her man and her six-year-old daughter would not ever be coming for supper… well… she went a little crazy. She remembered being admitted to a hospital, some needles, counseling (a little), and pills—many, many pills, as bright as candy on a cake. To this day she still believed Chris and Terri had visited her while she was cat-scratching at the ward's walls, telling her all would be well, and that they waited for her to return home.

Those two years had been the worst. Times were better now, but the sense of loss, of emptiness, remained. She had lost all drive, all desire to continue with her job at the bank, and over time, most of her friends. From that life, anyway. She stopped interacting with the old world. She walked Halifax's streets, doing things that needed to be done to survive, but sometimes just doing things. Taking things. Chemical things. Drugs that had summoned elaborate dreams where she and Chris and Terri still lived in their house, talking about what they would do after supper. In time, the dreams would hit her while she was wide awake and sober, fooling her with false realities. Four years after coming clean and swearing off drugs, the hallucinations still struck at times. Unexpected times.

Haley's hands dropped from her face and she considered the silence, wondering about the man in her scrounged easy chair.

"You're real," she announced.

The guy stared back.

She leaned forward and poked his forearm. He frowned at the unnecessary prodding, but otherwise didn't react.

"That's it, then," she said and rubbed her cheeks. "I imagined the road rash. Maybe even the car hitting you. Definitely the road rash. Not the first time. Won't be the last. I could tell you stories. Hoo-boy, could I."

She chuckled, showing chipped teeth in dire need of dental attention.

"They weren't real. Well." Haley stood and sighed with relief. "You hungry?"

No answer. She should have realized that by now.

"Well, okay, listen. I've got some things in the kitchen. Not much but…" She would share. "And maybe while you're eating, I'll slip on down to the shelter there and pick out some clothes for you? Some sneakers, too? Can't have you walking around town with your tackle swinging in the wind."

That brought about a smile, and for the second time, the man flashed a wan, uncertain smile right back at her.

"You stay there."

She got up and went to her modest kitchen, remembering the bloodstains. That sent a confused vibe through her person. There was blood on the coat. It sure as hell wasn't her blood.

The realization stopped her in the doorway. She looked back into the living room.

He returned her questioning stare.

21

The knock at the door summoned Kirk from the kitchen. He peeked through the peephole, saw a man he didn't recognize, and opened the door.

"You Doug Kirk?" the visitor asked.

Kirk caught himself staring. The man at his door stood roughly eye-to-eye with him, but the collection of scars covering his face could make a person wonder if he had dove headfirst into a wood chipper. A five o'clock shadow had bare runnels through it, reminding the Halifax warden of claws. A razor had done an equally fine job on the guy's scalp. The gray eyes were as pure as smoky glass.

"Yeah," Kirk said.

"Something wrong?" the man asked with a half-smile, showing white teeth.

"Just wondering… if I should call the cops now or later."

The stranger chuckled and shrugged his wide shoulders. He wore a fall leather jacket that might have been stitched together from the best cuts of a bunch of baseball catcher mitts.

"I get that a lot," the bright-eyed man said. "I'm Nick Dyer. I'm the last visitor to come calling, I think."

"Come on in," Kirk said and got out of the way.

"Just in time for lunch, I smell?"

"Yeah, sure," Kirk closed the door.

"Excellent, looking forward to some fine Halifax cuisine."

"You're from where?"

"New England, mostly. Milo, Maine, recently. Representing."

"Ah, well, all I have on are—"

"Roast beef and veggies," Dyer said, looking around the interior. "A feast."

"Not exactly cuisine."

"I was just sayin' that. Anything you got and are willing to share, I'm down with. There were no meals on my flight."

In the living room, Carma threw back the curtains to sunlight inside. Dust scattered and rode the currents. She turned upon hearing the exchange, and hitched her hands on her hips upon seeing Dyer.

Who nodded affably at her.

"You're Dyer?"

"I am."

"You're it, then," she said and lifted her chin. "We're all aboard. For better or worse."

"For the better," Dyer said and looked around. "Where's everyone?"

"Out hunting," Kirk said and earned a scowl from the pack leader.

"Out hunting," Carma repeated.

Dyer nodded in approval. "Yeah, okay. So where do you want me?"

"Hold on here. I've got people coming back soon. You'll go out with the next wave."

"Okay. Sounds good."

Morris walked out of the bedroom, buttoning up a black shirt that hung over a rumpled set of jeans much too short.

"Jesus Christ, you've got Big Foot in here," Dyer exclaimed softly.

"Fuck off, Nicky."

"Fun to see you, too," Dyer said, with that now familiar half-smirk. "You've shaved, I see. Can't say it's an improvement. You look like a bald testicle."

"Yeah," Morris scoffed and looked to Kirk. "You got anything bigger? Feel like I jammed my boys into a sock. Awfully tight in the crotch."

"No, I do not have anything bigger. And that's a favorite shirt of mine."

"You two know each other?" Carma asked.

"This guy?" Dyer pointed a finger at Morris. "Who doesn't know him on the east coast? He pops up every now and again like a fuckin' communicable rash. And most folks prefer the rash."

Kirk smiled at that.

"Morris likes crossing the border unannounced," Dyer said slyly. "Without notifying the proper authorities. And sometimes takes to snacking on chickens like they're noisy popcorn."

"I was drunk."

"So, anyway," Dyer continued, unfazed. "The first time I met him is still my fondest memory. Picture Morris, chicken feathers flying, freaking out some poor folks about twenty-five, twenty-six miles outta town. I pick up his scent and converge. Well. Long story short, excitement ensued. Ask me sometime about the scars on my chin and my ass. Over beers. Or a bottle of Captain Morgan. And why do I smell dead people?"

That left the other three wardens quiet.

"In the bedroom," Carma said. "Baxter Ryan."

"Baxter?" Dyer's good humor evaporated. "Baxter's dead?"

"I put him down," Carma said. "This is what we know…"

After a history recap that lasted almost ten minutes, the apartment door opened and Janice and Cyler returned from their hunts. The disruption left Dyer noticeably quiet, Kirk saw, and when introductions were made, the Maine warden remained affected by the news of Baxter's death.

Janice Glover's attention, however, was centered on the up and walking Moses Morris.

"Holy shit," she said, "the hell happened to you?"

"I got better," Morris deadpanned.

"Okay, let me rephrase that. How'd you get better so fucking fast?"

"Ladies don't swear," Morris said and walked for the kitchen, but Janice stepped into his path.

"And dead slabs shouldn't be walking. Last I saw you,

you were just a lump under some bloody sheets. Now look at you. As fresh as a daisy and modeling new clothes. Anyone else not find this goddamn unusual?"

"I think it's goddamn unusual," Cyler commented.

"Yeah," Carma said, "I think it's time you reveal your secret."

"What's going on?" Dyer asked, attention switching from one talking head to the other.

Janice gestured to Morris. "This guy was a bloody carcass this morning. I mean he was a chunk of meat. And now look at him."

Morris's back straightened, his features darkened. He wasn't enjoying Janice's line of reasoning and it showed.

"But wait," she said to Dyer. "To fully appreciate how much damage he took along with Ezekiel and Bax—who isn't with us anymore—go take a look at Ezekiel in the bedroom."

Dyer glanced at Morris, then back at Janice. Without a word, he slipped into the bedroom containing the recuperating Ezekiel. The Pictou Warden stared down at the smaller woman, and Janice stared right back, unafraid. Dyer returned as Mausler and Bryce entered the apartment. They, too, showed surprise at Morris's health.

Even Dyer studied Morris with a critical eye. "What've you been eating?"

"Nothing," Morris replied sourly, meeting Kirk's worried look. The question was a glib one, just a quip, but the Maine warden had no idea of how close it struck home.

"You've been doing something," Janice said.

"Damn straight," Ian Bryce said. "You should've been laid up for a few days at least. Not hours."

"Ezekiel is gonna take at least a few days with that throat of his," Dyer said, inspecting Morris's frame.

"I don't know what to tell you," Morris said. "I feel fine. I heal fast. What can I say."

"Hell, how can I get a part of that?" Sam Mausler asked. "Anything that can speed up the process is a good thing."

"Exactly," Janice added. "Which is why I want to know how come he's healed so quick."

Kirk cleared his throat. "Listen, we really don't have time for this. There's a monster out there and we only have a short time before he awakens. Morris heals fast. All right, but is that a bad thing? I don't think it is. And frankly, neither should any of you. Right now, it's the least of our worries."

That instilled silence about the room and a few suspicious glances.

"All right," Janice said. "It's not a priority right now. But Morris, we know something's wrong here. You think about that. If you got something to say, you better say it now. Especially since we're going after a monster. God as my witness, I can smell the indecision off you. It's unnatural."

"Back off, Janice," Kirk heard himself say. "You're talking to a warden there."

Janice regarded him, a question hooking an eyebrow, and the tension in the room swelled. "Why are you defending him?"

"I'm saying back off, is all. If Morris has anything to say, he'll say it. I was with him the whole time."

"Didn't you say you were in the truck the whole time? Which is why you got away without a scratch?"

Kirk winced inside.

"Something's off here," Janice said to Carma. "Something definitely not right. And Morris knows exactly what's not right."

Morris took a breath. "Look. Let's figure things out after we bag that bastard out there."

"Think you're up for it?"

"Always up for it."

A sharp smile unzipped across Janice's face then, suggesting she would be more than ready to hear his story.

"All right," Carma said, releasing the building tension in the room. "Whatever it is can wait. He's healed. We'll need him. We'll need Ezekiel, too, if he comes back from the dead in time. This hunt's only just started."

She glanced in Kirk's direction. "Let's eat."

The smell of food cooking steered them away, but Morris shared a look with Kirk. The wardens knew *something* was off. They wouldn't let it go until they found out what it was. Kirk and Morris knew it.

Carma met the Halifax warden's eyes as she walked past him. That one glance informed Kirk that the pack leader also knew something was off about Morris.

And Kirk knew she fully intended to find out what it was.

22

Haley held up a large brown sweater that might have belonged to a fisherman and inspected its lovely pattern. She checked the tag, saw that it was an extra-large, and stuffed it into a weathered green eco-bag hanging off the crook of her left arm. She moved to another clothes rack filled with T-shirts, noticing a few other people furtively moving amongst the aisles of goods. Of all the shelters in Halifax-Dartmouth, the one at the north end of Barrington was the best. An old brick and mortar community hall built in the early seventies, the basketball court had been transformed into an all-in-one clothing pit stop. Divided into women, men, and children's sections, one could peruse the aisles of clean, used clothing, take what they liked, and get the items checked off a list at a volunteer's table. The shelter used the same system for its distribution of food, and Haley reminded herself to bring home a few edibles if she could find them. The activity placed her in a good mood. She'd missed shopping for another person.

A pair of T-shirts went inside the bag. She picked out

some faded but serviceable jeans, selected two pairs of donated black sweat socks, which were new, and a pair of regular underwear. Picking up underwear for a grown man made her a little uneasy. She certainly wouldn't want a stranger choosing underwear for her, but an exception had to be made in the case of her unnamed guest. Perhaps he'd remember his name soon. Maybe his amnesia would be lifted by the time she returned home. That was something to hope for. Only then would she get a straight answer about how the guy's back had miraculously healed. A part of her still wondered if she was in some kind of elaborate hallucination, and he would be gone entirely once she got back home.

But most of her believed he *was* real. That he did save her. That his back *had* healed. And that he needed help. In any case, weird or not, she'd do a favor in return. Get him clothed at least, and turn him over to the shelter. Point him in the right direction, anyway.

She wandered over to the shoe selection—about five tables pushed together and displaying donated and secondhand footwear of various styles and sizes for all ages.

Elevens, she mused. She wanted elevens, and unfortunately there was nothing available. She found a pair of hiking boots that might fit her man—the reference set her eyes rolling—and plucked them from the table. The last thing she picked up was a large blue-gray parka, which she folded and tucked under her free arm.

With her shopping completed, she wandered over to the checkout table where Heather Scheelock and Mario Howe stood and chatted. Both volunteers were dressed for the season, and Heather, in particular, had a pleasant outdoor glow about her. Haley thought her nice enough but Mario could be a little too nosy at times.

"Hi Haley," Heather chirped while Mario offered a faint smile. "Did you find anything?"

"Yes, I did," she answered and pulled the articles of clothing and boots out of the bag. "Here."

"Getting colder out there," Heather said as Mario pulled the numbers off the clothing for inventorying.

"It is. It is. Hope the snow stays away this year."

"You got a friend now?" Mario asked bluntly, looking up from his clipboard and cocking an eyebrow at the clothing she'd collected.

"I do have a guest at the house."

"You know him?" he asked.

"Ah, he's a stray," Haley said. "Followed me home. Someone must have jumped the poor guy and swiped all his clothing. Had his back all cut up and bled all over my coat."

"Oh dear," Heather said, but her demeanor had chilled at the mention of a man.

"He's all right," Haley said. "He actually saved me last night. Some drunk asshole had me cornered. Who knows what might've happened if he hadn't come along."

"Oh dear Lord."

"What's his name?" Mario asked.

"I don't know yet."

"You don't know but he's at your house?"

"Poor guy seems to have a case of amnesia."

Mario exchanged a pensive look with Haley. "You want me to drop by? Maybe bring him back here? Might be safer for you."

Haley thought about it. "I'm fine. I'll bring him back here this afternoon anyway. Just have to get him some clothes first."

"You're going to bring him around here?" Heather asked.

"Yes. For supper."

"Good," Mario said and returned to his clipboard. "We can get a look at him then."

He wandered off toward a bin of used clothing that had been washed but not processed for the shelter's regulars, leaving Heather and Haley alone.

"You sure you're okay?" Heather asked, studying the older lady's face for signs of duress.

"I'm fine," Haley assured her with a bright smile. "The guy saved my life, I think. Or at least a beating. A car hit him and drove off. He's all disoriented. He wouldn't go to the hospital so I felt I had to do something to repay him. I wouldn't have done it if I felt threatened. Give me some credit."

"There wasn't any head trauma?"

"None that I could tell."

Heather nodded and smiled at the end. "That the coat with the blood?"

Haley realized it was. She nodded.

"Let's find you something better. I'll clean that one up and return it to the rack if that's okay with you."

"Oh, yes, certainly. Thank you so much."

Heather moved around the table and guided Haley by the arm. "You'll be back for supper later?"

"I will."

"And you'll bring him along?"

"I will."

"You're a good person, Haley."

"I know I'm a good person. I *am* a good person."

"Good. So you know it might be best for him to stay the night here."

"You have the beds?"

"We have a couple. How are you doing at your place?"

"They'll be tearing it down in the spring."

"You should come here, too," Heather said as she led her to the coat section. "When the snow comes. Don't be cold, Haley."

"I have blankets," she smiled. "But thanks anyway. I'm okay. That old house has been my home for the last few years. I'm attached to it. Be sad once it's gone."

Heather reached out and gave the old woman's shoulder a comforting rub. "You're a tough customer, you know that? I just don't know why you're still over there."

"You know why," Haley countered. "I like being on my own. I like the privacy over there."

"I just think it's dangerous."

It was, Haley admitted, but she knew the shelters could be dangerous as well. There'd been instances where unstable individuals had erupted into furies. Violent fits which required the police to intervene. At least at her house, she got to choose who stayed with her.

"Maybe when they finally destroy the house, I'll sign up for that 'roommates wanted' list. See if I can pick up a job somewhere and make another go of it. I think… I think I'm ready."

"Glad to hear it," Heather said and gave Haley's shoulder a squeeze. "And remember, supper's at five thirty. Chicken soup."

Haley would be there. Along with her houseguest.

"Now," Heather inspected the rack of ladies' coats. "Let's see, what about this one?"

The ancient Victorian regarded Haley in the overcast afternoon light, like a beaten boxer with a ruined smile, perched on a stool and recognizing an old friend. Paint peels littered the patches of yellow grass. Weathered clapboard that had withstood countless seasons and the storms that came with them hung in tatters, exposing tufts of insulation underneath and the odd bird's nest. The windows on the ground floor had been smashed, but the blankets held. One room on the second floor, facing away from the street, still had its windows intact, and that was where Haley slept on a pair of stacked mattresses.

An old beast of a house, but it had given her shelter during her dark times. Its days were numbered and it made her sad. She climbed the crumbling stairway to the front door and patted the doorframe's bare wood. She knocked before entering, just to give him a heads up. The knob was gone—had been missing when she first found the place—so she'd improvised, using a length of frayed rope looped through the resulting hole. She unwound the rope's end around a four-inch nail driven into the outside frame, fingers brushing the wood as she worked. She entered, closed the door behind and placed a pair of two-by-fours against the door, bracing it from within.

"There," she said and gathered up her shopping bag. "I'm back."

She wandered into the damp-smelling living room and there he was, lifting himself from the bare floor where he'd apparently gone to sleep. He studied her as if he'd been napping for years, yawned, and palm-screwed his eyes.

"You slept on the floor?" she asked. "The chair would've been more comfortable. There was a mattress upstairs, too, for that matter."

She caught herself, realizing the only mattress was her own bed, and felt the embarrassment explode into autumn blooms upon her cheeks.

"Well, anyway, I got you some clothes. And some boots. You were lucky."

The man sat and stared at her, and Haley wondered if he even understood the language.

"Here, then," she said and unloaded her goods into the easy chair. That got him standing, looking at the clothing with curiosity.

"Take that off and put this on."

He looked at her with the T-shirt and underwear in his hand.

"I'll leave it here, okay, and step outside."

She tossed the clothes onto the chair and retreated to the hall. "Get them on now, okay? You get them on and we'll head on back to the shelter. Get some hot food in you. I've been thinking you should stay there as well. For the night. I mean, thanks for helping me and all, but I don't feel so comfortable with you in the house. I think it's best, y'know?"

Silence from the living room.

"You'll be fine at the shelter. They have showers, and beds if you're lucky to get one. It can be crowded over there. At the very least they'll put some blankets on the floor for you. It's warm, but you'll have to put up with other people snoring and farting. But it's warm so that's nice. How you doing in there?"

No answer.

Haley peeked around the corner and saw the guy, standing like a dog waiting for a command, looking back at her.

"What are you waiting for?"

An expression of keen concentration, but otherwise no response.

"Well, geez, are you okay?" Haley went to him and studied his face. "I mean really okay? Say something, at least."

But he did not.

"You gotta put these clothes on. And take that off."

If he understood, he didn't show it.

"Oh Jesus Christ," Haley fumed and hitched her hands on her hips. "You can't go anywhere like that."

His deep brown eyes showed not a lick of understanding.

"I'm going to help you get dressed, okay? So don't freak out or anything."

With that, she opened the plastic containing the underwear and flapped them out before her. The snap of cloth made the man blink and frown.

"Relax. It's only underwear. Briefs. Drawers. Tighty whiteys."

Haley held them out and sighed again when he didn't react.

"You have to put them on yourself, okay? Like this."

And she squeezed into them herself, feeling like a fool the whole time, but it became clear he didn't know either the clothing's purpose or how to put them on.

"Okay," she said, and pulled the shorts off. She held them out to him. "Now you try."

To her surprise, he took the briefs, clumsily stepped into them and hauled them over his hips. Haley steadied him at times when he teetered, but in the end, he got them on.

"Excellent. All right, then. Let's try the rest. Take that off and put this on."

He made no effort to remove her sweatshirt.

"You aren't easy, are you?" Haley smiled. To her surprise, he smiled back.

Right before he pissed himself.

23

"You know there's something up with him, right?"

Janice sat upon Kirk's sofa with a cup of coffee. The steam from the black brew blew apart before her face as she talked. The guys who had been out on the morning hunt had crashed at various points around the apartment, and Carma decided to keep Kirk back and save him for the night. Kirk obeyed while she, Morris, and Dyer ventured into Halifax's urban wilds.

"Yeah," Kirk said in a low voice, sitting in the easy chair across from her.

"I mean," Janice continued, "you think about it, he and Ezekiel were the only ones in contact with that thing, right? We don't know anything about it. All we know is that it's a monster and on the loose and that shit's gonna fly come the next full moon. We have no idea if it remembers anything, or if, by some weird chance, it even knows what it is."

"Good point."

"If Bailey had his head shot off, who knows what could've happened to him, right? Who knows what he's capable of, and who the fuck knows what he might pass on to *us*."

That narrowed Kirk's eyes in thought.

"Yeah, that's right. What if something happened to Bailey when he got his head blown off? Something more than just having nothing on his shoulders. Maybe… maybe something was released in him and Morris contracted it when he fought it."

Kirk struggled not to squirm. "Ezekiel still hasn't healed."

"Not like Morris. Which makes me wonder if maybe Morris got bit or something. Something that might've infected him somehow, but… maybe in a good way? Which is weird but also thought-provoking."

"A lot of somethings."

"I know, right?" Janice exclaimed and sipped her coffee. She looked toward the picture window with the curtains opened about a foot and mulled. "A lot of things to consider. Be easier if you'd been in the same fight and gotten fucked up. Then we'd see how fast you'd recover."

Kirk smiled thinly at that.

"Morris is all right. Don't get me wrong. I don't think he's gonna freak out on us or anything, okay? He's grade-A hardass, but he's *our* hardass. We'll figure out what's going on with him," Janice said, studying him from underneath a lowered brow. "I know Morris, too. Know his reputation. And for the record, I don't think a case of rapid healing is a bad thing, I just want to know how and why he can do it. I mean, he was a sack of broken bones and skin when you brought him back, right? Who knows what his insides might've looked like. But he's out there now as if he downed a couple of beers and a handful of painkillers. Like a kid all hopped up on caffeine and sugar. All good to go."

"All good to go," Kirk repeated, shifting from one ass cheek to the other.

"It's just all weird, is all I'm saying. In need of an explanation."

"I hear you."

Janice took in another mouthful of coffee and studied Kirk for a few moments. "You know, you're all right. I can tell."

"You are, too."

When he'd first met her, Kirk didn't think she was anything to look at, but in the shade of the room, after the sense of urgency had abated somewhat, he saw that he was wrong. Janice Glover probably got more than enough attention with her untouched looks. Plain, perhaps, but there was a natural vitality about her that crept up on Kirk, and she was intelligent with a rock star's edginess. After an hour in her company, Kirk knew Janice didn't care what others thought of her, and that confidence in itself was as powerful as a magnet.

"You've been in Halifax a while, huh?" she asked softly.

"Yeah."

"Like it?"

"It's okay."

"We'll see what we can do to keep the peace. Got a damn impressive crew here. Carma in particular is one serious bitch who gets things done."

Kirk didn't doubt that in the least.

"Don't worry if she doesn't like you. I don't think she likes anyone."

"She liked me, once."

Kirk met Janice's eyes in an instant of skin-shriveling horror, realizing what he'd said.

"You and her?" Janice smiled slyly, nodding with approval. "You get around, don't you, Douglas?"

"I didn't say that."

"You didn't have to. Your face did."

Kirk puckered up sourly as if he'd just tasted ass.

"So you guys had a thing?"

Jesus. Kirk rubbed his forehead before eventually nodding.

"You and her? Wow. But it's over?"

"Long over."

"Is that why you're moping around this place? And the reason this place smells like a mattress pulled out of a sewer?"

Despite trying not to, Kirk shifted and the sofa chair's springs squealed softly.

"Don't worry, don't worry," Janice soothed, her smile dispelling the steam from her remaining coffee. "I won't say anything. Not like I'm best buddies with the woman. I'm not. Believe me. Alpha males, my ass. Try alpha *females*. I'll deal with the menfolk any day of the week. Are you guys on good terms or…? Have you spoken to her since she got here?"

Kirk sighed. "No."

"Uh-huh," Janice said, unblinking. "And she's not going to talk to you unless she really has to. Well, some things just became clearer."

"Where you from, anyway?" Kirk asked.

"Whole bunch of places. Recently Grand Falls. Know it?"

"No."

"Well, word of advice, if I were you looking to get her attention—"

"I'm not looking to get her attention."

The right side of Janice's cheek puffed out as her tongue prodded it. "If you were looking to get her attention, you should clean yourself up a bit. Shave the beard. Or at least trim it. You're not entirely a meat bag. There's potential there. Just put the time in, s'all I'm saying."

"Thanks," Kirk said and then glared. "But I'm not—"

"Yeah, yeah, but I'm saying if you *were*," Janice stressed. "Christ. Try and help a guy out. Not that you need it. Well, much."

"What do you mean?"

Janice didn't answer right away, content to study him. "You don't know anything about *weres*, do you?"

"Huh?"

"Or wolves in general?"

Kirk didn't quite know how to respond to that. Snores ripped from the bedrooms, filling the gap in conversation.

"It's gonna get bad, isn't it?" Kirk asked, hoping this time the subject stayed changed.

"This hunt?"

"Yeah."

Janice shrugged. "Strong possibility for it. Maybe we'll get lucky. Maybe we won't."

"My luck we won't."

"You been in situations like this before?"

Memories of Newfoundland flashed in his mind. "Yeah. Once."

"Where?"

"Newfoundland."

"Didn't hear about it. Not surprising, the way the network is. What happened?"

Kirk sighed. "A *were* went crazy. Killed some people and other *weres*. Morris and I were called in to put him down. More people got killed, but we got things done pretty quick. Just overnight, in fact."

"That might happen here," Janice said, and Kirk was thankful she didn't press for details.

"It might. You ever do anything like this before?"

"No. Nothing like this. I'm a youngster compared to some of you. Only sixty-seven."

She looked barely in her mid-twenties.

"I've had a few tussles with a couple of *weres* going a little crazy, but I straightened them out myself."

"By yourself?"

Janice took offense. "What? I look too much like a girl to you?"

"No, not at all, you look more than capable enough."

"What's that supposed to mean?"

Kirk kept his mouth shut.

"Relax," Janice smiled. "Giving you a hard time is all. Getting sleepy and I get cranky when that happens. I'll probably drift off here in a few minutes anyway. Gonna be some long days this week. Maybe even next week, too, if we're unlucky. Get some sleep if you can."

She stretched out on the sofa.

Kirk thought she looked comfortable, so he leaned back in the sofa chair, took a deep breath, and rested his head.

The knock at the door opened his eyes. Janice was already sitting up and staring, the contrast of white socks and black jeans reminding Kirk of cookies for some reason. He stood to see who had come a'knocking. To his surprise, it was two men.

"Yeah?" Kirk asked as he opened the door.

"You Kirk?" one of the pair asked, a land pirate with a well-trimmed goatee and blue eyes. The other one looked like an evil twin. Both were dressed in white overalls with a crest of some sort upon their left chest pockets. A waist-high container that resembled a huge fish box was between the men.

"Yeah."

"You got a package for us?"

A package? Kirk looked from one to the other and bade them enter. They rolled the container inside and the warden closed the door. Janice had risen from the sofa, watching the interaction.

"He's in there," Kirk pointed, indicating the room containing the fallen Baxter Ryan.

The two men went inside without a word and studied

the dead warden's remains.

"You got his badge?" one asked before spotting the weapon on the nearby nightstand. "Ah, I see it."

The second mover retrieved the weapon. He placed it in a thigh pocket while the first guy unfolded a great black plastic slip. The zipper shrieked as the mover yanked it open with two jerks. In a few seconds, he smoothed out the body bag beside the dead warden.

"We'll take care of this," the second mover said to Kirk and the assembled *weres*. "We'll take the sheets as well."

"You're taking him out in that?" Cyler appeared in the doorway, gesturing at the box.

"Do it all the time."

"Little obvious, isn't it?"

"It's a fish container," the first mover said with a frown. "You want us to roll him up in a carpet or something?"

Cyler looked skeptical.

The movers got on either side of the body. They hefted the corpse off the bed and deposited him into the black sheath. Kirk watched as they zipped Baxter up and transplanted him into the fish container, all without comment.

"Jesus," Janice said. "Nice to know how we're going out when it's time."

"You expecting a hearse or something?" Mover Two asked.

"Expecting a little more respect."

That drew both movers up and they stopped for an awkward moment, one actually pausing with the box lid in his hand. They returned to their work without comment and sealed the container with a few well-placed slaps and locks.

"Excuse us," Mover One said as he rolled the container into the hallway. Mover Two pushed as well with a glazed expression, as if hugely bored. They caught a corner of the door on the way out, and that summoned glares from both men. Then they were outside.

Mover Two faced the four wardens. "Call us again if you need us."

"Like fuck," Bryce muttered, and Kirk, taking the cue, slammed the door behind the pair.

"Jesus," a shocked Cyler said. "What a life."

"Just don't die, is all," Bryce said and returned to the bedroom. Cyler followed him.

Kirk studied the bare bed. The two movers had taken all the sheets. He'd fetch fresh ones from the linen. "You can sleep in here if you want."

"Think I will," Janice said, and walked toward the curtains. "Come here."

Kirk joined her at the window and they peeked down at the parking lot. Two minutes later, the movers rolled the fish box containing Baxter Ryan into view and toward what looked like a small, ordinary truck. They opened the rear and wheeled the container inside.

"Interesting," Janice said.

"Why's that?" Kirk asked, watching the pair jump out of the back and close the door.

"That truck," Janice indicated with a nod. "See that unit just behind the driver's cab?"

"Yeah. So?"

"It's a refrigeration unit. That truck is a moving freezer."

"Baxter was getting ripe."

"Where do they take him anyway?"

"Good question," Kirk said.

"That's one for Carma," Janice said, releasing the curtain.

"I'm going to sleep for a bit," Janice sighed and moved past Kirk. "You got them sheets handy?"

24

"Here he is," Haley announced, presenting a well-bundled individual to Heather Scheelock, Mario Howe, and the shelter's coordinator, Andy Houston. Andy was closer to Haley's age but with a lot more mileage. With his thinning hair and narrow glasses, the man resembled a frayed accountant more than a person who oversaw the running of one of Halifax's larger shelters.

"Hello," Heather beamed, extending her hand to the newest arrival—who didn't take it.

"He's not the quickest, is he?" Mario smirked.

"Smarten up, Mario," Andy warned, mildly peeved with the breach of etiquette. "Who knows what this man has been through. But to be clear, we will need a name for him."

"He never told me," Haley said, remembering how she had to clean him up after he soiled himself. The big guy never so much as whimpered as she wiped him down, changed his shorts, and then dressed him a second time with a firm warning not to do his business in such a manner again. To her surprise, the guy actually wilted under her scolding, which made her feel bad.

"How long have you known him?" Andy asked.

"Only since last night. He helped me out," Haley met Heather's eyes for a brief second, "and then he was hit by a car and left in the street. The driver sped off. Classic hit-and-run."

"Hm." Andy adjusted his glasses as he inspected the taller man. "Well, it's not uncommon for traumatized victims to experience memory loss. Suppressing or shutting the door, so to speak, on certain selective memories. And he could've landed on his head. Not too often we come across full-blown amnesia."

"Could we call a doctor?" Heather suggested.

"Better to bring him on down to the hospital," Andy remarked.

"I tried that," Haley said. "The hospital didn't appeal to him. He wouldn't go near the place."

"Well, he has to go."

"I tried, Andy. He won't. Refused to."

"Interesting." Andy studied the stranger again. "What's the reason behind that, I wonder?"

"Don't know. He saw the lights and wouldn't go another step."

Andy glanced at his watch. "Well, it's almost five now. How about we have him stay with us overnight, and we'll see what we can do in the morning, hm? Maybe his memory will come back during the night."

"You'll be fine with us," Heather said to the quiet arrival, giving his arm a quick rub.

"In the meantime," Andy declared, "we have to call him something. Names, people?"

"John," Mario offered.

"John's good to me," Andy nodded and Mario wrote the name on his clipboard. "From here on in, you're John. Doe, if anyone wants a last name. Stick with the tried and true. Heather? Mario? Show John to his cot for the night. And see to it he gets the basics. Suppertime is at five. You staying, Haley? It's soup again but it's good. The ladies really outdid themselves today."

"I'll stay," Haley said. "At least until he's settled away."

"No worries there. You know how we operate."

"You might want to watch him for accidents."

"What's that?" Andy asked, caught off guard. Heather and Mario appeared equally surprised.

"He had an accident earlier today. I had to clean him up before I brought him over. Only a number one, but a number two probably won't be too far away."

"Well, thank you for that, dear," Andy said and looked to Mario. "A job for you and me."

"Aw shit, Andy."

"None of that. The man has to know how to use the facilities, so we'll help him. Teach him if we have to. Until tomorrow when we can transfer him to a hospital."

"It's bad enough when the drunks barf all over the bathroom," Mario grumbled. "Or just outright shit themselves."

Andy reprimanded the man with an indignant look.

"*Defecate*," Mario corrected himself. "Sorry, I meant

defecate themselves. Sorry, sorry."

"There you go," Andy said. "Just think of this as a little preventative action. John isn't the disagreeable sort, is he? Doesn't smoke or drink? No harmful chemical habits we should be aware of?"

Haley realized that Andy had asked her. "No, not at all, as far as I know. And he did save me from a drunk. So his heart's in the right place. At least I think so."

"There you go," Andy declared with a note of sanctity. "Helping our fellow brothers and sisters in their darkest hour is what we're all about. Fear not, Haley, we'll take good care of him. Sit with him at suppertime if you like."

She brightened. That wasn't a bad suggestion at all.

For his profanity slip, Mario was nominated to instruct John on the finer points of effectively voiding within a public washroom setting. During that time, Heather got on the phone and called Social Services, the Department of Health and Welfare, and the Reeve's Institute for Mental Health. After a good twenty minutes, she hung up and reported to Haley and Andy that none of the three agencies could send someone over to assess the nature and extent of John's mental state, that the task was upon them to escort the individual to the official premises.

None of which surprised Andy, or placed him in a good mood.

An hour later, just as supper was being served and the shelter's regulars gathered in the hall partitioned off as a dining area, Mario guided a docile John to a table and sat him down across from Haley.

John appeared pleased to see her. Mario appeared disgusted beyond belief.

"Have some trouble, did you?" Haley asked.

"He's learning," Mario said. "He managed to use the toilet and wipe himself afterwards, but…"

Haley waited.

"But my God did he ever stink the place out," Mario blurted. "There were three others in the men's room and…" He caught himself, realizing that Haley had food before her and that John was already eating—grabbing at bread rolls and slurping loudly from his bowl of chicken soup and ignoring the plastic spoons and knives placed on the table.

"No, John, wait. Here, here," Haley said, reaching for him.

Mario backed away, leaving her to it.

Haley placed the man's hands on the table and demonstrated how to grip a spoon. Revealed how to dip and eat the soup and how to butter his bread rolls. John watched and quickly learned, which informed Haley that, despite having his face grilled and marbles rattled, at least he wasn't brain damaged. There was a brain in John's skull, a fully developed one, struggling to catch up with the lay of the land.

John recovered from his clumsiness and ate his allotted portions of two bowls and four bread rolls.

"Not bad, was it?" Haley asked over her empty bowl. "They have decent food here. Twice a day. There's a soup truck that heads to another part of town, but they load up from here. They're good folks. Publicly funded mostly, from what I understand, but with a few private contributions. This place saved my bacon. Saved it. You bet they did. I don't mind saying so."

She lifted a paper napkin to her mouth and dabbed at the corners.

John finished his meal and, after watching Haley, cleaned himself.

The gesture wasn't lost on Haley. "You remember doing that, don't you? Cleaning yourself? You remembered that from some time before."

John stared across the table at her, eyes bright, concentrating on the gibberish spewing from her mouth. She could see it. He was trying to remember, to understand, while glimmers of actions unconsciously rose to the surface.

The activity around John mesmerized him, so he studied the assorted characters eating at the surrounding tables. An older man, perhaps in his fifties, sat down with three others one table over and returned John's stare. A half smirk skewed his face and he glanced from John to Haley to John again while chewing on a forgotten bread roll.

John didn't look away.

The gray-haired man glared a question.

John glowered in turn.

"Something on your mind, son?"

Haley looked at her supper friend and then the guy at the table, whose own companions were drawn to the developing situation. All of them were older, clean but with thick beards, and probably could have just arrived from a far-north encampment somewhere.

"He can't talk," Haley said. "He's had an injury to the head."

"Not polite to stare," the older man warned.

"This bastard starin' at you, Gregory?" asked a man in a baseball cap sitting across from Gregory.

"Simpleton was. Still is."

"He doesn't understand—" Haley tried to explain but Gregory flashed a cautioning scowl.

"He understands. Ain't nothing wrong with him. I know the type. Overseen enough of the young fuckers to know a player when I see one. It's smart to play stupid, ain't it, son? Ain't it? You know what I'm sayin'. Trouble is, I *know* you know what I'm sayin'."

John didn't respond, but his jawline twitched.

"Yeah, I know," Gregory seethed with a snake's grace. "Just like I know you can talk, too. You might have them around you fooled but by Christ you don't have me."

Haley stood. John did the same.

"Where you goin'?" Gregory asked. "I might not like him but I like you. Sit down and let's talk. See what comes up."

The three others sitting with him snickered and shook their heads.

Haley ignored them and turned on her heel. "Follow me, John."

But John didn't.

"You best follow your mom there, youngster," Gregory said, leaning back with a chuckle. "Go on. Before you cause a scene."

"John," Haley insisted.

But the mute man didn't turn away. He kept his now menacing attention pinned on Gregory. John flexed his fingers. An upper lip curled in distaste.

The guy with the ball cap took offense. He stood and stepped directly between the two, breaking the connection. Bearded and shaggy, the guy was five inches taller than John. Mouth puckered, he grunted in John's face.

Haley grabbed John's arm and pulled him away.

"Don't you mind those guys. I'll report them to Andy. He'll take care of them. Sometimes you have to pick your fights."

She led John around the maze of tables and stopped at the corner of the kitchen. There Mario stood with his clipboard, surveying the supper hour like a penitentiary warden. Behind him, volunteers tended to two stoves and old countertops, preparing little sandwiches on paper plates.

"Mario, where's Andy?"

"Gone home."

"Where's Heather?"

"She's gone, too. And I'm only here until Len gets here, then I'm outta here."

Haley yanked on John's arm, arresting his slow but sure turn back in the direction of Gregory and his boys.

"We just had a problem," Haley said, making sure John was focused on her before going on. "The four way over there, by the wall."

"What about them?" Mario said, looking in that direction. "Ah, Gregory."

"You know them?"

"Know of them. Same story as a lot of these folks. He was a shipbuilder around the docks once. Got laid off, but if you ask around, he got fired because he assaulted a foreman for cutting his hours back. The guy with the ball cap is Adam Skoll. Not sure what his story is. The one on Greg's left is Bernard."

"Well, they almost got into a fight with John here."

"Yeah? About what?"

Haley hesitated. "John was staring at them."

"Was he?"

"Maybe a little, but you know what's going on with him."

"Actually, we don't, but Andy and I plan to get him to someone tomorrow who could examine him."

"Just saying they almost got into a fight."

"Noted. I'll talk to them," Mario said. "Give them a second warning."

"A second warning?"

Mario frowned, as if realizing he'd said too much. "Folks around here are fairly private. Loners. You know that. But a couple have come forth with reports that those guys have been stirring up trouble. Doesn't happen often, but every now and again, we do get a couple of troublemakers here. I'll get on the phone to the other shelters, too. See if they have a history or not."

"Thank you," Haley said. "I wasn't comfortable with them."

"Hearing that a lot, too," Mario said, tight-lipped. "Every so often."

"Where's he going to sleep tonight?"

"John?"

"Yeah."

"On the floor."

"Where are they going to sleep?"

"Same floor."

That horrified Haley. "You better make sure Len keeps them away from each other. Those guys might try something."

"They better not," Mario said. "Or they know what'll happen."

Counseling, Haley knew. Lots of it. And if they didn't get the message then, they'd get banned from the shelter. The place was a home for over two hundred regulars, according to Andy, with various sponsored programs in place to get people up, restoring their sense of worth, and integrating them back into society. The volunteers didn't want to expel anyone back onto the streets, but it was a last resort for the unruly ones.

"Where's his bunk?" Haley asked.

Mario nodded and left the activity in the kitchen. He led Haley and John past the dining area, past the long partition dividing the main floor into an eating area and a sleeping area, and followed a wall to a far corner. Army cots stacked two high lined the floor in an orderly fashion, covered in white blankets, pillows, and assorted clothing. About a quarter of the beds were full of people relaxing after their meal. Some read paperbacks, others read newspapers or old issues of *National Geographic*. Waiting in the corner, however, was a bare futon with a stack of gray blankets and a single, flat pillow.

"Here you go," Mario gestured with a hand. "Clean and warm. That thing's on a pair of pallets, so you're not completely on the floor. Space is a little tight but you're inside. And with a roof over your head."

John studied the sleeping space without a word.

"Well, that's it, then," Mario said and walked away, clearly miffed at the lack of a thank-you.

"You stay here now," Haley said to John, taking his parka and draping it over a nearby chair. "Relax and… well… tomorrow's another day. Maybe you'll start remembering things. These people will help you. They helped me."

She rubbed his arm, smiled gently and left him there. She walked along the wall until she came to a fire escape and pushed her way outside.

John watched her leave, saw the door open and felt the sudden invading draft. Then she was gone, the door closing. He stood there for a moment, the futon at his ankles, and waited for her to return. When she didn't, John glanced around the sleeping area, taking in the people settling in for the evening. Half of the fluorescent light tubes on this side of the partition wall were off, and some of the people who were reading had a clip-on lamp positioned right above their heads. Someone coughed, while another snorted, stifling what sounded like a cold.

The sounds were familiar, the smells sharp. John didn't think in words, but he was aware that he didn't like the various aromas wafting about, merging into a foul gas only he apparently detected. A young teenager with a magazine sat down on a bed and flipped his feet up. The guy took a second to reposition himself before unfolding a blanket, with which he then covered himself. John watched for a few seconds more before considering his own futon. He sat, studied his surroundings again, and arranged himself upon the padded softness. He liked the futon. The blankets were just at his feet. Learning from the youngster, John took the covers and awkwardly spread them over himself.

He liked the blankets, too.

The female, whom he associated with the name "Haley," was gone. He didn't know where she was gone, but the image of her living room materialized within his head. He wondered if she would be returning. As he thought about the female, his eyes grew heavy. The warm air was fragrant with those awful smells, momentarily repelling his drowsiness.

Things happened in his mind. The white screen took form at times and struggled to make things known to him, but a soundless snowstorm cloaked and buried them. John concentrated without knowing he was doing so, mentally tugging at wispy strands of memory, and failing to free anything from before that terrible, terrible time of waking up in a cold, immovable darkness. He didn't like to remember that place.

But thoughts of what he did to those people there replayed in his head. Pieces coming apart. The slippery ground. The noise.

Those violent scenes quieted his mind, shutting out the

awful smells emanating from the surrounding males and females.

Long enough for sleep to take him.

A boot nudged John's shoulder. Hard.

Three males stood over him. The one that spoke to him earlier was present, along with the guy with the ball cap, and another one, grim-faced and brooding.

The older man hunkered down and when John tried to raise himself to his elbows, the man pushed him back.

"Stay," he commanded in a whisper, smelling strongly of piss. "Stay right there, you unsavory bastard. You listen now. You listen. In the morning, that Andy feller is going to be asking you questions about me and the boys. You just tell him nothing happened. You tell him you figure nothing would have ever happened. You got that? You tell him or something *will* happen. Something that you sure as hell won't like. Understand?"

At that point, the older man nodded. John nodded with him.

"Good," he whispered. "That's good. Because it'd be a real shame if you had to slip on the washroom tiles while taking a shit. Split your head open. Those tiles can get slippery."

The man in the ball cap broke into a grin.

John didn't like any of them. They all smelled like piss. Warm piss that coated their hands and their lips. He didn't like them or their stink and he made it known.

"Goddamn," the third man said, "did this cocksucker just growl at us?"

"I think he did, Bernard."

"Don't like to be growled at, Gregory," said the man with the ball cap.

"Neither do I," answered Gregory. "Look at him. He's ready for a fight."

"He does look ready."

"Well, then quit it," Gregory glared at John. The old man stood and when he did, the other two backed away. "Quit it. And remember what I said, now. You remember."

The three men walked away, casting dark looks over their shoulders. They clumped past filled beds while soft snores cut the air.

John sat up and watched them. An anger rose as far as his gullet, wanting him to scream, wanting him to do *more*.

For some reason, he did not.

Instead, he cast off the blankets and rose, watching the shady outlines of the three men on the opposite side of the hall. They'd clustered around one bed. John didn't like them, and the urge to do things to them surged within his breast. The door distracted him, however. The one Haley had gone through earlier in the evening. He sniffed the air and couldn't find her scent.

She hadn't come back.

John looked one last time at the three males.

Then he picked up his parka, instinctively knowing its purpose, and went to the door with the glowing letters right above it.

EXIT.

The same door Haley had used.

Without looking back, John pushed his way through the door and cold air smacked his face.

*

A few minutes after midnight and Dax thought about calling it quits. The pickings had been downright shitty. Not one potential payoff strayed into his line of sight. Not one single individual looking as if they had something of value upon their person. Perhaps it was the park—people had been warned over the last few months about wandering through Regency Park after dark, and most of them had taken heed. Most folks stayed in groups if they were out and about at night, and not even Dax wanted to be out too late when it could start snowing any moment. He wiped his nose and rubbed his fingers on his jeans, knowing that snot stains showed on his parka under a strong light source. Dax lingered behind a thick elm, not five paces away from one of the smaller paved walkways that went off the main lane. Maybe it was his spot. Even animals had the good sense to stay away from an area after a few of the herd disappeared.

The trail he haunted meandered through some of the secluded areas of the park's designated twenty acres, and, seriously, no one in their right mind would wander alone through such a wooded area so late at night, unless they were coming off a drinking spree from the downtown bars. Or were just plain stupid. Either way, it had been the ideal place for a mugging, which was why Dax decided to cast his web there for so long. He felt his switchblade's handle, a sharpened sliver that could scare the shit out of anyone once extended. Except maybe a cop. Twenty-four-year-old Dax was strictly a small-scale mugger, a petty thief in the night, wondering if he should continue on with this particular career choice or start bootlegging booze for the Stewards across the US and New Brunswick border. The risk was greater than mugging folks, but the payoffs were much grander, at least according to his buddy Rocky Janes. Rocky didn't shit in people's hands for fun. If he said there was opportunity there, there was opportunity. And Rocky had already put in a word with the Stewards on Dax's behalf. There was money in bootlegging and, as far as crime went, Dax didn't see the transportation of alcohol (and sometimes cigarettes) between the two countries as breaking any laws. As far as he was concerned, all he was doing was supplying folks with product while stiffing the government of their taxes. All it was. No crime at all in his mind, really, just governments pissed off that they weren't getting their share.

That alone was enough to make Dax consider taking up the trade.

Someone moved along the paved walkway, a telltale scuffle of boot rubble on asphalt, announcing the arrival of a potential victim. The clicking drew closer. He tensed up and looked to the pavement, eyes well-adjusted to the dark, just waiting for a dark outline to step into view. When that happened, Dax would go to work. If he was lucky, maybe it was a rich old bastard with a full wallet, two or three pints into the night.

The steps halted, started up, and stopped again. The guy certainly *sounded* loaded. Probably a student from one of the nearby universities. Dax didn't mind that at all. He'd wait until he saw the person before pouncing, remembering the story of poor Ruben Hart who hadn't checked beforehand before jumping into action, and pulled a knife on four basketball players. The police found Ruben's broken, unconscious ass hanging from a tree the next morning. Dax was smarter than that.

The footsteps wandered past the elm and stopped, practically parallel to where Dax waited, his back pressed against the same tree trunk. Most people wandered on by without a glance, but this character *knew* he was there. That alone was a bad sign.

Fuck it, Dax thought, and let the *snick* of his single blade do the talking.

The late-night walker didn't flinch at the sound.

"You run and I'll catch you," Dax warned, leaning around the tree. "Fight and I'll stick you. Hand over your money and we can both call it a night. Whaddaya say?"

The stranger didn't answer. Worse, the winterized outline didn't hand over his wallet.

Dax peered left and right, checking that they were indeed alone. If need be, he already had his escape trail plotted, and only an Olympic sprinter on a good day was going to catch Dax if he had to run.

"God*damn* I'm tired of you already," Dax muttered, and stepped toward the man on the pathway. Dax grabbed him by his fluffy parka, whipped him around and forced him off the path, into the dark. The tree halted them both, but by that time, Dax had already placed his blade's edge against the guy's left nostril.

"Don't move now," Dax warned, focused on the narrowed slits of his victim's face. The guy was a little taller than Dax, not that it mattered. As long as they were alone, he didn't give a shit. "Don't move. You do and I open up your face. You hear me? I'll cut a line right up the middle and flick the excess away. Start with your nose and if you're lucky, I won't blind you. Now, hand over the fucking wallet. Or your purse or whatever you carry your goddamn money in. Do it now."

He pressed the flat of the blade into the guy's nostril, the fine tip pointed north toward a right eye.

"Well?" Dax demanded.

The man didn't move.

"The fuck you on?" Dax spat and shook the man by his collar. He repositioned the knife, holding the edge to the guy's throat. "You don't make a move."

Dax fished through the pockets. Dug two fingers in and out with practiced ease, and came away with nothing.

"Well, shit," he panted. "Can't believe this. You don't got anything on you?"

Nothing. No answer. No sign of even being heard.

Dax rested the knife against the man's nose once again. "Getting real tired of talking to myself. I'll tell you what. You answer the next question and I'll let you live. How's that sound?"

There, in the deep dark of night, narrowed eyes glinted

distrust and, for a split second, Dax thought he saw anger.

"Don't think of anything, you cheap prick. Don't think of a goddamn thing. I'll stick you three times before another thought. You just *do*. Now, what do you have on you?"

The guy snorted. Actually *snorted* at Dax.

"You smart-assed fuck," Dax whispered.

And cut him.

He drew the blade across the outer curve of the man's right nostril, parting that knob of skin like a cancerous tumor about to pop. The guy grimaced. Dax's blade came up firm against the base of the bone, but then he was flying through the air and landed, facedown, on the frozen grass. His knees screamed and it took him a good ten seconds to realize that he'd flown about ten feet and landed on his chest. One kneecap had landed on something incredibly hard, and Dax rolled over with a groan to see that his own jeans had been torn from connecting with a sizeable rock. Blood glistened, and a wave of nausea swept through him. He groaned again, tried to straighten the hyperextended knee, and a super-charged blast of pain stole his breath.

Hands gripped his neck. Those hands lifted Dax into the air with a curt gurgle.

Directly before the bleeding face of his intended victim.

You fucker! Dax wanted to say, but all he got out was a strangled hiss of nonsense. His vision narrowed into a tunnel, then a tube. He kicked at his captor's legs, but Dax never really got anything behind it. The pressure on his neck and the weight of his own body sapped what strength he had left.

Narrowed eyes studied Dax.

On the brink of passing out, twisting and turning in the air, Dax saw the dreamy flash of teeth.

A split second before his entire nose was bitten off.

25

The next morning, Carma surprised Kirk by telling him he was traveling with her in his truck. In the same breath she instructed Morris, Bryce, Janice, and Nice Dyer to hang back at the apartment and rest up for the evening shift. Ken Cyler and Sam Mausler would scour the streets in the south and west while Carma and Kirk would head north and east. When duties had been assigned, the pack leader led Kirk out the door.

"You two be good now," Janice called out to them. Carma closed the door on her, but the parting words alarmed Kirk. Carma, however, didn't even acknowledge them. He followed the pack leader to his truck, keeping two steps behind her. Outside, a fog trapped the city in a dream.

"You drive," she said.

They pulled out of the parking lot and hit the highway, heading for the city's north end. The dash clock said quarter to ten, and the morning traffic glut had begun to work itself loose.

"Take your time," Carma said, propping her elbow up

on the door's sill and looking ahead. "No rush."

"Didn't think I was rushing," Kirk muttered, applying brakes as a sedan's tail lights flared up ahead of him.

"Just sayin', is all."

Kirk cleared his throat. "So, what about you then? All's going well? You must be doing something right to be pack leader of a bunch of wardens."

"I do what the elders tell me. Simple as that," Carma said.

"I do what the elders tell me and I don't get a promotion."

"And I get things done."

"Ah."

Carma stared out the window and studied the throngs of pedestrians dressed in fall fashions and armored against the cold. "How do you ever live here?" Carma asked him.

"Aren't you in a city now? Toronto or somewhere?"

"I am. Still don't like it."

"It's not so bad, once you get used to it."

"That why your apartment smells like a barn?"

Kirk frowned at that.

"And you look like a bum?"

He took a deep, stabilizing breath and checked his mirrors. "I'm in disguise."

"It's a good one."

"Thanks."

Kirk reached for the radio and switched it on. Music blared through the cab so he quickly turned it down. "I'll be moving on in a few more years. Maybe I'll go somewhere up north. Maybe Cape Breton. Somewhere I can lose myself."

"In a bottle?"

Kirk frowned. "That hurt. I don't drink like that. Barely drink at all. Only certain times. Like when I'm reading. A few beers help me better appreciate the classic lit."

"I remember."

"Just because you don't drink doesn't mean the rest of us are fucked up."

"Oh, I drink. Simply not to excess."

"Yeah? That's new. Wine, right? Some fruity bouquet? Or something with a spicy flare?"

"Jack Daniels. Shots. Straight over the tongue and freight elevator to the gut."

Kirk eyed her. Christ. She'd changed.

"Never did like cities," Carma said, eyes roving left and right. "Never did."

"I tolerate it. Easier to lose yourself here than the wild, I think."

"Again with the losing. You still at odds over what you are?"

Kirk didn't respond and that alone was an answer.

"After all this time and you still haven't come to grips with it?" Carma questioned in a wondering tone.

"Guess not."

"Think you ever will?"

"Don't know."

"You better. And soon."

Kirk shrugged. "Might not."

"We're not monsters."

Kirk noted a winterized mother wheeling a baby chariot

along the sidewalk. "I keep telling myself that."

"We're superior."

"Higher up on the food chain?"

"Much more than that."

"I keep hearing that as well."

"You think too much. Clean yourself up when we get back. It'll be a step into getting your head straight."

"I think we talked about this once before."

"Mm-hm," Carma nodded.

"I turned a guy."

That took her attention off the road. She turned her head and balked. "You what?"

"I turned a guy." Kirk checked his rearview mirror. "A year ago. In Newfoundland."

"You created a *were*?" That impressed her. "What were you thinking? The elders must've been pissed."

"They, ah, yeah, were. Really pissed, since I put him in place as a warden."

Carma hid her smile with a hand. "Jesus Christ, Kirk. Holy shit. Well, why not? If you're going to shit in the head office's flowerpot, might as well water them, too, right?"

"I wasn't going to stay on the island."

"What's wrong with the island?"

"Nothing's wrong with the island, but I wanted to be here. I was born here."

Carma kept her thoughts to herself.

"I had to change the guy," Kirk continued. "He was going to die anyway. He helped me and Morris clean up a mess over there. An old bastard by the name of Borland. Up to dark shit. Transformed dogs into these… half-breeds. Ross—that's the new warden over there—he got hurt by one of them and who the fuck knew what was going to happen to him on a full moon. So I turned him."

"And he was okay?"

"He's accepted it."

"You explained everything to him?"

Kirk paused. "Most of it."

"Most of it. So that's what's eating you? You're feeling guilty?"

It was his time to be quiet.

"So many years and you haven't changed," Carma said wistfully. "You're too fucking noble for your own good, you know that? Guilty because you saved a life by cursing it. Well, guess what? *You* might think we're cursed, but not everyone shares that opinion. I certainly don't think I'm cursed. Or a monster. Your guy, Ross? There's going to be a little anxiety about coming into the pack. A little grief as friends and neighbors and family pass on, but he'll get used to it. Hell, he might already have. You talk to him recently?"

"Yeah."

"And?"

Kirk inhaled sharply. "Says he's doing fine."

Carma let it rest for a while. After a long silence, she asked, "What happened to Morris?"

The hairs on Kirk's neck bristled. "Just like he said."

"This Borland character. You get into a tussle with him?"

"Yeah."

"He claw you? Bite you?"

"Yeah."

Carma glanced sideways at him. "Did you get hurt?"

Kirk took his eyes off the road and met her gaze. "No."

"Are you like Morris?"

Cars passed by and one indicated it was changing lanes, so Kirk allowed it to get ahead of him.

"Douglas?"

"I don't know," Kirk said. "Maybe."

"Maybe?"

"Yeah. Maybe."

"Jesus Christ, Douglas."

"I don't know for sure."

"There's one way to find out," Carma said pointedly.

"Yeah. I guess."

"You feel any different?"

Kirk thought about Baxter in the back of his truck. Remembered the pointed boot, and that moment when a part of him just wanted to bite. He remembered the three unmoving bodies lying side by side, packed into the box like pork cutlets in a tangy sauce.

"I feel fine."

The intensity of her stare heated Kirk's profile. She was wary of him. He could sense it just as plain as she could smell the lies. A set of lights ripened to red and Kirk applied the brakes. Carma had twisted in her seat, and Kirk noticed that she left the top two buttons of her denim shirt undone, showing off a T-shirt underneath, and a very fine-looking neck.

A cop car zipped through the intersection, heading northeast on Duffus.

"Cops," Kirk said, thankful for the interruption.

"Follow them."

He flicked on his turn signal and when the lights turned green, the car behind allowed him into the lane. He pulled onto Duffus Street and hit the gas, looking over car roofs and spotting the cruiser far ahead. Carma leaned ahead, holding on to the dash as if coaxing more speed from the vehicle.

The patrol car arrived at a two-vehicle collision, a classic T-bone where the drivers stood beside their wrecked rides, snapping pictures with their cell phones.

"False alarm," Carma said.

"Looks that way."

"Drive on."

Kirk passed the site, thankful that his lane wasn't affected by the crash.

"You know what a monster is? The literal definition?"

"Go ahead," Kirk said.

"Well, there are several definitions. And some of them are unquestionably true. But people created and defined the word. People. Them. Am I one of them? I look like them but am I monster? I'm not. I'm a *were*. I'm better than them for a number of reasons we've already discussed. You read too much classic lit. That'll warp your perceptions about what is and isn't. You saved a guy's life by bringing him into the fold. You ask me, they're the ones who are cursed, not us. Not us."

"We still eat them," Kirk pointed out.

"We do," Carma nodded. "But so what? Cats eat mice.

Are they monsters? Eagles will make meals of rabbits. Are they monsters?"

Kirk frowned, not bothering to respond. He'd heard it before from her, or at least a similar speech delivering the same message. "Where to now?"

Carma told him where to go.

*

Back at the apartment, Morris got up from the sofa where he'd fallen asleep, upon the insistence of his bladder. He went to the washroom wearing the same clothes as yesterday, and relieved himself. His face stared back at him in the mirror as he washed his hands. Once finished, he pulled this and stretched that, inspecting himself in the mirror. His neck felt great, his cuts healed. The speed amazed him.

When he opened the door to leave, a scowling Ian Bryce stood in his way.

Morris matched the ferocious look. "Something on your mind?"

Bryce took his time answering. "Yeah."

"Well?"

"You're not right," Bryce said with stark frankness.

"Guess I'm not," Morris said and got into the man's personal space. "So fuck off."

But Bryce, all burly three hundred pounds of him, didn't move. "I'm watching you, Moses."

"Watch my ass all you want. But you get the fuck out of my way now, or as God is my witness, we'll wrestle."

The tension swelled between the two wardens, the glares

deepened, and Morris knew that the Quebec warden wasn't about to back down.

"Bryce," Janice called from the living room. "Stop poking the fucking bear and get your mutual hairy ass away from him."

That diffused the swelling hostility between the two. Morris stepped through the opening but glared howitzer strikes at the warden.

"He giving you a hard time?" Janice asked, lounging on the sofa. Her white socks twitched.

"No," Morris said and picked up his coat.

Janice exchanged a quiet look with Nick Dyer camped out in the easy chair. "Where you going?"

"Out," Morris said. "Without your fucking permission."

A wry smile crossed Janice's face. Dyer was expressionless, studying the Pictou warden.

Morris pulled on his coat, taking his time, and regarded all three of the present wardens in turn. "Getting tired of being watched in here."

Without another word, Morris turned and walked past Bryce, delivering a stern check into the man's shoulder. Morris didn't look back as he let himself out.

It was a long time before anyone spoke.

"That one's off," Bryce said. "I can smell it."

"We're all off in here," Janice said.

"Don't fuck around. Shit's going on with him."

"Don't need to smell that to know it," Dyer sighed.

"Whether something's off with him or not, he's still a warden," Janice said. "And we still have a hunt going on.

Everything else is secondary."

"I'm calling it in," Bryce said.

Janice and Dyer exchanged looks again, but neither said anything as Bryce left them.

"We're still talking though, right?" Dyer said, sizing up Janice's stretched legs.

"Mm-hm," Janice answered.

"Then all's well."

That prompted Janice to meet the Maine warden's eyes. Dyer smiled at her.

She smiled back.

*

Bryce swung the bedroom door closed and went to the window. He stood and waited, watching the parking lot for Morris to appear. When he did, Bryce retreated a step and took out his phone. The number he dialed was a number he'd known for a very long time, one for emergencies.

"Yeah, give me a call back when you can," Bryce growled into the phone as Morris turned one way and then the other, watching traffic zip along. Bryce closed his phone and not ten seconds later the device vibrated.

"Yeah. This is Bryce. Listen, we have a second concern developing here. Anyone call in about Moses Morris?"

He listened, observing Morris from the crack offered by the curtain.

"Well, yeah, I'd say," Bryce said. "He's healing a lot faster than he should be, and he's not talking too much about it. I mean a lot faster. Like four or five times fast."

Morris walked a few steps and made a show of taking a deep breath.

"Oh, really?" Bryce said and shook his head. "She didn't? Interesting. Well, now you know."

The voice on the other end of the line spoke again.

"Will do," Bryce finished and closed the phone.

As if hearing the click, Morris turned around and looked up at the bedroom window.

26

The overcast morning kept Haley in bed a good hour longer. She liked to sleep, liked to dream, and, despite her squatter existence and nagging anxiety about waking up to the sound of construction crews about to demolish her home, she slept quite well. In her dreams, she still had her family. In her dreams, she laughed, loved, and grew old with her husband. Saw her daughter overcome her fear of spiders, grow up, and marry. In her dreams, Haley's perfect grandchildren, a girl and a boy, visited her almost every day.

Haley loved to sleep. Slept to dream.

Gray light seeped around the blankets nailed over the windows, invading the room and urging her to rise. She lingered, luxuriating in that comfortable warmth from a pile of old blankets. The thought occurred if she should get a prescription for sleeping pills and take them all at once. Dying like that seemed like a good way to go, a peaceful way to go, except she was fearful of taking her own life, fearful of crossing over to the other side by her own hand.

She rose, mouth pouted, eyes narrowed, and sleep-stomped to the washroom. Thick socks muffled the noise. She arranged her hair with half a mirror—the other half had been smashed out long before she had made it her home. Her bladder urged her to move quickly as there was no running water for her flush box at the house. She'd have to go down to Halifax Place to use the public washrooms. Or the public park. Both were a hurried (and sometimes frantic) ten-minute walk from her front door.

She straightened out her clothing, took the one stale muffin she'd left in a take-out box, and pulled on her boots. Her back cracked as she pulled away the timbers barring the entrance of her house. Haley wondered why she even bothered with the crude attempt at security. If someone wanted to get in, really wanted to get in, it wouldn't be a chore to do so. Her castle would crumble pretty damn quick, in fact.

She gathered up her environmentally safe shopping bags and filled them with three empty plastic jugs. She would fill those with water. All set, she thought, as she pulled open the front door.

Right there on her step was John, bright-eyed and hopeful.

His sudden appearance surprised Haley, but it wore away into a smirk.

"Get homesick, did you?"

John smiled back and grunted.

"Didn't like the accommodations at the shelter?"

His left cheek twitched at the question, but he didn't answer.

"What was it? The snoring or the farting get to you? Well, anyway, I don't blame you. There're good things and not-so-good things about the place. But I figured you should know about it. And now you know. You waiting for me? I'm heading for a washroom, right now. Fill up some jugs and then maybe come back here. Maybe head down to the shelter for lunch. They have soup and sandwiches for lunch down there. All the ham and cheese you could ask for. Interested?"

No response. Just like a big old puppy.

"Figures. Come on, then," she said as she closed her door and fastened the length of rope around the nail.

"Here," Haley said and handed him the pair of shopping bags. "You carry these."

She stopped, noticing bloodstains on John's blue-gray parka.

"The hell happened to you?"

John didn't answer.

"Well, you can't go walking around like that," she said, stressed, noting that he didn't look hurt at all, except for what might have been a scar on the left side of his nose. She hadn't noticed that before. Haley shook her head and turned back to the door.

"Come on in," she groaned and unraveled the rope from the nail. "People see you like that, they'll think you took the coat from a gunshot victim. You didn't take the coat from a gunshot victim, did you?"

John didn't say a word.

"Good answer. You stick with that and you'll do fine. You better not get into any trouble with the sweater I'm going to give you. *Loan* you. On a very temporary basis. Till we can find you another coat. Won't be from the shelter though. They get testy about handing out more than two coats to one person. We'll have to go shopping for you later on."

Haley entered her home with John on her heels. She realized what she'd just said. She turned and faced the big man, studying his unconcerned features, long enough for John to stop and stare himself, no doubt wondering what was going through her head.

"Well, what the hell," Haley said in resignation. "You're housebroken now, anyway. Might be good having a guard dog around here. For now, anyway. But you get weird on me and I'll scream like a five o'clock whistle. Understand?"

If he did, he didn't show it.

"Yeah, thought so. Get your ass in here and let's get you into a sweater. It'll be cold, but that's your punishment until dark. Goddammit. I can dress you up but can't take you anywhere."

Not fifteen minutes later, she had him out of the stained coat and in her spare sweatshirt. He let her dress him, offering no resistance. The man was like a big old rag doll still in possession of its bones. She tossed the coat in the kitchen sink and wondered if the little detergent she had on hand would clean it. That would be a chore for another time.

Right now, she had to get to a washroom.

"All right," she announced as she tied off the front door once again. "Let's get going. Momma's gotta pee, big time."

They arrived at the shelter just after noon, when the lines for lunch were dwindling. Haley talked to the volunteers on behalf of John and loaded up the trays with lunch leftovers. The soup was hot, the sandwiches a little on the skimpy side, but were all good and kindly offered.

"Eat up," Haley told him as they sat at a table. "When it starts to get dark we'll head on over to the M and M Mall. That's Martin and MacDonald. Some call it MartyMac. Which has a nice ring to it. MartyMac Mall. See if we can't find you a coat in the dumpsters. Sometimes a few of the clothing shops have clothes that aren't stitched properly or have one too many zippers. Some kind of defect that makes the coat unsellable. Doesn't happen much but we'll take a look. Otherwise, we have to make the longer trek to another shelter that's way down on the south side. Better to check the places you know before we have to make the hike over there. And don't you forget what I'm doing for you, either, buster. You'll get chores for this."

John ate, couldn't get the spoon into his mouth fast enough. Or the sandwiches, which he sucked down in single bites. Haley watched and remembered her unborn grandchildren.

Heather appeared at their table and beamed at both. "Hi Haley. Hi John. How are you guys today?"

"Hi Heather," Haley said. "I'm good, but this turkey—well, no change."

"Come back here tomorrow, okay?" Heather said, "There'll be a social worker stopping by. She'll run an assessment and maybe put in a request. Fill out some paperwork. Maybe she can get him into a smaller clinic and not a full-blown hospital. Work him into it slowly."

That would at least be a start, Haley thought.

"Any plans for today?" Heather asked brightly.

"No." Haley answered, knowing the woman meant well. "Maybe take a walk in the park."

"Is he going with you?"

"I guess so."

"Good. And better stay away from Regency. Police found a body up there this morning."

"What?"

Heather nodded. "Something, 'eh. I walk my dog over there, too. Police are all over that area this morning."

"My Lord."

"Drug killing, probably. One dealer offing another. I'm sure we'll hear all about it later this evening. You guys'll be around for supper?"

"We'll try to make it but I do have some plans today," Haley said. "Haveta take this guy shopping again."

"I'll tell Louis to put some food away for you."

That brightened Haley's spirits. "That would be wonderful, you sweet dear."

Heather smiled back. "No problem. You're a semi-regular. Well, have a good day then. Hope to hear you talking soon, John."

John watched her leave.

"You finished?" Haley asked.

There was nothing left on John's tray.

"Go to the washroom and use it. I'll wait for you at the exit over there."

Haley got up and John immediately followed, sweatshirt specked with soup stains. A thought struck her then, as he rose to attention, a memory of the other night when he saved her ass from rape and maybe even worse.

"You, ah, you didn't hear anything about that murder, did you?" Haley asked.

John looked at her, waiting for more.

"Didn't have anything to do with it?"

Not a glimmer of comprehension. No guilty look. Just that hopeful shine of a person expecting a surprise. Or a treat.

"You're like a big kid," Haley sighed and pointed to the men's washroom. "Over there. I'll be over here."

And to her shock, John went to the designated washroom door.

"Holy shit," Haley whispered, watching him disappear inside. A good sign for sure.

John entered the washroom and went into a stall, ignoring the one guy leaning over one of three sinks and inspecting his beard. John checked on the toilet paper, as the one called Mario had demonstrated, and fumbled with the front of his jeans. He sat down on the toilet (again as instructed), tucked himself inside the seat, and did his business, staring at the glyphs and numbers on the back of the stall door. His mind remained a white screen, but every now and again he became aware of certain impulses. Movements that were very natural to him. Recalled memories, perhaps, familiar scenes that rippled in his mind's fabric, glimpsed but not quite understood. Images of a nature he couldn't quite grasp but knew were important. John didn't know where they came from, was incapable of analyzing his condition, but when they appeared, he recognized them as significant. He spaced out for a good ten minutes, lost in smoky recall. He came to with a jolt, realized he'd finished. He stood up, fastened his jeans, and opened the stall door.

Hands. He had to wash his hands. Mario had showed him how.

There, blocking the washroom door, were the three amigos. Gregory, Adam with his baseball cap as if it had been permanently glued to his head, and Bernard.

John stopped within the stall.

"C'mon out of there, cornshitter," Gregory rumbled, dislike narrowing his eyes.

Adam Skoll quickly grabbed John by the sweatshirt. Seams ripped. He threw the mute man against the wall, knocking over a full garbage can as he did. Bernard Shoop pinned one arm while Adam pinned the other, breathing into his profile. His breath smelled of ham and cheese.

"Now, I don't like you," Gregory said with his hands hooked into a belt and stopping not two steps away. His skin smelled of salt and brine, like he'd been sprayed by an Atlantic storm front. "And frankly, I don't want to see you coming around here no more. The woman you're with? I like. You? Not so much. So tell you what, chief. You leave nice and quiet here today, just saunter out the exit like you did last night, and I won't kick your ass. As a bonus, Adam here won't break your fingers. And Bernard won't break your arms. Which, I haveta admit, I was looking forward to seeing. You ever see a chicken with its wings all fucked up? It's funny."

Gregory leaned in closer.

"But if you do say anything to anyone. If you do keep whatsherface from coming around here, well, Gawd as my witness, I'll make certain you won't use this again."

Gregory's open hand grabbed John's crotch and squeezed, buckling the man's knees and producing a gasp of pain. Adam and Bernard kept John upright, refusing to let him fall.

"Got quite the pair," Gregory muttered, smiling at his companions. "I might be a little jealous. Course, if you can't use it, then what's it good for, am I right?"

He squeezed harder, crippling his captive even further.

Bernard snickered.

"You hear me?" Gregory whispered.

John's head remained lowered.

"I said you hear me?"

No response.

"Goddamn it," Gregory spat and gripped John by the shock of his hair. "If it's one thing that bugs me it's being fucking ignored."

The older man yanked John's head up and his voice crystalized in his throat.

John had bared his teeth.

And they'd become fangs.

*

The background noise of shelter inhabitants chirped in Haley's ears as she waited beside the east exit. She watched the homeless guests sitting at their tables, chatting away, and noticed the washroom door swing open. John walked out, looked somewhat distressed, and marched toward her. He rapped a table with his hip, swinging the piece out of position, and slowed at the impact. He grimaced but ignored the questioning looks of the guests in the dining area.

"You okay?" Haley asked as he neared her.

But John marched past her and opened the door in a rush.

Haley regarded the onlookers, met the wondering faces of Heather and Louis, and briefly considered the closed washroom door. Before anyone could ask, Haley went out the exit and hurried after John's departing form.

She didn't hear about the blood pool, or how it had seeped out from underneath the men's washroom door not five minutes after she left. Nor did she hear about how Mario himself discovered the gruesome remains of three men.

Haley had other problems.

27

Ominous gray clouds pressed down upon the city, squeezing daylight from deepening shadows. Kirk and Carma returned to his apartment parking lot and saw Morris outside with his midnight duster on, looking like a homicidal doorman.

"How you doin', sunshine?" Kirk asked as he got out of his truck.

"Fuck off."

Kirk shot a sideways glance at Carma.

"Where do I go?" Morris asked her.

"Head back on up to the northern tip of the city. Work your way back here. Call as needed."

Morris walked off, heels clicking on drying pavement.

"He's not happy," Carma said, pulling open the door. "Not even by Morris's standards."

"I could go after him."

"And do what? Listen. You think Morris is the kind to cry on your shoulder? Or in the mood to do so now? Or ever? No. So get inside before I let the door close on your ass."

Despite wanting to follow the Pictou warden, Kirk didn't mind following her orders. He liked being bossed around by Carma. The difficult part was not letting it show.

They walked through the building, not meeting any other residents, and reached the apartment door just as the three others stepped out.

"Where to, boss?" Janice asked, with Nick Dyer standing just behind her. The movement wasn't lost on Kirk.

"Same as earlier."

"Wouldn't another area be better?"

"No," Carma said. "Halifax and Dartmouth's a big city. Lots of places to look. So get looking. Comb the same area. He might just pop up."

Bryce distanced himself from the hallway huddle, apparently eager to get to work. Janice and Dyer followed, but nowhere in the same hurry.

"Supper's ready," Dyer said before he got too far away.

"Thank you, dear," Carma replied and went inside. The smell of hamburgers lingered in the air, and Kirk saw a plate-full resting on the kitchen counter.

"He wasn't joking," Kirk said. "They did up a nice little feed here."

Carma didn't respond. She kept her back to him.

"Something wrong?" he asked.

"Nothing."

Kirk left it at that. He saw the time on the wall and considered his phone. Since their talk in the truck, Ross Kelly lingered on his mind. A bad feeling had seeped into his chest, and Kirk wanted to clear it by checking in on the man.

"I'm going to make a call," Kirk said, while Carma stood before the television. She didn't answer him. He left her alone and peeked in on the prone form of Ezekiel, still unconscious.

Rubbing his chin, he dialed Ross Kelly and wandered inside the room.

The newest warden picked up on the fourth ring.

"That you, Dougie?"

Kirk winced. "Yeah, that's me."

"You worried about me over here?"

The man was sharp. "Something like that. Just a quick call. How's the island?"

"Fine," Ross replied. "As far as I know. It's a pretty big island. Not that I'm rushed to get out there and explore it all in my new capacity as sheriff."

"Good. That's good. Ah…" Kirk stopped by the bedroom window and pulled back the curtain just a crack. In the parking lot, Bryce stormed off in one direction while Janice and Dyer went off in another. Together. That raised an eyebrow.

"Listen… never really talked about it before but I wanted to let you know, I'm sorry. For bringing you into all of this."

Silence on the other end. "Bit late for that, ain't it?"

"Yeah."

"I'm learning as I go here."

Kirk suspected he would.

"But… it's not all bad," Ross added. "Not at all. I… don't mind it, to tell the truth."

"You don't?" That knotted up Kirk's forehead. "What?"

"No, I like it. At times. I mean… I guess I was looking at leaving way back when all of this happened, y'know. Had to. Now, everything's changed. I mean, the pay is still shitty, but whatever, y'know. I get to stay here. In this town. For a while at least."

"For a while."

"And even then, after I leave, I'll get to come back."

"Yeah. You will." *Eventually*, Kirk thought.

"Things will be different, I know, but that's life anyway, y'know? I could mope around about it, but I'm not like that. Don't you worry. I've spent many a long night puzzling over things and thinking. And it's like anything else. It takes getting used to at first, and then it's what you make of it. I'll make the most of it. I mean, really, some of those midnight runs through the bush are just glorious, I gotta tell ya."

"They can be."

"And Kirk?"

"Yeah?"

"Listen. All things considered, you saved me here. More ways than one, y'know. In the beginning I used to think I was fucked with all of this. Now? Not so much. Just the opposite, in fact. So don't be worrying about me. I'll be fine. I'm doing fine. Matter of fact, got something going on here that might even us out—if you're feeling a little guilty, that is."

"Sounds good," Kirk smiled. "What is it?"

"Ah, not right now. But I'll tell you. Certainly before you come visit, anyway. We'll sit down and have ourselves a smile."

Kirk pinched the bridge of his nose. "All right, Ross. All right. Good to hear. And thanks."

"Thanks for callin'."

He broke the connection and hefted the phone. Kirk stepped back from the window, letting the curtain close, and considered the open doorway beyond.

"Douglas?"

"Yeah?"

Carma appeared. She dialed a number on her phone. "The news is on. Police found a body in a park."

28

The temperature plummeted as night descended upon the city.

Sensing it was only around five o'clock or so, Haley lowered her head into the cold and meandered along exit roads leading to the glowing Mecca that was the Martin and MacDonald Mall, an architectural wet dream of irregular angles and curves, gravity-defying arches and platforms, all under a glass and steel roof that shimmered at night like the moon on a calm bay. A modern-day coliseum of feral consumerism stacked four levels high in places. Haley stopped on a nearby hill to marvel at the structure's lights, the sole attraction that kept pulling her back. The building's glittering exterior reminded her of Christmas. And, as luck would have it, management had already placed Christmas trees out front, magnificent spires of bright, multicolor goodness that left her feeling warm despite the temperature. Haley loved the lights, the beautiful, beautiful lights. They were so calming. She could camp outside and stare at them all night.

"See that?"

John stood beside her and saw. A corner of his mouth curled into a smile. That was good. Just after leaving the shelter, vibes of negativity had radiated off him like a quivering red needle on a boiler gauge, edging into an area dangerous and palpable enough for Haley to cease talking to him. Whatever had happened back on Barrington had seeped out of him like bad gas. Perhaps a hunt for a coat would improve his spirits. Haley hoped so. She wasn't bringing him back to her place if he was pissed.

"That's where we're going. Just on the other side of that parking garage and around the back. It's a loading and dumping area. A lot of the shops have garbage bins back there. On some Wednesdays, when they get new stock in, you'll find something interesting in those bins. Not always useful, but interesting. There might be a coat down there for you. Or something warm. Save us the trouble of walking over to the other shelter. Wanna check things out?"

John actually looked at her suspiciously then, as if wondering what glorious madness she was about to reveal. At least, that was how Haley interpreted the expression.

"I got this."

She reached into a pocket and produced a small flashlight, which she demonstrated as functional with a quick click on and off.

"Come on," Haley said and eased herself down over a yellow slope of grass. "Be careful you don't slip here. It's a bitch in the winter. One slip and you could slide on your ass right out into that."

She pointed. At the hill's bottom was an exit road curving away from a main drag. Cars turned off the street and coasted toward the parking lots.

Haley was halfway down the slope when John decided to follow.

They timed their crossing just right, able to sprint over the off-ramp pavement when no cars were passing through. Horns sounded near the mall and a man yelled *Hey Lorri*! which turned Haley's head. The shopping paradise loomed closer, the bright glowing signs mesmerizing, displaying popular chains and designer outlets. People bustled along the mall's front end, on their phones, in groups, or walking alone. John stopped at the fringe of light, on slick pavement that led around to the back of the superstructure. He stared at the bright lettering, puzzling over its meaning. Haley pulled him away by the hand and led him down another short incline, toward the mall's less glamorous side. A wide open space came into view, paved and painted with lines, between the shopping center's back wall and a looming hillside that had its slope cut away to better accommodate the expansive zone. What once was a slope had been removed and replaced by brickwork and wire mesh, rising some thirty feet or so into the dark. Globes of lights appeared, spaced at regular intervals and perking up the building's concrete hide.

"Almost there. Stay out of the light. We only have a short time before someone sees us. Depending on who's working and their mood, they might come out here or just straight up call the cops."

Haley pointed to a grim bouquet of security cameras, perched high above on the walls at regular intervals.

John frowned at the devices, sensing their danger.

A wide slope edged downwards at a comfortable grade. John looked up, seeing how the hillside climbed all the way up to a protective fence, hiding both highway and the traffic slowing down to catch the shopping center's off-ramp. Loading bay doors for various outlets lined the left wall, each one designated by smaller signs bathed in white light. Metallic dumpsters rested against the wall, their bulks gleaming under nearby fluorescent glows and stretching onwards in a bumpy line of braille. The containers were of various lengths, some only square boxes while others were almost as long as a school bus. They varied in height, from five feet high to a more daunting six feet.

"Here we are," Haley whispered, creeping toward the first bin. "The first treasure chest."

John followed her along, eyeing the metal box. Overhead, traffic rumbled by like missiles running on fumes.

"This one," Haley said and stopped before a dumpster spattered with warning signs and phone numbers. With a little grunt, she tried flipping the lid off and failed. "Well, shit. They have a padlock on it now. Come on. There's another one. This section has a couple of men's shops. Or did, anyway. Let's see if we can find you something warm."

The next bin was also locked, but the third wasn't. Haley threw the lid back with some effort and peered inside.

"Your first dumpster dive," Haley announced with a little smile, nodding at the garbage collection of boxes and bags.

"Okay, root through the boxes first. Don't worry about the garbage bags. And don't litter. That really pisses off folks. And, really, the city doesn't need it. You start on that end and I'll start over here."

With that, she got a foot up on a protruding piece of metal and leaned into the bin, until her butt was aimed at the night sky. She pawed through the refuse, peeking here and there, discarding everything. John watched her for a few seconds, stepped up to an opposite corner, and tentatively retrieved a cardboard box. Several blue packing slips were stuck to the front.

"That one looks promising," Haley said.

John peeked inside the box before turning it over and giving it a shake. Nothing fell out.

"Happens," she said. "And for the record, this is a long shot. Don't be surprised if we don't find shit here. Actually, be happy if we don't find shit."

She smiled and glanced at the security cameras. The dark fixtures stared back with baleful scrutiny, melting her humor. "Work fast. We might not have much time."

With that, she sped up her search. At one point she climbed into the bin to get to a few boxes out of reach.

"What's the date?" Haley asked herself and stood up. "I know of a few apartment complexes that might have some goodies tossed to the curb. Some places have monthly trash nights for heavy things. Furniture and such. Some people toss out clothes then, too. Whole wardrobes sometimes. Not bad when you don't think about why they're tossing out perfectly good clothes."

She got a leg over the dumpster's lip and swung herself out with a groan.

"This isn't for me anymore. I should be…" She trailed off and turned her face away from her companion, hiding a second's worth of grief and regret. "Come on."

The next bin was too high to climb into, so Haley told John they'd come back for it. The dumpster after that had no lid at all and didn't appear full. A good two-thirds of its mass was cloaked in shadows. Haley stopped and peeked over the side, her expression lighting at the contents.

"Okay, I'm too short for this one so you go in and dig. There's some stuff at the bottom. Lower yourself down in there and look for anything useful. This might be the one. Once found a dress in here."

John looked at her.

"Go on," Haley said and indicated he crawl over the lip. "In you go. Said I'm too short. These tall ones are a bitch to climb back out of when you're inside."

Unsure of himself, John gripped the dumpster's top and hauled himself up. He got one leg over, then the other, and dropped on cardboard. He looked to Haley for direction.

"Get moving," she said, finger twirling at the floor. "Hurry. This one's going to take a while to really get through. I'll keep watch."

John nodded, whether consciously or not, and hunkered down. He kicked at some of the larger scraps of refuse and uncovered a few things of note. A pair of gloves. Styrofoam popcorn filler, but nothing that interested him. A long plank had various bent nails hammered at different angles, so he moved that to one side, sifting through clumps of damp paper that he didn't like to touch or smell.

"See anything?"

John grunted.

"No? Well, take another look."

At her insistence, John lowered himself into the bin once again.

Misplaced plastic containers, baby clothing, cracked lamp fixtures. He uprooted a drying blanket and frowned at the stink. There was a small chair with two broken legs and a mess of what might have been an empty tub of yogurt. John turned in circles and scoured the area around his feet.

A child's doll sat not four feet away on a pile of cardboard, arms open and button eyes smiling. The toy interested him and, for whatever the reason, he stepped toward it.

And slipped.

He fell backwards, feet shooting out from underneath, hands rushing behind him to cushion the crash.

A nail, hammered into that dangerous length of wood and straight enough to be spiteful, punched through the meaty middle of John's left hand and popped out the other side. That shocking spike immobilized him at the bottom of the dumpster as if in the grip of a terrible electrical current while the bin's opening perfectly framed the night in dark lines. John inhaled sharply, held it, and bellowed. He jerked his hand right then left, but the nail refused to let go.

John's squeal reached an agonized pitch.

"What's wrong?" Haley blurted, peeping over the dumpster's lip.

"Hey!"

A door along the mall's back end opened and two uniformed individuals emerged, their heavy-duty belts jingling. A man and a woman, none too pleased with the pair of two-legged raccoons on their doorstep.

"Oh, hi," Haley said, dropping back while John remained inside, still wailing.

"The hell you guys doing?" the man asked as he dug his heel into the door's base, lowering a metal leg to prevent the door from closing. The woman approached the dumpster and glanced inside.

"Just looking," Haley said, her attention split between the two guards.

"The one in here is hurt."

"Goddammit," the male officer fumed and pulled a radio receiver off his tactical vest. He turned, and Haley glimpsed the words 'MALL SECURITY' stamped across his back. "Gene, you there?"

"Sir, are you all right?" the female officer yelled, attempting to out-yowl a screaming John.

"You just stay where you are," the man warned, glaring at Haley. "What's wrong with him, Patty?"

"Hell if I know. Looks like something done to his hand."

"Goddammit," the man declared again before barking, "Gene, you there? Answer me!"

"Sir, can you get up?" Patty said, surveying the edge of the dumpster as if it were a cliff side. "Sir, answer me when I'm speaking to you. Can you get up?"

"Ma'am, just step away from the bin there," the male

officer directed. "You're trespassing on private property and have to leave the area immediately. If you refuse I'll call the police and have them arrest you for trespassing. *Gene!* Answer me!"

"Sir, are you able to stand?" Patty repeated while her partner droned out his memorized warning.

John abruptly stood, his shoulders clearing the dumpster's height, and he straightened his back. The sudden move made Patty step back, one hand going to her belt.

"Joey," Patty said in alarm.

Joey and Haley both looked to the dumpster as John yanked the troublesome plank from his hand and clanged the wood off a metal wall. He screamed at his palm before side-jumping out of the bin, clearing the lip with ease. He landed between the security staff.

"Jesus Christ," Joey exclaimed, drawing one leg back as if making to kick.

John charged him.

The security guard whirled into a powerful back kick, buckling John at the waist and stopping him in his tracks. Air escaped John and he staggered back a step just as Patty cracked an extended baton across his back.

John straightened, face contorted with hurt.

Joey punched him across the face, driving him to the pavement.

"John!" Haley shouted, hands gnarled into fists at her sides.

"You attacked me first," Joey got out, chest heaving from the shot of adrenaline. "You attacked me. You came at me and I defended myself."

"I saw it," Patty said, arm cocked and ready if the homeless guy wanted to go another round. "I saw it."

The homeless guy did.

John stood like a spring breaking free of a worn sofa. One hand lashed out and dug into Joey's neck and hoisted the gurgling security officer off his feet. Joey's strangled cry was nipped just as Patty cranked John's lower back with the baton once again, seeking to free her partner.

John hissed at the impact, spine arching to the brink of hyperextension, but absorbed the blow. He bounced Joey off a concrete wall and whirled upon Patty as she jabbed the baton deep into John's midsection. The blow dropped him to his knees, gasping.

A firm believer in subduing an attacker, Patty clanked the baton off the back of his head.

She hammered him again as his knuckles kissed asphalt, and a third time when he lifted his grimacing face and looked her straight in the eye.

"Stay down," Patty hissed and cracked him a fourth time across that snarling, mad-dog expression, splitting the skin of his forehead in a burst of berry juice. "Stay *down*."

John swatted her across her midsection with the back of one hand, the blow so fast she didn't have time to react. Patty flew into the dumpster's metallic girth, ringing it like a church bell.

"You fucker," Joey slurred, propped up on one elbow and trying to rise.

John rushed and grabbed the security man, brought Joey

in close, and bared teeth that elongated into fangs. Joey's face went slack and he kicked at John's lower legs, frantic to escape.

One boot caught John in the knee.

The shot infuriated him.

He slammed Joey's head against the concrete wall, squashing the life from the guard in an egg burst of skull matter. A surprised shriek spun John around, his hand dripping with horrific pulp.

Haley stood at the light's fringe, her hands clamped to her face, her eyes about ready to burst from their sockets.

John huffed, cavernous lungs working like a freight train, the cords on his neck prominent and bulging. His eyes had become black. His teeth daggers. And his fingers.

Knives extended from his fingers.

Haley barely possessed breath to scream and so released a mangled wheeze of unchecked terror. She spun away drunkenly, attention split between the man she thought she knew and the best escape route. John wasn't really John at all. He wasn't even a person. And that was enough to break through the communications jam between her brain and her legs.

Haley ran.

She only made it ten strides when the claws clamped about her neck.

*

Returning from the shitter a full five pounds lighter, Gene Malkin, the on-duty security supervisor, stopped and stared at the bank of security screens. The displays showed the fight as it happened behind the mall, in pale, cheap-ass quality Gene often complained about to the mall manager, right up to Joey getting his face squashed into a concrete block. Gene's jaw dropped and hung on the breeze as if the hinges had just been freshly greased. The color in his cheeks bled out in a drain-sucking rush, as the screens displayed Joey's killer rushing after the fleeing bag woman and grabbing her around the neck.

Joey's killer smashed the bag woman into a trash bin's side. The resulting tomato-like spurt of her head paralyzed Gene to the core.

That was a person, a voice chatted in his skull.

Something caught the murderer's attention, and he half-turned, dropping the dead woman as he did so.

Oh shit, Gene thought as all of his sphincters, known and unknown, tightened at once.

The door. The *open* door.

The lights and smells and all within lured Joey's killer toward the yawning mouth of the open door, hesitantly at first, as if wary of a trap. The sharp camera display recorded every movement as a silent, high-quality movie.

Gene grabbed the telephone on his desk. He jammed the receiver to his ear and punched in the quick and dirty number to the Halifax police department, his eyes never leaving the screen as the man who had executed at least two people—one of whom was a valued security staffer and his friend—slowly entered the mall's back door.

"Oh *shit*," Gene said, breathless, his heart already

exceeding recommended RPMs. The killer disappeared from the camera's frame.

"Yeah, we got a crazy person here in the Martin and MacDonald," he barked when a voice answered the line. "You heard me. We got a fucking murderer in the Martin and MacDonald Mall, so send over whatever you got. Fucking *now!*"

*

The water dripped from the mop bucket's wringer when Jake Redmond pressed his weight down on the lever. He eased off, adjusted his mop, and squeezed again, hearing a pee-like trickle. Damn food court and the fuck-heads who ate there didn't give a damn about the effort he or Connor or Christine put into keeping the place clean. It was just whoops sorry about that, with some lame excuse and a shit-eating grin. Almost as if it was on purpose, and those were the only ones who hung around. With a thousand-plus souls herded through the food court in the run of a day, something hitting the floor was an almost guaranteed event, but it still got on Jake's nerves. What really twisted his pearly danglers were the assholes who decided to mix things up a bit, just for shits and giggles. And if he ever found the prick who had left two pounds—two whole *pounds*—of pure, patiently collected canine scat on a table, well, Jake would probably be arrested for shoving his mop up their asshole. There was no justice.

A sharp scream broke his thoughts and he looked to the door of the janitor's station.

The fuck was that now? Jake's shift had started in glorious fashion with a whole pizza, ass-up, on the tiles only fifteen minutes ago, and now what? Burritos? Sub sandwiches? Baby barf?

He hesitated, considered flat-out ignoring the scream, and then felt bad for even thinking about ignoring it. Jake placed his mop against a wall. Five seconds later, he opened the door.

A big guy in a sweatshirt stood there, hunched over as if about to tackle someone, and that was all Jake knew. The man grabbed him by the shirt and whipped him face-first into the nearest wall. The impact wasn't as spectacular as Joey's, but it was messy enough that Jake went down and did not move again.

John roared at the unmoving man, livid that he had been challenged. He took hold of an arm and vigorously twisted it left and right before releasing the broken limb. A long, well-lit hallway proceeded a good twenty meters before turning a corner. Three closed doors dotted the passage but John ignored them, acutely aware of the grand spectrum of aromas issuing from deeper within the mall. John—but part of him was sensing he was no longer John—thought about the one called Haley. He didn't like what he'd done to her, but a building, all-encompassing rage immolated that regret, compelling him onward, urging him to do more. Telling him he *could* do more. Much more.

He pounded a wall and the chalky crumple of wallpapered cement echoed briefly. Voices lurked around the corner. Many voices.

John was pissed off enough to see what they were.

His claws raked the wall as he walked by, leaving tattered curls in his wake.

Images blurred through his mind's eye, and the word "Bailey" came to him. Bailey was his name. His true name. He rumbled with recognition, and felt the mounting pressure of gathering memories just behind the thinnest, straining membrane of total recall. Bailey remembered mesmerizing fragments, unable to grasp the grand scope of it all. He remembered violence with ease, and inherently knew he exceled at destruction. His hands had changed and he stopped to examine them at the corridor's corner. Voices filled his ears and wrenched his attention away from the red sickles weaponizing his fingers. Bailey eventually turned the corner and beheld another tunnel of white. At the end, however, a crowd—a herd—of people walked through the mouth, appearing and disappearing in seconds.

Bailey went to them.

He emerged in an enormous food court that sat perhaps three hundred people at the very least, eating, drinking, chatting—their noses in shopping bags, rummaging through the evening's purchases. Some laughed and some sat hunched over, feeding in earnest. One of them, the closest to Bailey, looked up when he appeared at the mouth of the hallway.

Bailey slammed the chewing head into the table, splintering the plastic surface.

That got the attention of the masses and for a fleeting moment, the entire glass and steel and fabricated wood cavern focused upon him in stunned silence.

A team of security guards, metal batons already extended, appeared at the fringes of the food court and weaved through the people, closing in on the apparent hostile shopper.

Bailey roared, throwing his hands wide and startling the nearest shoppers.

Several humans hugged their children close, staring at Bailey with wide-eyed dismay bordering on outraged hatred. A few even stood and pointed Bailey out to the approaching security team. A pack of teenagers stood and watched with gameplay delight. A man—a big man wearing the latest winter style—got up from his table with two others and faced Bailey.

The man reached out a calming hand, his reddening expression twisted into a scowl. "Hey, dude, the hell's the matter—"

Bailey took the hand and its attached arm and flung the man ten feet behind him as an afterthought.

The man's two other companions stood. One dark-haired with a braid, the other wearing a black-and-white snowflaked toque.

Bailey raked the face of the dark-haired one, shredding flesh. The blow drove the man to his knees while thick fluids, bright under the fluorescent lights, gushed over his chest. The second man got in close enough to punch Bailey, cracking his jaw to one side. Bailey slashed the puncher's stomach, opening the sweater and the skin underneath. The puncher dropped to his knees, cradling his midsection as he bent over as if in worship. The tiles turned red.

That was enough to incite the stampede.

The spooked herd of humans dropped their plastic trays of mush and fled. Shrieks spiked the air and melded into a single off-key note of chaos. Children stumbled amongst the tables, crying and squealing and impeding the rush of men and women. Some fell in their haste, others were knocked off their feet. The mob flooded the exits and the corridors, stampeding away from the food court frenzy.

The security team struggled against that thrashing tide, closing in on the man with the bloodied hands and Halloween makeup. One security guard gave up and ran with the rest, hauling a pair of teenage girls to their feet from where they had frozen at a table.

Bailey watched them go, roared so they would move faster. His limbs thrummed with newfound strength, and he sensed the awkward yet undeniable righteousness of it all. His jaws snapped and he ripped the nearby tabletops free.

Four new challengers fought free of the retreating herd, not so easily frightened.

Two women and two men. One man could have been an athlete of some measure, tall but bulky with fat rather than defined muscle. The women were just as tall but slender, their drawn faces brave and focused, their batons extended like singular claws.

"Get down on the floor," one of them yelled. "Get down on the floor now!"

Bright-eyed and showing teeth, Bailey did not obey.

"Get down!" the smaller man insisted with a pointed finger, brandishing his own club. Three more guards appeared at the absolute corners of the emptying food court, racing to reinforce their companions. Bailey snarled, warning them to stay back, and looked to one of the table units to his left, complete with seats, all suspended by a singular post of considerable thickness.

"*I said get down, goddammit!*"

Instead, Bailey crouched, reached out, and fastened a hand around the table's thick support column. Claws clicked on the smooth surface. He paused, securing his grip, while black eyes narrowed to slits.

Just before he ripped the unit free of the floor.

29

The police had Regency Park cordoned off when Kirk and Carma arrived, so they parked across from a lengthy stone wall that marked the park's southern border and waited for night. Officers milled about the crime scene, collecting evidence and taking pictures, while the multiple yellow ribbons that cut up the area seemed to be missing a bow. Carma scanned the site as parked cruiser lights whirled, shooing off the dark. People filled the sidewalks, all hopeful and patiently waiting for a peek.

"Okay, you stay here," Carma told Kirk as she unbuckled. "I'm going in."

"You're going in there?"

She frowned. "Yeah, I'm going in there. Don't repeat everything I say as a question. It's annoying."

"Cops are everywhere in there."

"It's a *park*, you turkey. Plenty of places for me to hide. No one will see me coming or going and I'll sure as hell smell them before they hear me. Besides, it's dark."

"Turkey," Kirk muttered.

"What?"

"You called me turkey. That's an improvement over what you used to call me."

"What did I used to call you?"

"Dumbass."

Carma held his gaze for a moment before allowing a wry smirk. "Did I call you that?"

"You did. Several times."

"Huh. Wow. How about that."

"Yeah."

"Keep the radio on," Carma said and cracked the door open. "Give me an hour at least. I should be back then."

"And if you aren't?"

Carma shook her head in annoyance. "What do you mean 'and if you aren't'? Christ, Doug. And don't you dare tell me to be careful or I swear to God I'll slap the living stupid out of your ass."

She closed the door only to open it a second later.

"Dumbass."

Kirk smiled wanly as Carma slammed the door and trotted off. He watched her look both ways before crossing the street, her hands deep into the pockets of her winter coat. She resembled a woman from abroad, trudging through the icy winters of Sweden or Norway. She reached the sidewalk and soon disappeared past clots of onlookers. Her plan was to enter the park far and away from the masses, where there were no streetlights, where no one would be looking. Carma was an old pro at stealth. No one would see her coming or going.

That, and Kirk *was* a dumbass.

He sighed and strummed the steering wheel with a thumb, taking in the parked police cruisers and vans that glutted the park's main entrance. Maybe she would be lucky and catch a whiff of something. Kirk was hopeful. They still had plenty of time before the next full moon, but something seemed off about that. He didn't know what it was, but a bad feeling crossed his heart, dampening his spirits.

His eyes drifted back to the main entrance of the park. Police officers moved with purpose amongst the cars, women and men in uniform and outfitted with protective vests. At one point in his life, Kirk wanted that very job. He wanted to protect the city's people, wanted to enforce the law and bring evildoers into the light. As he watched the police walk about their vehicles, his expression softened, shifting into a dreamy glaze, and he remembered those childhood days. Then puberty hit, and his world spun out of control. His *were* blood matured, and he later became chosen as a warden, a protector, of the weak and defenseless human herds. A glorified sheep dog that kept the wolves at bay, ensuring that only a few were ever preyed upon during the year. He could do that part of the job, but it was the other part, the *were* part, that worried him. He'd seen feeding werewolves firsthand and didn't share their taste for blood, refrained from partaking in the scheduled hunts. Hunts that he supposed were sometimes necessary, even though he despised the thought of them. He imagined there were parts of the job the officers didn't care for either, but he couldn't think of what they might be—beyond what they were dealing with at the moment. The uniform looked noble and every bit as gallant as a suit of medieval armor.

Kirk rubbed his throbbing temples and settled into the seat, savoring the smell of Carma even as it dissipated from the truck.

His cell phone rang in the cup holder. Kirk watched it vibrate for a second before picking it up and checking the number.

Morris.

Debating whether to ignore it or answer, Kirk plunged ahead and flipped the phone open.

"Yeah?"

"Kirk."

"Yeah."

"You alone?"

"Huh?"

A pause on the line. "I asked if you were alone."

A group of five police officers stood in close quarters amongst their cars and vans. One of them was talking, the others listened. Kirk wished he could read lips.

"Yeah, I'm alone."

"Where's Carma?"

"How'd you know she was with me?"

"Good guess."

"Well, you can guess where she went, too."

Silence for a bit. "I need to talk to you."

"Can't talk on the phone?"

"No."

"All right." Kirk shifted, unease creeping in, threatening

to sour his guts. "I'm at the park."

"I know."

A set of fingers rapped on the passenger side window and Kirk jumped. After recovering from the scare, he glared at the Pictou warden and shook his head. A grim Morris opened the door and got inside.

"Is that shit I smell?" Morris asked.

"If it is, you're cleaning it up."

"Ha."

"All right, so you're here," Kirk said. "How'd you know we'd be here?"

"Didn't. Cops were zeroing in on the place while I was a couple of streets over, so I just followed my nose. Got in amongst the ambulance chasers and the death peekers like any curious passerby. Was waiting for night to come on when I spotted your truck. Saw her so I stayed out of sight and smell. Where'd she go?"

"Carma? Into the park to see if she can catch a whiff of anything."

"Good. I saw her get out."

"All right, well, she's gone and I'm here and you wanted to talk. Start talking."

Morris looked at the truck's passenger door and slowly flicked the lock.

"Okay," Kirk noted. "So we're both safe and sound now. Good for us. What the hell do you want?"

Morris drew a hand over his face and stared ahead. "I had to get out of the apartment. It was too bad. Too tense."

"Yeah."

"You know what I mean, right?"

Kirk shrugged. "Maybe. Didn't we talk about this before?"

"I did, but you didn't," Morris said. "You're just too sensitive."

Kirk studied the warden's profile. "Yeah."

"So you know what I'm talking about?"

Kirk nodded.

"You don't eat people. I know that. Turns my guts in a way, but I'm past that. So what do you do? Since you're something of a vegan."

"I eat what I can."

"Like what?"

"Roasts. Beef. Pork."

"You cook that?"

"Yeah. Sure."

"Nothing raw?"

Kirk realized his fingers had stopped strumming the steering wheel. "Sometimes."

"And that takes the edge off? Since you won't hunt people? Or try to avoid it at least?"

A huge drop of rain spattered the windshield, followed by several others.

"Sometimes."

"Only sometimes."

"Yeah."

"The smell," Morris began with a sigh, "the smell of Ezekiel was driving me crazy."

"Me too."

To his surprise, Morris didn't pounce on the admission.

"This Harvest Moon," the Pictou *were* began, "I partook. Killed a guy. Like everyone else. Just like all the other wardens. Well, except maybe you, y'goddamn hippy dicksmack. Hunted two days before the moon, actually. That didn't take the edge off at all. I knew then that I had a problem. Felt the pressure building, y'know?"

Kirk hung his head, nowhere near prepared to hear such details but forcing himself, knowing very well what Morris was describing.

"That first one? I devoured him. Bloated myself. Thought that would do the trick, y'know. Except… except it didn't. Which I thought was really weird. So three nights later I hunted down and killed another. A hitchhiker. What the hell, right? Another missing person is all. Anyway, damn near ruptured myself that time. Thought that would take care of things."

"Jesus Christ, Morris."

The Pictou warden held up a hand, invoking silence. "Except it *didn't*. Not in the fucking least."

"I don't wanna hear anymore."

"You have to hear."

"No, I don't."

"Kirk, I got no one else to talk to."

"Talk to Carma—she's pack leader."

"Yeah, but she wasn't in Newfoundland."

Kirk slumped in his seat.

"We were on the *island*," Morris said, fixing him with a glare as flat as unpolished marble. Rain speckled the windshield. "We both ate *weres*. What I need to know is if you're getting these cravings, too."

Kirk couldn't find his voice.

"Well?" Morris asked.

"No," Kirk finally whispered.

"You're lying."

"The fuck I'm lying, look at my face."

Morris did. "Then what is it? I mean, I had to get out of your place because Ezekiel was just lying there and I was damn near drooling to chew his face off. Just finish him off like leftover chicken on a dinner platter. I still get those cravings. That's the scary thing. Ever since the island I've felt great… but I've had times like this. They just came and went or I went out and took down a deer. But that's…it's like living off candy. Or just noodles. I mean, you can *do* it, and it'll keep you alive, but it's not really filling you. Not really nourishment."

Kirk stared at the warden, transfixed by the revelation. He squirmed in defeat. "Yeah. Me too."

It was Morris's turn to stare. "So you do get the cravings? The same cravings?"

"Yes."

"You lying sack of shit."

"I just said I do."

"You had me thinking it was just fucking me this whole time!" Morris blurted. "I was going crazy. You heard me say I was going crazy. That's fucking low, man. Fucking low."

"I was going to confide in you?" Kirk fired back. "We don't exactly get along, Morris. We've been through shit but…"

"Kirk, we're in the middle of shit. We're at the fucking *epicenter* of shit."

The rain had grown into huge clumps of wet snow that blew apart upon hitting the windshield.

"So what do we do?" Kirk asked.

"I don't know," Morris said, utterly defeated. "I have to think about this. It's all too much."

The truck's interior felt like a deep freeze, but Kirk kept his hands off the heating controls. The cold was the only grip on reality he had at the moment.

"You think the elders know?" Kirk asked.

"Since we already told them we ate *weres*? Like the day after? And now with Bailey? Yeah. I'm pretty sure they know something."

"You can control yourself?" Kirk asked him.

"Yeah. I mean, I think I can. As long as I'm away from the others. It's the blood that does it, I think. Funny thing, though."

"Yeah? What?"

Morris considered him. "I don't get anything off you. Back at the apartment, even Nick and Janice and all those guys were smelling like spicy roasts to me. That, or burritos. Somewhere in between the two. And I mean that. I had to get out or I was going to snap. But here, now, with you? Nothing. It's either because you're a piece of shit and I know it, or because the urge has passed, or because you and I both ate *weres* and a part of me knows it and doesn't want anything to do with you. Or it recognizes you're like me. Like our own little secret club."

"I don't get anything like that."

"Strange," Morris said.

"Not yet, anyway."

They sat in silence, time passing in measured flicks on the dashboard clock.

"All right," Kirk finally said. "This is what we do. You stay away from the others so you don't go crazy. Keep a safe distance. See if this passes."

"I don't think it will."

"See if it passes," Kirk stressed. "Might be like an addiction, right? Maybe over time, it'll all go away. Maybe all we both need is a weekend parked over a toilet bowl, sweating and yakking our guts out. We got other things to worry about, anyway."

Morris nodded but he seemed distracted. "Yeah. Okay. We take care of Bailey first."

"One thing at a time."

Morris reluctantly agreed, his hands knotting into fists between his knees.

"I don't think he's anywhere near here."

"I don't know," Kirk sighed. "I just hope we find him soon. We got a few more days until the next full moon. We just stay positive. Stay focused."

Morris smirked and threw his head back. He clawed at the lock, opened the door and got out.

"Where you going?" Kirk asked.

"Fresh air. Nothing better to get the thoughts moving along. Thanks for listening. Partner."

Morris slammed the door and walked down the street,

glancing at the gathered police officers.

Partner.

Kirk didn't like being called that.

30

The first police officers responding to the Martin and MacDonald Mall belonged to the Central Halifax Police Force. Four CHP cruisers responded within minutes of the security supervisor's call. The officers pulled up around the main entrance, forming a barrier of sorts, just in time to witness the final trickles of a massive human flood. People were wailing, some carrying or struggling with those rendered unconscious from the sheer press of bodies being channeled through the bottleneck exits. Some individuals were unlucky enough to be trampled. Constable Nancy Keiller took one look at the bewildered stragglers emerging from the mall's shattered doors and radioed for Emergency while her driver, Constable Phil Beach, slammed the car into park and jumped outside. Other officers clambered out of their vehicles and held up their hands in a fleeting attempt to instill some semblance of order. Citizens stopped within an arm's reach of the assembled authorities and machine-gunned them with eyewitness accounts of a terrorist attack from deep inside the mall. Some claimed that several terrorists had opened fire in the food court. That story was soon refuted by shoppers who were actually present in the eating area, explaining that a single distressed man had appeared in Halloween makeup and with blood on his hands. All witnesses verified that a handful of the mall's security staff had moved in to surround the infuriated and violent individual.

Nancy Keiller, outfitted in light body armor and a tactical vest, stood tall behind her cruiser's hood, looking into the fully lit interior of the shopping mall. She scanned for stragglers and threats, and couldn't see anything beyond the clear glass of the entrance. The hallway was clear although littered with debris.

"See anything?" Phil asked beside her.

"No. Get everyone back behind the cars. Get on the horn and report the situation. Bring in support. There's no way we can cover all the doors to this place."

Phil ducked into the car and made the call. The other officers stood behind their cruisers. Their weapons had been freed but not drawn, though hands rested upon the grips of their standard-issue Smith and Wesson pistols. One of the officers realized a wall of frightened people had formed behind the police presence, so she pulled out a bullhorn and ordered the masses to back away to a safe distance.

A single individual ran toward the mall's glass doors, a young man, perhaps nineteen or twenty, tall and skinny and dressed in clothing that he might've picked up at an army surplus store. He belted his way through the entrance and stopped before the cruisers, eyes blazing.

"Hey! *Hey*! There's a guy in there killing people!"

Nancy urged him to get clear. She waved the guy over, his hair a salute to mullets, and he ran to her.

"There's a crazy bastard in there," he cried, "and he's killing people! He killed two mall security guys and was squaring off against the others. He—he squashed one with a fucking table!"

Nancy collected him around her cruiser and Phil crowded in, his attention divided between the mall entrance and the survivor.

"Slow down now," Nancy instructed him. "Take a breath. Did you see anyone else?"

"No ma'am," he blurted. "Nuh-uh. I was in the food court and hung on while everyone else ran, just to see what was going on. Then shit got downright dirty. I mean dirty. There's one guy in there causing all this. Mall security went in there and last I saw, about five more folks were running for the food court. They all had their clubs out. Some had that spray can shit. They were shouting. There was a lot of screaming."

"Did the attacker have any weapons?" Nancy asked.

"Weapons? Nah, nothing, just his hands. And the guy was strong! I mean he ripped a fucking food court *table* out of the floor with his bare hands! I heard the crackle of the floor tiles and saw him lift the table over his head. When he killed that security guy with the table I took off. Last thing I saw were uniforms being thrown around, and I mean fucking *thrown*."

"Are there any more people in there?"

"Huh? Ah, yeah," the young man said, speaking as if suddenly very tired, and folded his hands above his head. "At least the guards. I saw other people running for other exits. Not only through this one. I mean, people were just bolting in every which direction to get clear. Just everywhere."

Nancy met Phil's eyes before focusing on the survivor. "Sir, I want you to stay near Officer Beach here, okay? Stay here and listen to whatever he says. There are going to be other police units arriving soon and they'll want to hear your report too, okay?"

The guy nodded.

"Phil, I'm going in."

"Who you taking?"

Nancy looked around her squad. "Everyone, except you and Vicky. You two keep watch. I don't think you'll have any trouble keeping the crowd back."

"No," Phil agreed, examining the banks of shoppers gathered amongst the parked cars on the mall's expansive lot. To no one's surprise, hardly any vehicles were leaving the lot. No one wanted to miss the show.

Nancy called the officers to her cruiser for a huddle. "I'm going in. There are enough eyewitness accounts confirming that there's only one unarmed attacker, if you don't count a table as a lethal projectile. There's a number of mall security staff unaccounted for. They don't carry anything heavier than batons and mace. I'm not asking for anyone to come with me, but I'd appreciate company."

"I'll go," Nolan Matthews said, a big intimidating cop from the south shore.

"I'll go, too," said Jesse Ferris, a Bridgewater native.

"I'm there," announced Vicky Lyons from Yarmouth County.

"You won't," Nancy informed her. "You stay back with Phil and keep an eye on the entrance. Make sure no one follows us inside. Support's no more than five minutes out anyway. In ten they're gonna see this place from the space station."

"Only one guy in there," Phil added. "One strong guy."

"Probably all souped up on some loaded shit," Jesse muttered.

"No doubt," Nancy agreed. "Ashlie, you got that Taser?"

"I do," answered the young woman from Wolfville, a fourth-degree black belt in Aikido.

"Get it ready. Will, you coming?"

The tall officer from Dartmouth nodded grimly.

"All right, then, weapons free," Nancy said. "Ashlie, call in the paramedics. Meet me here and we'll all go."

Jesse popped open his cruiser's trunk and retrieved a shotgun. With the weapon pointed at the pavement, he jogged back to the assembled team. When all were ready, five of them drew their handguns and marched to the main entrance. They moved inside in a crouched line, all aiming in various directions.

Vicky called for a team of first responders on her radio while Phil Beach watched his fellow officers disappear down the mall's well-lit corridor.

The main walkway, with its festive decorations and signs brightly displaying CHRISTMAS SALE, hummed with the vast emptiness. If Nancy hadn't known it was actually just after six o'clock in the evening, she would've thought it was closing time. Except for the shops and their opened gates. And the debris spread over the mall's beige tile floor. Everything that had been placed on display outside of each shop was now kicked down and strewn haphazardly across the mall corridor. Soap baskets, boxed chocolates, paperbacks and hardbacks lay in a frenzy, caught in a violent storm surge of thousands charging at full panicked speed. Christmas trees had been overturned and stomped on, bulbs kicked and crushed, garlands hung in tatters. Some of the lights remained on, casting a dim twinkle across the floor tiles.

The fleeing shoppers had torn the living shit out of the place, and Nancy believed that anyone who didn't get out of the way of the rush would have been trampled by the unchecked herd. Her fellow officers reviewed the carnage with neutral expressions, the scene resembling a street party that had gotten way out of hand. The five officers held their tight formation as they crept past wrecked entrances of popular brand shops and gummed-up clothes racks. The overhead lighting remained unaffected, soft, yet bright, offering the best shopping experience to the mall's customers.

"Food court's on the second level," Nolan said quietly, pointing his gun to the floor with both hands. A broken bottle of an expensive perfume wafted by, issuing from a stomped pack and a dribble sprinkled with sparkling shards. The officers soon reached a juncture where the corridor split north and west. A tower of wide stairs decorated with bright holiday lights rose and offered a quick route to the next floor. Squashed bags and boxes littered the gap between the steps.

The sound of sobbing emanating from the west stopped the team. An accompanying undercurrent of moaning drifted from the north, weak and eerie, like a ghost that lay gut-shot and bleeding.

Nancy stopped and held up a hand, indicating she was headed for the cries of distress. They found survivors, shell-shocked and confused, rising from the deep wells of smartphone kiosks and fallen walls of handmade Christmas wreaths. The slow-moving few who had either been slapped out of the stampede's way or had decided to wait until the shocking, heavy gust of flesh had passed. Some had their backs pressed against the walls just inside the storefront thresholds. When they saw the peacekeepers, their cries stopped for only a second before increasing in volume, calling for help.

"Will," Nancy ordered before peering up the north corridor.

The young officer rushed to the nearest civilian—a gentleman of perhaps seventy-five years—and tended to his wounds.

Nancy pinched her radio's receiver attached to her upper left shoulder. "Phil, I'll need first responders in the north corridor. ASAP. All along the strip here. People are coming out of their holes like rabbits who'd just gotten out of the way of a tank."

"Roger that."

She released the receiver and looked back to the glowing set of stairs. That would take them to the food court level but still a good ten-minute walk away from the crime scene. Her other choice was to advance to the escalators that emptied right into the center of the food court, which didn't bode so well with her.

"Will, you stay with these people," Nancy ordered. "See who can walk and get them out of here. Make the others comfortable and watch over them. The rest of us are going up."

"Roger that."

Nancy studied the faces of her three fellow officers. Their expressions were stern and ready to use lethal force if needed. She'd known them for the better part of nine years and couldn't ask for a better team.

"You all good?" she asked, knowing the answer.

Affirmative nods all round.

Nancy indicated the stairs and its starlight glow. "Let's bag this bastard."

They ascended.

31

A rush of activity amongst the police cruisers parked at the mouth of Regency Park caused Kirk to sit up and pay attention. In seconds, half of the cars started and pulled out into traffic, sirens blaring and lights flashing in a hypnotic swirl. The flurry of cars and bodies dispelled the gloomy funk Morris had left Kirk to deal with, replacing it with a growing sense of urgency. Kirk watched as several cars streaked away into the night, wondering where they were going and sensing that Bailey wasn't going to wait for a full moon. Somehow, Bailey was going to start that very night.

He grabbed his cell phone and debated dialing the wardens at the apartment. The remaining officers appeared agitated to some degree, elevated to a heightened level of alertness. Kirk studied the city park, in the direction Carma had gone. Could it all have something to do with her? He doubted it.

The door opened almost ten minutes later, causing Kirk to flinch.

Carma hauled herself aboard the truck. "See where those cars went?"

"Of course I did."

"Know a place called the Martin and MacDonald Mall?"

Kirk wasn't so quick to answer. "Yeah."

"Get us there. I was in the park bush sniffing around when I overheard some cops. They have a three-twenty developing at that mall. I have no idea what a three-twenty is but those cops thought it was pretty important."

"It's something," Kirk agreed and started the engine. "About a half dozen squad cars scorched rubber pulling away from the park so fast."

"Follow the flashing lights," Carma ordered.

So he did. The police, however, did not slow for traffic lights as normal civilians should, and Kirk soon lost them within the city.

"You find anything in the park?" Kirk asked while they waited for a set of lights to turn green.

"Someone died in there," Carma deadpanned, digging her cell phone out of a pocket. "Smelled blood the instant I went over the wall. Nothing else, though. Ground was damp but it had already been covered by the cops. Couldn't get close to the exact place where blood was. No trails or scents. Nothing. Just the blood."

"Should you alert the others?"

"About what? This? Let's wait until we see what's going on. Could be anything."

Kirk *hoped* it was anything. He thought about telling her about Morris but the lights turned green, so he drove on, weaving his way through the cold cityscape. Huge elms flashed by, their bare limbs reaching desperately to the sky.

Neither Kirk nor Carma spoke as they flashed through the streets. In time, the white dome of the Martin and MacDonald Mall illuminated the skyline with an extravagant collection of Christmas lighting and brand-name shops. Police cruisers sped down ramps and through parking lots. As Kirk and Carma drew closer, they saw a large mob standing behind parked squad cars, faces turned toward the mall. The police had cordoned off two large entrances on the south side with their vehicles.

Kirk pulled into a parking space where he had a somewhat clear view of the mall's largest entrance. Red, white, and blue police lights swirled across the mall's concrete walls as officers placed wooden barricades several meters back from the glass doors.

"Holy shit," Carma whispered.

"Yeah."

"They're sealing the place up."

"Something's up."

"You stay in here," Carma ordered and cracked open the door. "I'll check it out. Soon as I get an idea about what's going on, I'll be back."

"Be careful."

Carma glared at him. "What did I tell you about saying that?"

She slammed the door.

Kirk meant it all the same. He gripped the steering wheel and tapped out a nervous beat, straining to make out the shapes teeming behind the police barricade. Soon after, several ambulances pulled into the parking lot and stopped behind the cruisers. More activity as Kirk glimpsed first responders leaping out of the vans and tending to several injured people. His stomach clenched before he turned one way and then the other.

A pair of police officers opened up a set of doors to one entrance, allowing a line of armed officers and paramedics with gurneys to enter. The sight of all those men and women going into the mall only tightened Kirk's frayed nerves. Bailey was in there. The Halifax warden knew it. Bailey was in there and he was on the loose. Kirk rubbed his chin and scanned the cars surrounding his truck while dazzling police lights splayed over the thickening crowds.

Minutes later, the paramedics and their police escort returned with a collection of injured civilians, running through the opened doors and stopping in the midst of the waiting ambulances.

Kirk fidgeted.

He hoped Carma would return soon.

32

Sergeant Sean Decker of the CHP swung his size-thirteen boots out of the van and onto the asphalt. He rose into the night's winter breeze like a grim watchtower and turned his steely eyes and considerable bulk toward one of five entrances to the Martin and MacDonald Mall. Halifax police officers—his fellow officers—guarded the withdrawing paramedics bearing injured civilians. Decker's eyes narrowed into slits of concentration as his men and women withdrew thirty meters to an assembled wall of police cruisers and wooden barricades. The interior of the mall shone with festive splendor, making one wonder if there really was a killer on the rampage within those bright halls.

All reports concluded there was.

About nine members of the mall's own security had been decimated before the remainder fled. The supervisor—thank God Almighty—had the situational awareness and good sense to call in the police before vacating his post. Decker didn't blame him in the least. Mall cops weren't trained for such movie-style ultraviolence. Decker himself wasn't sure of what was in store for him, but as a veteran of three tours in Afghanistan with the RCR, including participation in both Operation Medusa and Falcon Summit, he wasn't about to underestimate the level of destruction a single crazy person could achieve, especially within a commercial setting. What brought him onto the scene were the reports of a blood-crazed individual who had attacked civilians and security professionals alike, and was probably responsible for the loss of communication with four of the CHP's own. According to the report, shots had been fired, which didn't bode well on Decker's mind. He made it a point to remember the department's four hundred and seven members by their first names, a feat he knew kept his brain matter sharp. He knew who the CHP had inside, knew their faces and personalities. And if he was called down to a conflict at eight at night, where those fellow officers may very well no longer be alive, well, he was going to make it his prime objective to not only apprehend the culprit inside, but also to personally drub his boot heel into the murderer's face.

Whoever was responsible, Decker would make certain he or she would be good and goddamn sorry for ever stirring up shit with his crew.

A flood of halogen light bleached his armored uniform as Decker stood and studied the beast of a mall before him. He was the commander of the Emergency Response Team for Halifax-Dartmouth, a specialized unit that was called in for scenarios deemed too dangerous for the regular constables. The ERT was the equivalent of the American SWAT, and dealt primarily with hostage and terrorist situations.

Decker stood behind his cruiser, helmet cradled in one arm, eyeing the mall's entrance like a medieval, axe-wielding executioner sizing up the bared neck of the condemned. He was a tall, imposing brute of a man, forty-five years of age, clean-shaven and alert, sheathed in black body armor. His tactical vest carried an intimidating array of spare magazines, canisters, plastic cuffs, and knives.

The warning beep of a truck in reverse broke his thoughts, chirped for several seconds, and stopped in a mechanical huff. Decker still didn't move.

"Sergeant Decker."

He turned and met the blue eyes of another officer. Decker nodded. "Sergeant Potter."

"You've been briefed about what's going on here?"

"I have. Anything to add?"

"One of my guys was assigned to get the remaining civilians out while four other officers went deeper into the mall. He later reported multiple gunshots, handgun and shotgun. Those officers have not replied to our calls since then."

Sergeant Potter paused and studied the glass doors. "That's it. That's where we both got called in."

"You have this place secured?"

Potter nodded. "Six entrances. One loading area that's a dead-end alley with a bunch of service doors. I've deployed teams around each. Snipers are assigned to the main entrances. The windows around the food court are covered in decals of some sort. Some fancy decorations the mall put up. Long story short, they can't see inside. Regardless, nothing's going in or getting out without my say-so."

Decker glanced around. "Anything on the roof here?"

"Nothing yet, but I'm going to get people on it."

"Power?"

"We have a line on that. When you're ready to insert, say the word and I'll have the whole mall shut down. The doors on the far right can be pushed open. All the others are automated."

Decker took in the information. "All civilians free and clear?"

"We're not sure. Go with about ninety-two percent probability. Regarding the power, we throw the switch and it all goes down. The security supervisor here says the cameras have battery backups, so there'll be a recording."

Decker considered that. "Half my team have mounted cameras, anyway."

"More the merrier." Potter paused. "You wanna wait for the feds? As backup?"

The tactical leader shook his head, confident they didn't need the support. "It's only one guy."

"Assumed he's armed," Potter pointed out. "He wasn't in the beginning, but those officers were."

The cold air dropped perhaps another three degrees in that instant.

"We'll go in through the back," Decker explained slowly. "Make our way through the mall. Get to the second level. Make sure there are no other civilians present, and do a store-to-store search on the way to the food court. Try and come up behind the guy. Tag him while the lights are off."

If Sergeant Potter had any reservations about the plan, he didn't make them known.

"When you're ready, then." Potter nodded and turned to a pair of officers at his back. Decker turned as well, facing a long white van striped with police force colors which had its ass pointed at the front doors. *The kennel*, he called the van, and inside was the best pack of hounds he had the pleasure of serving with this side of Kandahar.

Decker strode to the van's rear and rapped on its double doors. They opened and Decker pulled himself inside, taking a moment to accept a helmet from a seated officer. He pulled it on, fixed a radio mic directly over his mouth, and studied the assembled unit, all clad in identical uniforms and outfitted with the same gear and hardware as himself— body armor, helmets, and balaclavas to conceal their faces when it was time to roll, Smith and Wesson's strapped to thighs, MP5s held at port, and a couple of Remington shotguns. There were probably more than a few boot knives in the mix as well. After Decker closed the rear doors, he accepted his own Heckler and Koch submachine gun, sat down, and checked the weapon.

Eyes twinkled in the van's dim light.

Ready to swing the wrecking ball. Decker regarded his team. "Ladies and gentlemen, we've been invited to a shit kicker's hoedown, thrown by a single, unknown, squirrel-crazy assailant who has decided to royally fuck up this fine November evening. By all accounts, he is operating alone and, as of the last hour, possibly armed with police firearms. Central reports five officers went inside, one of whom was tasked to escort injured civilians out of the building. He's the only lawman to return from the mall. The other four have not returned or reported in. These people are in addition to an unknown number of missing civilians and security personnel. Shots have been fired. We're going in on my word and we are green to use deadly force. If you see a tall man dressed in a bloody sweatshirt and Halloween makeup, fire at will. Suspect was last seen in the food court. All entrances are covered but we'll be entering here, walk through the mall under the cover of darkness, and search shops as we approach the food court from the east to make sure our boy doesn't try an ambush or scoot behind us. All clear?"

"Clear," answered eleven operators.

"Questions?"

Not one.

"Get your sets ready."

Upon the command, the men and women hauled on third-generation night goggles over their helmets. Half of them wore video cameras upon their helmets, recording the coming event for later review and, if necessary, to prove if use of deadly force was justified. Decker looked them over, all ready to bounce on command. His unit comprised himself and eleven highly trained constables, male and female. All were accredited officers with years of experience and were still active members within their respected law enforcement branches. During special nights like these, however, they got called in to perform duties considered above normal policing.

"All right then," Decker said, and pinched the radio mic fixed to his helmet. "We're ready."

Five minutes later, the lights within the mall and the surrounding buildings and houses for a ten-block radius winked out, leaving a scorched-earth patch of blackness that marred an otherwise elegant city nightscape.

33

When the lights went out, Kirk's fingers tightened on the steering wheel. A great black void had suddenly opened where only seconds before the mall's superstructure glittered and shone with pre-Christmas merriment. Tiny lights blinked on amongst the crowds behind the police-erected barricades. Kirk struggled to see anything and told himself to relax, even though he'd already picked up his cell phone.

This is bad, he thought and craned his neck, straining to discern anything along the shopping mall entrance. Five minutes later, Carma opened the door and climbed aboard. "Cops are going in with a tac-team."

She settled into her seat and punched numbers on her phone. "Janice? Yeah, get down to the Martin and MacDonald Mall. No, we're not coming back. Get a cab. Martin and MacDonald. We're parked… where are we parked?"

"South parking lot," Kirk answered. "Look for H-section. No one around us anyway. Everyone's up front where the cops are."

Carma relayed the information and snapped the phone shut.

"Well, looks like he didn't wait for the full moon."

"Looks that way."

"I saw about a dozen special forces rushing to the door," Carma reported, staring at the mall. "Armed to the teeth. The story from the crowd is some guy walked into the food court and started throwing people around."

A surprised Kirk regarded her profile.

"Sounds like our guy, *n'est pas?*" Carma asked

"Shit."

"We're going to have to go in there," Carma said. "When everyone gets here. We'll go in as a pack. Find him and take him down."

"That's a SWAT team going in there." Kirk swung his attention back to the mall. "They might have a chance."

"There's no chance. Best they could do is hope they blow its head off again. Or torch him. And I didn't see anyone carrying anything that looked like a flamethrower."

"It might be something else," Kirk muttered. "Maybe a terrorist inside."

"It's our boy," Carma said in a resigned tone, thudding against her headrest. "And he's taken the center of the ring. Of the arena. Waiting for his challengers. You've been to this place before?"

"I've shopped here, yeah."

"Then start thinking about how we can get in there."

34

An armored train of bodies bristling with automatic weapons swept through the front entrance and steamed into the wide corridor beyond. The lead man carried a black shield the size of a small door with the word POLICE stamped across the front, just below a generous viewport. A hunched Sergeant Decker, goggles and balaclava covering his face, stayed at the heels of the shield bearer, sweeping his MP5 wherever he looked. The remaining officers followed in a line where each person covered a section of the corridor with their weapon. The night goggles utilized the minutest light fragment and intensified it, transforming pitch black conditions into a haunting, aurora borealis green. Flattened packages and toppled display stands littered the floor in strikingly detailed images of lime and shade. Christmas decorations and signs heralding super sales hung in tatters. Marching through the deserted corridors as Decker and his team were, an eerie sense of wrongness nestled at the back of his skull. Something terribly wicked had occurred within these walls, and Decker's unit was going to locate and deal with it.

"Coming up on the staircase," he whispered into his headset mic, broadcasting it to the members of his unit as well as the police outside.

Three unit specialists turned their weapons upon the staircase while the force slunk and curled around the base like a voiceless dragon of war. The shield bearer ascended first, angling the barrier upwards. The train followed on his heels, spiraling upwards, rubber-sole boots padding over the steps in a soft tattoo. They regrouped on the next level in seconds. Decker lifted a fist and the line stopped, looked and listened, weapons aimed. The closed doors of a nearby tavern were on their right. Deserted tables arranged upon an indoor terrace glowed in green. Three corridors that led north, west, and south looked as forbidding and desolate as abandoned underground bunkers. Nothing moved in the night-vision optics. Nothing could be heard.

"Reached the second level," Decker reported in a whisper. "Initiating sweep en route to the food court."

"Affirmative. Be advised, One, suspect could be on the move."

No shit, Decker thought sardonically, but what he said was, "Roger that."

He slapped the shoulder of the shield bearer, pointed in one direction, and the lethal train got moving. Decker held up a fist and swung his arm, pointing to the closed door of a tavern. The team stopped, divided, half covering all angles while the other half attempted to enter the tavern. One officer tried the door.

"Door's locked, skipper," a female officer whispered over the radio.

"Regroup," Decker ordered. "Move on."

The team reformed and, near soundless, they trekked along the east passage, paying heed to every set of opened doors. A jewelry shop twinkled like a royal tomb. Decker held up a fist once again and stopped the unit. Half the line entered while the others ringed the entrance, guarding against attacks from the outside. Operators snaked through the aisles with grim efficiency.

Decker glanced over his shoulder and glimpsed his team illuminated in green-black. Three of them slipped through a doorway at the rear of the shop. Decker returned to scanning the wide corridors. The immense mall was dead. Soundless. The surface of the moon possessed more life. Decker figured a person could probably hear a cockroach scurry across the tiles a football field out. The distinct absence of noise didn't bother him. He was the fist of God with his team around him. Fingers flexing on his MP5, his attention settled upon the food court somewhere ahead. With the lights off, targets usually panicked and made noise. This one wasn't making a peep, which suggested the individual had either moved or was keeping quiet.

And if he was keeping quiet, he knew someone was coming, and might very well be waiting for them. Decker would assume so.

In a short minute, the operators emerged from the jewelry store's back room, signaled *all clear*, and rejoined the team. They crossed the floor to an outlet for novelty goods, where an inflated drunken elf hung from the ceiling just inside the doorway. Decker trained his weapon upon the elf, daring the merry fucker to utter a single syllable. His team split again and he led the other half into the joke shop. Debris cluttered the floor, slowing the sweep as he had to pay attention to what was underfoot.

Goddamn shitbox, he fumed, checking his corners before proceeding into the next aisle. The first beads of sweat seeped into his balaclava.

A sheep's guilty bleat shattered the silence and Decker whirled about to see a team member holding up a hand. A second later, the officer picked up the noisemaker—a plush toy that moaned a second time upon leaving the floor—and placed the offending device upon a shelf. Decker exhaled. *Goddamn* noisy *shitbox*. Well, he figured the gig might very well be up with the smiling sheep and its dose of parliamentary language.

Feeling just a little more wired, Decker directed his unit through the remainder of the store and deemed it empty. They proceeded to the drugstore next door with a log jam of overturned displays upon its threshold. A splatter of what might have been vitamins and greeting cards covered the floor.

The tactical team repeated the search, found nothing, and moved to the shop across from the drugstore. Decker didn't like all the open shops. There were too many places to hide. Too many back doors to storage areas. If a determined individual didn't want to be found in such a setting, the hunter would have to be even more determined. And thorough.

And Decker considered himself to be one ruthless and methodical bastard.

The corridor wound to the left and arched to the south, passing more shops and more evidence of mass flight by the mall's dwellers. The unit members maintained silence as they stitched their way through every outlet, stoic and resolute.

The team member carrying the shield stopped and pointed. Decker peered over his lead man's shoulder. A green and black lump lay in the middle of the corridor, a body, its feet pointed skyward and the head aimed at them. Decker's heart rate increased ever so slightly while he scanned the shops left and right. One was a men's clothing shop with a spilled heap of boxes and sneakers covering the floor. The other store sold used and new console games.

Tendrils of foulness reached them, wrinkling Decker's nose. He recognized the smell.

"Body ahead," he whispered into his mic and positioned half his team facing the corpse while the others cleared the caves to the left and right. When they regrouped, Decker gave the signal to proceed. The squad advanced upon the body like a hurrying caterpillar, gun barrels bristling.

The smell hit them hard.

The team forced their way through that eye-watering stew of ripe blood and offal as if it were a wall of horrid, permeable jelly. Boots padded through a wide pool of fluid, thick and warm enough to make one think they were walking through a basement flooded with paint. When they reached the body, Decker placed a hand on his shield man and stopped the team. He crouched and didn't bother with the useless gesture of checking for vitals, seeing how both the victim's arms had been removed and were nowhere in sight. The dead man wore a mall security uniform. Decker took a moment to absorb the morbid sight at his feet, knowing full well it would take a pair of trucks to rip a human being apart in such a manner.

To their credit, the other team members didn't say a word, but Decker sensed a swelling abscess of disbelief.

"Pulled him apart," a voice whispered in Decker's ear with a telltale note of dread. Potter. Safely situated in the command van, far and away from the front line. "Pulled that poor bastard apart. Holy Christ our Savior."

Decker agreed with the assessment, but he didn't care for the dismay in the sergeant's voice, not over the open line where all of his team could hear. Decker looked away from the carcass and saw the corridor opened into the ominous cavern of the food court.

He spotted two other bodies.

One hung over a table like a sacrificial offering to dark gods. The sight of the green-black body chilled Decker's steely nerves. The corpse lay on its back and appeared to be one of the missing police officers. The front plate of ceramic body armor worn by the man had been ripped free like loose packaging, and the cloth and flesh underneath opened and ravished like a cooked crab. As still as an evil sculpture, the sight disturbed Decker.

The sergeant chopped at the air, starting the team into an open aisle between a flat labyrinth of prefabricated tables and chairs. Another corpse lay at the end of the lane some twenty feet away, the torso visible from the waist up, the face turned away from the tactical team. A third body lay ten quick paces to the team's right, lying on a pair of chairs and opened like a grisly purse.

Decker panned his weapon side to side in a smooth motion, searching for targets. The team slithered along the aisle, leaving boot prints upon the floor. He leaned to his right, looked over a low wall, and noted the sizeable drop to the first floor. The escalators gleamed but from his angle, he couldn't see anyone on them. The team halted next to the body tangled in the chairs and Decker involuntarily studied the dead security staff.

"Holy shit," one of his team members whispered.

Decker did not reprimand the officer.

The body resembled a messy banquet. Fluids dribbled from the table edges. The wafting smell prompted Decker to glance away, ready to signal his people to move.

A cup scuffled across the floor, bringing the tactical team to a standstill. They centered their weapons on the nightmarish space on the far side of the gaping pit containing the escalators. Decker blinked as sweat trickled into his eyes, not appreciating the sting or its timing. A second rattle sounded from across the way, quickly stilled as if grabbed with a heavy hand.

Decker slapped his lead man on the shoulder to move out when a man appeared on the other side of the escalator pit, the torso rising from between the assembled tables like a soundless green ghost. In the magnification of the goggles, the man appeared half-naked, broad across the chest with muscular shoulders, and possessed a hyena's leanness. The ghoulish black-eyed individual sniffed the air with doe-like curiosity and quickly caught the scent of the tactical team.

Upon which the man's mouth split apart with alligator mirth.

The unexpected transformation chilled the hot coils of Decker's guts and made his brain hesitate in a double take. Worse still, the guy held something, something which dripped in thick rivulets.

"Light him up," he whispered softly.

The team opened fire, the deadly stuttering of automatic weapons shattering the mall's crypt-like silence. Light streaked across the escalators and zinged through the space once occupied by the grinning, half-naked suspect, who ducked out of sight the instant the first shot was fired. A few rounds drilled spidery holes into the table surfaces while others bit off corners.

Decker slapped the shield bearer on his shoulder and the train chugged forward, guns quiet but poised to speak. They double-timed it through the aisle, stepped over the body with the twisted head, and rounded the wall toward the fiend's location. Decker hunted for a target, seeking to place a full burst in the monster's heart.

His breath caught in his throat at the figure streaking through the gaps between tables, surging around the corner like a torpedo.

Straight into the shield bearer.

Decker swung his weapon around to fire as the goblin-man gripped the edges of the police shield and yanked it up, taking the officer whose arms were strapped to the shield.

The team member yelped as he was tossed into the tactical squad lined up behind him. A boot caught Decker hard across the forehead. Stars exploded in his vision, driving him to one side as the mall killer flashed by and crashed into his squad.

The third man in the tactical line got tossed screaming over the wall and into the pit.

The fourth officer had his head torqued to one side with a scream and a crackling of kindle, dropping him in a heap.

The fifth and sixth fired their weapons into the attacker's rushing form, the automatic chatter drowning out their collective shouts. Tracer fire lasered through the dark. The mall killer swatted them both aside with savage force. One officer flew through the glass pane of a sandwich shop, smashing the window in a twinkling cascade. The other operator flipped over the wall surrounding the escalator pit and disappeared from sight.

From there, all cohesion in the unit collapsed.

Team members yelled and screamed as the monstrous entity in the shape of a man ripped through their ranks with all the speed of a tumbling line of dominos. Some fired their weapons, the curt burst like drum machines caught in a screeching of guitars. Ejectors pissed away brass casings in shiny arcs. One female had her head gripped and smashed clean through a nearby table, leaving the helmet's outline in the fiberglass surface. A male officer had his jaw nearly flayed from his face with one slap. Another male officer fired a burst at the attacker's bare shoulders, missed, and was grabbed by his neck and crotch and pitched into the remaining team.

The sounds of combat reached Decker from a very distant place as he struggled to regain his senses. His helmet and goggles had been knocked aside, skewing his vision. Outlines disappeared in sprays, like figures struggling on a ship sailing through rough seas. A gargled cry brought Decker back online. He quickly righted his helmet and located his MP5. He untangled himself from the table and chairs, and rose with his weapon braced against his shoulder.

The tac-leader flinched at the carnage surrounding him.

Seconds, he couldn't have been down for anything more than five or six, yet his entire team lay sprinkled around the food court in spectral images. Arms and legs had been snapped backwards. Bodies twitched. Groans and bloody coughs spritzed the air. One officer dragged himself along the floor, leaving a lengthy streak that slowly filled in behind him. The man was giggling, faint but wheezing, shaking his head as if clutched by an insane joke. He pulled himself another foot, actually nuzzling a discarded shotgun, before becoming still.

Decker scanned the level, seeing another tac-member lying boots up and halfway through a sandwich shop's display case. He forced himself to ignore her, ignore the fallen, because he had to, because the killer lurked within the food court.

A moan, low and sobbing, spun Decker around on his feet. He aimed in the escalators' direction and moved the waist-high partition, gun first, and peered down. Some twenty feet below stood the half-naked mall killer, crouching over one of two fallen officers. The figure tore at his victim's face and pulled things out in viscous arcs.

The team leader fired, opening up from the second level's edge, lighting the dark.

The burst cut across the mall killer's bare back. Fleshy pieces spattered against the floor. The half-naked man roared and jumped out of sight. Decker ceased firing and fumbled at his vest. He swapped out magazines and hastily loaded in a fresh one.

"Command—One," he spoke into his mic. "The team is down. The whole team is down. I'm—"

He stopped and tapped his headset. No response. He reached for his mic and realized it was no longer on his helmet, but hanging below his jaw and presently inoperable. *Shit.* Decker scrambled to the nearest officer, a woman named Tessa Bell. He examined her for a moment, deciding what to do. He lowered his face to hers and plied back her mic so that he could speak into it.

"Command—One. The whole team is down. I'm the last. Over."

No response.

Sweet Jesus, Decker grumped, *where the hell did the brass buy these shitty headsets?*

"Repeat, team is down and I'm last man standing. Target has been hit. Repeat, target has been hit. I'm going after him. Send first responders in through the food court's entrance. Officers are in need of immediate medical attention. Decker out."

*

In the mobile command center parked at the center of a line of police cruisers, Sergeant Potter experienced a lance of anxiety. He gawked in disbelief at the banks of computer monitors. The screens were transmitting but showing nothing, while the mics had stopped entirely after a clearly heard *light him up*.

Then a maelstrom of shit as gunfire erupted through the speakers, followed by a bout of death metal screaming, and then…

Then nothing.

As if the entire tac-team had been swallowed whole.

Potter slapped the shoulder of one of his operators.

"Get me the Feds."

*

After attempting to radio in, Decker pulled back from Tess and studied her green-glowing features. He slapped her cheeks. She didn't respond so he lowered his cheek to her mouth and waited for a breath.

Nothing.

Anger welled up inside the team leader. He stood, bolted to the low wall encircling the escalators, and looked down to the first floor. Nothing moved. Nothing so much as breathed but he had to confirm the kill. He saw the shots ripping across the lower half of his target's back, blowing out a kidney. The mall killer was probably directly beneath him, bleeding out facedown on the tiles.

Decker ran to the escalator and descended two steps at a time, his footfalls ringing out in the dark. The gloomy body of Rich Duran appeared on the metal stairs, his face a loose portrait of peace. Decker checked on the officer and confirmed his death, since his head plied almost flush to his left shoulder. The team leader crouched and proceeded cautiously, reaching the base of the escalator and the last officer the mall killer had been working over before Decker had shot him. Mel Thompson, an eight-year police veteran. The team leader turned away from the ruined face whose eye sockets resembled the holes of a very messy bowling ball.

Decker swept his gun right to left, lingering on the potted plants and overturned benches decorating the first floor. A gym was just to his right while a mountain bike shop was across from it. He stopped and listened, his senses fully returning.

The stink of blood swamped his nose and a second later, he spotted a blood trail. A grim look of intent hardened Decker's features. He moved around metal benches and large pots, avoiding the brush of plastic plants, and snuck along the inky blots. The mall had returned to its tomb-like silence, as if aware the hunt was still in progress. That suited Decker just fine. This wasn't a sand-blasted wasteland with pebbles underfoot. He held his MP5 firm against his shoulder and stared down the sights.

The oil spots led into the gym.

Decker crossed the floor, keeping low, and made like a floating phantom as he proceeded inside the sports club. Benches. Rows of free weights, from little wrist burners resembling doggy chew toys to huge plated pork barrels no mortal could ever possibly lift. A jungle of exercise machines and cycles assembled on a rubber-like material that covered the floor. Decker had no trouble seeing the ghoulish markers spattered across the surface. He moved between multiple shoulder press machines, addressing his angles, when a muffled slap from deeper within the gym froze the team leader in place.

Decker stayed in place for several fleeting seconds, wondering if his attacker was about to charge again. If he was, he'd have a clear field of fire. When nothing appeared, he unlocked himself and huffed along the blood trail toward an open hall at the center's rear.

The word POOL was stenciled in big black lettering upon a closed door.

Decker placed his back against the door and pushed against it, immediately greeted by thick humidity. He entered, gun barrel first, the goggles rendering the Olympic-sized pool in a stygian hue, the waters shifting uneasily like a sinister cauldron just beginning to boil.

Decker checked behind the door and scanned the chamber's vast interior. White porcelain armored the room, brightening the goggles' vision. A foam kickboard, shaped like a headstone and longing for a name, rode the water's dying ripples.

The blood trail continued into the men's changing room at the pool's far end. Decker took a breath and tiptoed to the entrance without an echo, a ghost of vengeance aiming to blow the head off his quarry. There was no door to the changing room, just a twisted passage that switched back. Decker placed his shoulder to one corner, leaned ahead to see around the next, and darted forward to what he suspected was the last. The blood splotches were notably smaller here.

The mall killer stepped into view just as Decker turned the corner. The beast shoved Decker's weapon upward just as his finger tightened on the trigger and the MP5 blurted out one loud verse, blowing holes in the ceiling and making it snow chunks. The mall killer grabbed Decker by his tactical vest and lifted, crashing his head against a ceiling beam. The half-naked form then whipped the tac-leader against one wall and then another like a mat being beaten free of dust.

The beating stopped and a hand clamped down on Decker's throat, hard enough to open his eyes, and powerful enough to crush the officer's windpipe like a drinking straw. Decker heard the crinkling of his trachea a microsecond before mind-freezing pain. In his dying vision, the decorated police sergeant noted the killer's face elongating once more into that strange goblin mask.

Lengthening fangs enveloped Decker's mouth.

Bailey—as he inherently realized was his name, or a step closer to his true identity—held his prey against the wall as he chomped and chewed through cheeks and crackling bone, pausing to spit out meddlesome teeth. The man tasted good, as did they all, but there was something missing. This one had hurt Bailey, which made him angry, angry enough to punish his attacker. And as he consumed great wet chunks,

Bailey was aware of his wounds closing, healing, zipping up as if they'd never existed. *Meat*, he realized, meat did this. But his mind attempted to reveal there was even better meat to be had, flesh that would make him even stronger. Faster.

Bailey knew he was missing a vital element. With his expanding mental capacity, deep-rooted instincts, and a bottomless well of memories teasing him with its knowledge, Bailey suspected it was only a matter of time before… what? He didn't know exactly, but he knew his newfound strength and energy were a clue to greater things. He was *meant* for greater things, a higher purpose, and he sensed a… *history* rich in such hunts. Yet as hard as he tried to glean more from his subconscious, the farther he pushed away those tantalizing fragments of true self and purpose.

He released the dead man, letting the husk drop with a thud.

More, the impulse filled his mind and chest and lured him from the changing room. The face of Haley appeared in his mind, the woman who'd helped him for the past few days. Perhaps good things would happen to him if he ate her? What she'd done for him, her efforts to help, meant nothing to Bailey. He realized he needed no one.

He only needed meat. And perhaps time. All would return to him in time.

His mouth and hands dripped as he walked along the pool.

There was meat nearby, in the shape of men and women. He could smell them.

He wondered how they would taste.

35

Muffled gunfire erupted on the far side of the Martin and MacDonald shopping center, turning the heads of the wardens gathered around Kirk's weathered old pickup. The reports split the cold peace of the night, but Kirk knew there was a developing war zone inside the mall, an enclosed arena they'd have to enter if they were going to kill Bailey.

"Shots fired," Sam Mausler said, listening.

"How many entrances does this place have?" Carma didn't look in the mall's direction. She was on her phone, scouring the internet for floorplans.

"Uh," Kirk wasn't sure. "There's a back way. A back alley with loading bays. Right over there and below us. Big open space with its back against the hill there. Only one way in."

"Cops got that all covered by now," Ken Cyler said. "Especially the back alley."

"Probably a way to the roof," Janice said, studying the topside of the structure. "Might be a ladder."

"We'll deal with the police when we have to," Carma muttered, the indifference in her tone alarming Kirk. "Most people are gathered around the main entrances anyway, looking for a show. We won't have to worry about them. All right. I have floor plans. It's a big place. Kirk will be key. We'll start from the back alley and look for a way in. Maybe there's a ladder to the roof. We take out anyone in our way and find our way inside. We change and hunt Bailey down. All clear?"

Heads nodded. Kirk looked around. Morris still hadn't reported in and refused to answer his phone.

Carma read his mind. "Morris is on his own and will answer to me once this is over."

"Now, when you say deal with the police…" Kirk started, but Carma stopped him with a look.

"Subdue them. Try not to kill them."

"Thanks."

"Everyone clear on that?" the pack leader asked.

Everyone was.

"Then let's go. The dance is waiting."

With that, Carma led them through the dark gridlock of parked vehicles, avoiding the mass of onlookers facing the mall where the police blazed spotlights at the main doors. The wardens traveled along the blacked-out periphery of the parking lot, moving to the shopping center's loading area. Lanes leading into the zone had been blocked by police barricades, but beyond that were pockets of darkness along a lengthy wall. Carma stopped on a grassy hill overlooking the loading area, a high protective fence at her back that hid flowing traffic. Kirk pointed to that particular section of wall dotted by dumpsters. Parked not fifty meters away were a trio of squad cars, cordoning the area off. There quite possibly was another barricade on the other end, but that didn't concern the pack leader.

"Sam," Carma said. "You and Bryce take care of that."

The pair of *weres* nodded and started down the hillside.

"And Bryce?"

The shadowed face looked at his pack leader.

"Don't surprise me," Carma warned, holding his gaze.

For a moment Kirk thought the big warden might have something to say to that, but after a few fleeting seconds, Ian Bryce broke the stare and followed Sam down the incline toward the cruisers, going the long way to avoid a deep drop-off.

"He has a reputation?" Nick quietly asked Janice.

"We all have reputations, but yeah," Janice nodded. "He's got a bad one. And by the way, Carma, would you say this is a fairly modern building?"

"What's your point?"

"My point is they probably have security cameras. See those black knobs mounted on the walls? Just below the top of the roof?"

Kirk squinted and saw them, grateful for his heightened vision.

Carma sighed. "Power's been cut."

"You sure about that? They could have backup of some sort. Maybe even batteries."

"Cover your faces then, until we get inside," Carma said without hesitation. "Regardless, once inside, we go as wolves. Cameras will only see a bunch of big dogs taking down an unarmed man. We'll be long gone by the time they realize what happened."

Carma looked to Janice. "Wouldn't happen to have ski masks on you?"

Janice glowered and shook her head. "Just sayin' is all. Don't bitch."

"Point taken and noted."

"We'll go in without Morris," Carma said in a low voice. "Much as I'd like to have him in there. We have a shrinking window of opportunity here. And remember, Bailey instinctively knows to go for the throat, so watch yourselves."

Kirk sighed at the thought and glanced around the steep embankment, scanning the area for the Pictou warden. The mall's parking lot looked like a concert setting in the distance, with spotlights and cell phone flickers. There was a short clatter of activity below, barely heard, bringing his attention back to the squad cars.

Sam and Bryce had done their jobs.

"Here we go," Carma said and padded down the slope. The others followed, masked by the night, keeping their balance as they descended toward the mall. As they drew closer, some of them pulled their coats over their heads while others merely covered their faces with their hands. They met Sam and Ian crouched amongst the police cruisers. Kirk spotted six unmoving officers, their dark heaps piled into their vehicles, before following Carma and the others to the back wall.

Carma stopped at a lowered loading bay door that

stretched from the base and up some ten feet. She pushed the barrier, causing it to buckle with a rattle. She looked up, coat pulled over her head, and padded over to where a security camera was mounted below the roof. She inspected the device before returning to her pack a minute later.

"Red light blinking. Keep your faces covered."

Kirk buried his face in his straightened arms and pushed into the door, creating a sliver of a gap at the base. Bryce jammed an extended baton into the crack and heaved all of his considerable strength into pulling. The inside lock gave way with a metallic pop. Kirk and Ken lifted the door two feet, the sound like the subdued rattle of a locomotive.

The pack scurried across a threshold of cold concrete.

Once inside, Kirk placed his back to the loading bay door.

"Where are we?" Janice asked, standing amongst stacked shelving units of boxed goods.

"Unloading area for one of the main stores," Ken Cyler reported. "Probably dry goods and shit."

"Strip," Carma ordered, quelling any further small talk. "Kirk, you're on guard while we change. Don't let anything in here."

As she gave orders, Carma had already dropped her coat. Kirk turned away, not wanting to see her peel away her clothing.

The silver knives—the wardens' badges—were placed next to each owner's pile of clothing. They would use their jaws to kill Bailey. Outer and underwear dropped to the concrete floor in whispers and soft thuds. Kirk plodded along in the dark, finding the outline of a second door. He located a knob and gave it a turn, grimacing at the barest click. He put his shoulder to the metal surface and cracked the door just a sliver. The air smelled a little stale, but nothing sinister like a lurking *were*.

Grunts of pain erupted behind Kirk. Cartilage popped. Sinews stretched like bowstrings and thickened. Fleshly matter split and spattered the floor. A soft yelp pierced the air.

Kirk had heard it all before.

Growls rose behind him and a part of the Halifax warden sighed, longing to join and hating himself for even thinking it. *I'm not a monster, I'm not. I'm… I'm a peacekeeper. A protector.*

Minutes later, heavy paws padded on concrete, stopping behind him. A waist-high snout exhaled upon his hand. Kirk saw the transformed face of Carma, sleek and black and beautiful. There was no mistaking her, a supernatural gift of nature and a deadly wonder. She regarded him as the others formed behind her in a wedge. The wardens were huge in wolf form, three to four times bigger than regular animals, their mass doubled. Their jaws could crack open skulls and snap bones. Raw power on four legs.

Carma studied Kirk with Zen-like patience while the pack gathered behind her, panting with anticipation.

"Good luck," Kirk whispered.

He got a sarcastic growl.

"Yeah, well, good luck anyway."

He pulled the door open, revealing a midnight jungle of clothing stands and racks.

The werewolves surged past him.

36

The wardens streaked through the darkened clothing store, rustling boughs of shirts and jeans. A scent of blood drew them into a wide corridor littered with shopping bags and discarded purchases. The skeletal frames of metal displays, overturned as if gunned down, splayed themselves in between abandoned kiosks.

Carma padded through the clutter, the wafting hook of blood leading her. The others stayed on her flanks, watchful, waiting for her lead. She turned right and trotted through a wide walkway, following the wreckage left in the wake of a human stampede. The tang of blood, rich and wicked, grew fuller. Carma increased her pace and ran along the corridor, past the front of a deserted bank and a wall of dead ATMs. The werewolves followed, claws clicking on polished tiles, speeding past empty booths and eager to close with the arisen abomination called Bailey.

The dull splendor of an out-of-focus tempest on the very edge of a dream slowly materialized. The structure solidified into metallic stairs, looming over them in a ghostly spiral.

Carma stopped with her paws upon the lower steps and gazed upward, testing the air. The others gathered around her, snouts lifted to the second level. Ian Bryce circled them all, his movements anxious and impatient. Carma ignored him, waiting seconds longer, before deciding to move. She climbed the stairs in leaps, Janice and Nick Dyer on her heels.

A skylight far above them framed a patch of night in a long rectangle as Carma reached the second floor and turned south. The smell of blood hung thick on the air currents like foul portents. Bailey had killed. The werewolf had killed many, judging by the powerful smell filling the mall's upper levels.

She trotted along, on guard, attempting to discern other scents from the blood, trying to separate the individual spices already absorbed in a stew, and failing. So much blood. And it was only getting stronger. The others smelled it as well; its heady aroma quieted them.

Carma turned right at a juncture, the aroma intensifying, and she showed her displeasure in a confession of teeth. The wardens fanned out at her sides, just behind her, in a line of four-legged gunslingers. Their superior hearing picked up a sound, low but steady, like a muffled drum.

A heart.

Relaxed. Sated.

Carma led her wardens toward the ever-nearing heart of the slaughter.

*

And as the werewolf wardens picked up on Bailey's scent and heartbeat, he caught theirs in turn. He lifted his face from the partially devoured slab upon the floor situated behind a wall of wood and glass. The overpowering fragrance of blood made it difficult to detect with certainty, but Bailey could sense danger approaching, different from the previous attackers, with their noisy pipes that stung. Bailey's nostrils flared at the curious blend of flesh and bone and fur. The smell summoned a familiar yet indistinct memory from another time, one he believed he lived in and even ruled. A hazy hunch of long ago, where he'd hunted and killed with those similar to himself. Bailey stood, his jeans drenched in the life juices of the human dead. That time had been with friends, however. Those that approached were not friends. Certainly not like the female called Haley.

They wanted to hurt him.

Perhaps even kill him.

Like the others.

That split his mouth in a snarl. Marble eyes twinkled in the dark as he heard their soft padding, coming closer, invading his territory. Just like the others, showing no respect at all for what he was or what he'd done. Or what he could do.

Talons clenched into frenzied fists.

He went forth to greet his hunters.

<h1 style="text-align:center">37</h1>

The outer door rattled, jarring Kirk from a session of undiluted self-loathing. He turned and walked back to witness a pair of boots at the door's exposed base. A figure dropped to the cement floor and Morris rolled through the gap.

"The fuck have you been?" Kirk blurted.

"They gone in?" the Pictou warden asked as he sprang to his feet.

Kirk shook his head in wonder at the balls on the *were.* "Yeah, they are."

"So why are you still here?"

"Waitaminute," Kirk held up a hand. "Where the hell have you been?"

"Out walking. Thinking."

"And you decided to join in now?"

"You rather not at all?"

"No time for this shit, man."

Morris studied Kirk with an air of suspicion. "No time, huh? So why are you still here?"

"I was about to change."

"Yeah," Morris said. "I bet. You were all in a hurry. Guarding your girlfriend's panties out here."

Kirk rubbed the bridge of his nose. "You ready to go?"

Morris snorted. "Are you?"

"Yeah."

"Then let's get going." Morris threw off his leather duster and ripped open his shirt. "They're going to need it."

"What do you mean?" Kirk asked.

"Something's been bothering me this whole time," Morris said, pausing. "I mean, this is pretty bad, right? What's happening here. Really bad, right?"

The question hung on the air as Kirk nodded with impatience.

"I've been thinking about who Bailey really is. Whoever he is, he's alone, so he must be pretty badass, right? If he was planning on killing me."

"Yeah, okay, so?"

"Well, then, how come the elders only sent eight wardens to find this guy now that he's reborn? Huh? Why is that?"

"Eight's a fuckin' army."

"Eight's not a fuckin' army," Morris groaned. "Eight's a smokescreen. A show of nothing. The way the world is now? All widescreen and high definition and hooked to the interwebs? This town should be *crawling* with wardens. Wardens *and* wolves arriving on planes and driving up in trucks and cars. There's been plenty of time to get them all here. Seriously. Should be a huge fucking convention here with everyone with their noses to the pavement, sniffing out

Bailey's ass. But there isn't. Bailey's been on the loose now for a couple of days and the wardens in that mall are all that's coming. That's it, Kirk. Why do you think that is?"

"I don't know. Why?"

"Because someone wants us to fail. The goddamn elders want us all to die."

That struck Kirk cold and senseless. "What?"

"You heard me. I say Bailey was sent to kill me, and I think Bailey is still meant to kill me. These wardens? Enough to get us all motivated, but seriously, we're hunting a fucking monster in there. A monster. The elders know it and they know Bailey is more than capable of killing all of us. Eight wardens? That's nothing. All replaceable. Small price to pay and perfectly acceptable. Especially if it means getting rid of us."

Kirk remained speechless, Morris's rant making a lot of sense.

"That's right, man," the Pictou warden said. "I was right all along. The elders want you and me dead. And it's because of what we did on the Rock. Because of what we ate and what we are. We're something else now. Maybe like what Borland was. And whatever *that* is, the elders sure as shit don't like it."

All Kirk could think of was Carma, that she might be in danger.

He shrugged off his coat.

38

The pack edged closer to the fragrant cave known as the food court. The area reeked of death and cooling blood, blood enough that it almost left Carma dizzy. She couldn't locate Bailey's scent, couldn't smell anything but the rich soup ahead. She'd thought she picked up on his trail but it had evaporated the closer they got to the food court.

A body lay before them, a grim lump marking the outer edge of the food court's vast expanse. Carma slunk toward the carcass, her senses buzzing. A male, not long dead. She lifted her head and peered into the arena before her. Mauled bodies lay strewn about, in dark, unmoving husks, garnishing the place in morbid splotches. A black pool surrounded the body before her and her supernatural sight could easily distinguish where the outer edge of blood stopped and the floor began.

The others halted on her flanks and sniffed the air. Looked and listened. Nothing stirred. The temperature inside the building remained warm and the food court was a congealing tomb. She edged past the body, leaving paw prints in the tepid tar coating the floor. The others spread out behind her, and as a group, they drifted to the left of the ubiquitous tables and chairs and garbage dumpsters. Ian Bryce snuck by, closed in on the remains of a pair of armored police officers, and prodded their lifeless arms with his snout.

Ken Cyler hopped onto a pair of tables and inspected another dead police officer, his spine snapped. A second later he stood vigil and peered around the food court. Janice and Nick Dyer fanned out ahead of Carma, leaving an elegant, almost floral design in the blood underfoot. Corpses lay scattered everywhere, some sprinkled with discarded weapons. Automatic machine guns. Carma didn't know the make.

Janice sniffed at a female corpse, this one in a shredded uniform, and scanned the area beyond her. Nick Dyer sniffed at the dead woman's boot and crept to the next body—half-naked and apparently dunked in ink.

The warden's eyes narrowed, catching an alien scent.

The thing called Bailey snapped forward like a closing bear trap. He grabbed Nick by the throat scruff and nipped the airways shut. Bailey held him with one arm, choking off the warden's warning, and dragged him along like a distressed mule. Bailey finally lifted the werewolf off its paws and took three long steps before vaulting over a low wall, disappearing below.

Carma rushed to the edge and looked down in time to see Bailey blur out of sight underneath the overhang. Janice raced to the escalator landing and bolted down the stairs.

Ken Cyler and Ian Bryce followed her.

Carma didn't bother with the stairs. She jumped.

And as she fell, Nick Dyer flew through empty space just below. He crashed through a storefront's display of flowers. Glass fell and the warden struggled to stand, a dark gush issuing from his neck.

Carma landed as Janice leaped onto the escalator. They grouped around Dyer, seeing dark rags hanging from his exposed throat.

The wounded warden's claws scraped on tiles. Janice nudged the furry mass once before it ceased moving entirely.

The wolves gathered at the base of the escalators, beholding the *were*-thing called Bailey, the seemingly undead creature they had been charged to kill. It backed into a gym, its eyes and teeth stained in shadow most dire. Bailey had coated himself in blood, fooling the wardens' superior noses. They would not be fooled a second time.

With the air of eager executioners, the five werewolves converged on their prey, flooding the gym.

Bailey retreated amongst the various machines and racks of dumbbells as growls grew in the confined space. Black eyes bore down on the abomination, promising a quick death. Janice rushed in, eyes bright with malice, her back arched, fur spiked, and lips rippling.

Bailey turned and grabbed the iron bar from a nearby bench press, a length some seven feet long.

Janice leaped as the pack's circle collapsed upon their quarry.

With a speed unimaginable, Bailey set his feet and

swatted the streaking mass of fur from the air, sending Janice flying across the room where she crashed into an unyielding shoulder press machine. Bailey whirled the bar like a quarterstaff, smashing Ian Bryce's snout a split second before upper-cutting the jaw of a lunging Ken Cyler.

Bryce skittered across the floor.

Cyler flew into a wall.

Sam Mausler launched himself at the bare-chested Bailey, who released one end of the bar to catch the werewolf by the throat. Bailey's outstretched arm buckled upon impact, and Mausler's hind legs swung forward, clawing at a meaty thigh and drawing bloody runnels in denim and muscle.

Bailey screamed, crushed the warden's windpipe, and flung him into a leaping Carma. The wardens collided like a pair of bowling balls before crashing across a rack of dumbbells.

As the wardens regained their feet, Bailey attacked, stabbing the bar into the face of the closest warden. Bryce glimpsed the metal just before the blunt spear broke his front fangs and lanced a good foot down his gullet. Bailey swung the choking warden around, swatting two more furry forms away, and flung the impaled werewolf into the shoulder press machine.

The wardens' attack faltered, and the two-legged abomination pressed its advantage.

Dripping blood, Bailey slapped the snapping maw of one warden away, ripping one eye free of the beast's head in a shower of skull stew. He punched another head and kicked a furred torso with a yelp. A werewolf leaped but Bailey ducked and the *were* sailed into a row of stationary bicycles.

Bailey scurried around Bryce, attempting in vain to disgorge the maddening spear jammed down his throat. Bailey grabbed the iron, gripped it, and pushed down another half foot.

Bryce convulsed.

Bailey left the shivering werewolf and stopped at a Christmas tree rack of forty-five-pound plates. He pulled the heavy discs off as if they were ceramic saucers and hurled them at the remaining wardens.

One disc caught Carma in the face, dropping her cold.

Another crashed into Janice's ribs.

Two slammed into Ken Cyler, shattering a hind leg.

Teeth bared, Bailey soon exhausted his supply of missiles, so he grabbed for the nearby kettlebells, taking up fifty-five pounds of cast-iron in each fist.

Carma lunged for Bailey's knee just as he swung a cannonball into her face and broke one side. With uncanny speed, he turned and brought a kettlebell straight down upon the brain pan of an attacking Janice, sending her to the matted floor. Bailey knelt and hammered her skull twice more, pounding the warden's head with his improvised mallets and shattering bone.

A dripping Nick Dyer, risen from the dead, sped toward the abomination with his jaws open. He jumped as Bailey turned and struck the *were*-thing square in its chest. The pair tumbled back and over a low rack of dumbbells. Nick landed on top and raked flesh, raising inky geysers. Bailey released his kettlebells and grabbed for a throat, but Nick evaded and plunged forward. Bailey caught him by the soaking mane as the Maine warden chomped down on a shoulder, sinking teeth to the bone.

Bailey bellowed and rolled over, taking the warden with him, and together they tumbled across the floor, each attempting to mangle the other. Bailey landed on top and shoved the werewolf away, spun, and backhanded Sam Mausler flying at him through the dark, sending the creature through a glass pane in explosive fashion.

Carma slid across the floor in a skitter of claws and glass, stopped herself, and squared off against the standing man-beast. If the pack leader realized she was the last werewolf standing, she didn't falter.

Bailey crouched and hissed at the one werewolf, swiping at air, daring the warden to approach.

Carma growled and snapped, edging closer.

Bailey blurred forward in a burst of killer speed, clamping a clawed hand over the werewolf's muzzle while grabbing the scruff of her neck. Bailey reared back and whipped Carma through one of two reception desks.

The pack leader didn't rise.

With the final foe down, Bailey reeled about in drunken fashion, blood dribbling from his war wounds. He spotted the convulsing Ian Bryce caught in the early transition from wolf to human form, a forearm's length of iron bar still shoved down his throat, his paws struggling for purchase on the shaft.

Bailey walked over to the wounded werewolf and

stomped on its neck, leaving the body in shivers.

Methodically, the *were*-thing dealt with the rest of the fallen pack.

*

The sounds of bones shattering reached Carma's ears in a red fog that clung to her vision. She attempted to rise but her body refused, so she rested on her belly, knowing something terribly wrong had happened to her head. It didn't hurt, not much at all, but a crippling nausea had clutched her innards, wringing them and causing a high-pitched death drone in her ears. An unending buzz disrupted by Bailey and the sounds of things being pulled, being squished, and being torn. Her head twitched and shivered, yet she made out the tracery of a doorway that twinkled at the absolute edge of her vision. The sounds of butchery increased behind her, a yawning tunnel of carnage that drew closer to her heels.

Carma pushed with her hind legs, unhooking herself from splintered planks. She inched her way through the widening pool of her blood, smearing the tiles underneath. She pushed herself a head's length, stopped, and cursed herself in drunken agony for doing so. The screaming grew louder behind her, an ever-widening chasm of sound and fury that instilled fear. Carma pushed herself forward again with a whimper, identifying the rectangle as a portal. She didn't know where it led, as long as it was *away*. She grunted, a spawny red frothing her determined sneer.

A loud crackling made her good eye flicker white as she

glanced to one side in reflex. Unable to see anything, the noise drew another whimper from her and her claws clicked. Faster. She had to escape. Had to recover.

A hand grabbed her ankle, causing Carma to whine. It yanked her back a good mile, or so it felt, and the doorway disappeared. An eager hissing filled her ears as if a mass of snakes had invaded them.

Her free foot flailed at her captor and was slapped away. Her entire rear quarters were then lifted off the floor. The world spun, and she faced a hand possessing fat meat hooks as fingernails.

Resembling a demon that had clawed its way free of a tar pit, Bailey grabbed Carma's skull and twisted the pack leader onto her back. She didn't resist.

A low growl perked their ears.

Bailey looked up while Carma didn't have to, recognizing the scents.

Two fresh werewolves plodded into the gym, but it wasn't Kirk the *were*-thing focused on.

It was Morris.

The monster fixed upon the Pictou warden with an expression of puzzled wonder, as if realizing it should know him. Bailey didn't move, seized in a vice of hesitation, and attempting with all his might to remember.

Morris never appeared more determined, marching toward the standing *were*.

Bailey tossed Carma away like an empty bottle, where she bounced off an exercise bicycle.

And Morris charged.

The werewolf barreled into the standing monster, who attempted to catch the *were*'s neck and failed miserably. They tumbled backwards as a ball of angry energy, spinning around on the ground like a flesh and fur turbine freed of its metal housing.

Morris had his head slammed into a wall of iron plates. His hind legs cut bloody runnels down Bailey's abdominal wall. Bailey howled, turned and shoved Morris's wide head through the second reception desk, the panel wood shattering with an arctic ice crackling. Forgoing any further offensive, Bailey staggered back, reeled and made for the door. One hand cupped about his lower extremities.

Kirk struck the monster before it cleared the threshold. His jaws snapped against the side of Bailey's head, snipping off an entire ear, and then they were crashing into the framework of the doorway. Metal buckled. Glass popped. Kirk chomped down on a shoulder and shook his head, rattling the fallen *were*-thing until Bailey jammed a handful of fingers into his face. One talon popped an eye, the pain electric, and Kirk howled and kicked the *were* away.

Bailey rose, no longer smiling, the right side of his head a grisly display of mauled flesh. Both shoulders appeared wrecked but his right one possessed a wound resembling a snowman's smile. Bailey attempted to lift the limb but couldn't move it. He grunted, turned, and intended to stomp on the werewolf at his feet just as Morris crashed into him.

They rolled outside of the gym. A three-foot-high floral display halted their tangled path.

Bailey landed on the bottom, his good hand gripping Morris's neck.

The Pictou warden snarled back and pushed forward.

The strain drew a grimace across Bailey's face. He panted, wheezed, and stared into Morris's canine eyes.

For a fleeting second, they stayed that way. Breathing. Trembling.

Then Morris started digging, shredding the bare chest and abdominal wall of the monster underneath him. He clawed with all the frenzied energy of having discovered a tasty bone, ripping out a black tide. Bailey screamed and thrashed but soon relaxed, his expression softening, his grip on Morris's neck relaxing.

The reborn *were* twitched when the warden's claws hooked backbone.

And when Bailey's hand dropped away completely, Morris buried his muzzle in the man's chest cavity and ate his enemy's heart in two savage bites.

In a semi-conscious daze, Kirk heard the commotion. He felt like a hornet's nest had been shaken and stuck to his head. *Jesus Christ,* he seethed in agony, realizing he just had an eye hooked out of his head a second time in the same year. He rolled over, vision skewed, but still managed to see Morris's immense and shadowy mass hunched over Bailey's body that jerked and twitched with morbid life. Perhaps it was the gravity of Kirk's wound and the skewed sense of time, but it seemed to the Halifax warden that Morris took a long time before pulling his head clear of the hole in the dying *were's* torso. The werewolf paused, jaws dripping and eyes aglow like the tips of hot iron pokers. He took a step and considered the *were* beneath him. The warden snorted in the fallen monster's face and prolonged the inevitable by revealing the jaws that would take Bailey's life.

Kirk knew what was coming next, but was distracted when a weight thumped across his shoulder. Carma collapsed at his side, the bashed side of her face like a bloom kissed with a flash of napalm. She nuzzled his shoulder and he shied away in pain. Determined, she whined a protest and planted her body tight to his.

You don't know anything about wolves, do you? Janice's raspy voice asked him.

Kirk's heart sputtered with dreamy shock at such an unexpected connection, before settling into a deep and powerful rhythm. Carma's warmth diverted his hurt like a rock splitting mad torrents of white water. He weakly nuzzled Carma's forehead, and licked at her face's good parts.

And in doing so, Kirk completely missed the execution of the reborn *were* called Bailey.

39

Taken from the *Halifax Metrus Journal*, dated November 16, 2015.

The city of Halifax is in mourning from the horrifying killing spree that paralyzed the city and centered all its attention upon the downtown Martin and MacDonald Mall. Halifax-Dartmouth police have confirmed that several sets of human remains have been taken from the Martin and MacDonald Mall, where the city is still reeling in the aftermath from the rampage of a disturbed individual identified only as John. An official number of victims killed in John's one-man rampage has yet to be determined. Meanwhile, the province's chief medical examiner is expected to release further details later today regarding the identity and background of the assailant.

On a related note, mystery still surrounds the whereabouts of several naked survivors of the mall attack, all of whom had been found unresponsive with life-threatening wounds. They were being transported to the city hospital for immediate medical attention, but their ambulances never arrived. The ambulances were later discovered parked on the side of the highway, their lights turned off and the first responders in mass shock. EMT personnel claim that their patients became fully animate mid-transit and quickly overpowered them. Eyewitness accounts reported several suspects dressed in paramedic uniforms carrying away bodies upon leaving the parked vehicles. Police report that investigations are ongoing into the whereabouts of these missing individuals, and that anyone with information as to their identity and location is strongly encouraged to contact the authorities.

*

The surviving wardens lay low for the remainder of the week.

The mood at Kirk's apartment was one of muted sadness as some of the law bringers, far too gone to safely regenerate for fear of rising as another Bailey, had to be put down. Sam Mausler had been torn apart by Bailey and his bleeding body had been the hardest to conceal while returning to the apartment. Ken Cyler had also been brutalized, his head flattened. Janice Glover's own head had been half crushed, resulting in her being put to final sleep with a silver blade. Kirk remembered their brief conversations while picturing her plain but attractive features, liking her perhaps most of all. Nick Dyer stood by her unmoving form as Carma administered the killing blow, and even though he mostly kept his emotions in check, flickers of misery leaked through around the edges.

After that, phone calls were made and meals were prepared.

For the first day, Morris was the only one in any shape to complete the several tasks around the apartment. The beds and sofa were filled with the regenerating *weres*, and Morris walked amongst them, guarded them, with an air of reluctant duty. Kirk could see it. Anyone could.

Sleep eventually suppressed the buzz-saw pain of Kirk's eye, and the Halifax warden knew nothing until the next morning, He opened his eyes and realized with a mix of relief, awe, and several strong blinks that his missing eye had regenerated. He paused at the edge of his bed, rose, and walked out into the kitchen.

Morris was at the front door, leather trench coat covering his broad shoulders. The Pictou warden rolled his eyes when Kirk noticed him.

"Hoping to make a clean getaway?" Kirk whispered.

"No hope needed," Morris answered. "Watch."

"Hey, before you go, thanks for everything."

Morris stood and considered that, the darkness of the hallway lending his hard features an almost poster-like quality. "If it wasn't for me, none of this would've happened. If I'd bagged that bastard in the first place, Janice and the others would still be alive. And none of these other bastards or the head bitch would know of my miraculous healing abilities. Or yours."

Kirk didn't comment.

"You're better," Morris pointed out and cracked open the door. "You got the watch. I'm gone."

"Okay."

"Seeya around."

"You heading home?"

Morris stopped on the threshold. "Don't know yet. Figure it's best to stay low to the ground for a little while. Maybe just think. Everything I said to you? That all needs more thinking. A lot more. You should try it sometime."

"Maybe I will."

Morris smirked.

"You have my number," Kirk reminded him, letting him know a call would be welcome.

Morris's brow wrinkled in a frown. He left without another word, closing the door with a soft bang. A wry smile spread across Kirk's face. He expected no less.

Thoughts turned to breakfast.

"He's gone?"

Kirk turned to see a disheveled Carma standing in the hall, fresh from the spare bedroom. She wore jeans and a wrinkled T-shirt. Hair partially hid her sleepy eyes. The side of her face was a swollen mass of angry purple, but even now Kirk could see it had gone down a little since last night. She was lucky she had an exceptionally tough skull.

"Yeah," he answered. "You up now?"

"No."

"How you feeling?"

"Like shit." Carma yawned. "You got your eye back."

"Yeah," he smiled. "I did. Works, too."

"You got kitchen duty," Carma informed him. "And guard duty."

"I know."

"I'll be expecting steak and eggs. Around ten-ish."

Kirk nodded.

"Good. See to it, temple-slave."

Temple slave. That brought him back years, when he and she were more than what they were now.

"Carma."

She stopped.

"You… wanna talk? About anything?"

Carma regarded him, the busted side of her face hidden in shadow. "About what?"

Kirk faltered.

"That snuggle at the mall?" She rolled her eyes. "Jesus Christ, Douglas. Don't get hooked on that. Think about steak and eggs. Ten-ish. Chop-chop. Quicker we're fed the quicker we're all outta here. Including me. Like a bat outta hell."

She left him standing in the hall.

The next day a disposal crew stopped by early in the morning and carried away the body bags containing the dead wardens. Nick Dyer followed the black sack carrying Janice Glover and did not return.

The day slunk along, heedless of the slow-moving hours. A watchful Kirk sat in the living room most of the time, ignoring the snores from Ian Bryce, who slept on the floor behind the sofa, his throat badly bruised as if he had been strangled by a length of steel cable. Somehow, the cramped space and being partially out of sight made him feel secure. He couldn't talk at all, and could only drink his meals, which made for the loudest time in the morning since Kirk had to heap everything into a blender. Kirk didn't care, as long as the dog was up and moving around soon. Ezekiel had even started talking the night before, showing disappointment at how events played out, and indicating he'd be strong enough to travel in a day or so.

Carma appeared from the spare room every four or five hours, rising to use the bathroom. She didn't look in Kirk's direction, and the second time he didn't react to her at all, sending his own message. He could ignore a person as well, no problem. But his defiance eventually rusted away to a melancholy frame of mind.

He spent the night at the window, watching the traffic rush by like low-flying comets.

The gray light straining through the drawn curtain roused Kirk to another day. He rubbed his face, realizing he'd fallen asleep. With a grunt he got to his feet, entirely healed, and puttered into the kitchen to prepare the first meal of the day. He fried up steak and eggs, making the mental note to eat nothing but granola for the next ten years. The snap, sizzle, and smell from the frying pan would draw the others. Kirk prepared a plate, slopped a pair of eight-ounce steaks and a hill of eggs onto it, and then dumped the works in a nearby blender. The loud grind of the machine made him wince.

Once done, he poured the contents into three beer mugs

and carried them into the living room.

Bryce pulled himself out from behind the sofa like some great serpent. He slunk to the coffee table's corner, sniffed at the food, and drank slowly. He fixed Kirk with the evil eye all the while.

Kirk knew what was going through his mind. He ignored it and returned to the kitchen. On the way, he glanced toward the closed door where Carma slept.

The door, while closed, was open just a crack. He hadn't noticed that before. He stopped, hesitated, and pushed it open with a finger.

Carma was gone.

Bed made. No note.

*

The bus would take Carma to New Brunswick, and from there, she intended to reclaim her car from the terminal's parking lot and drive all the way back to her territory. She settled back into her seat as the bus pulled away from the station. About half the bus's burgundy seats were filled. Carma sat three rows from the back and propped her head up on the nearby sill while watching the Halifax cityscape blur by her window, keeping pace with her thoughts. A light snow had fallen, dusting the concrete and steel in feather white.

Minutes later, Carma reached into her coat and pulled out her cell phone. She hefted it, then flipped it open. The number she called she'd called many times before, and already called the morning after the battle at the mall. The elder had ordered her to make contact after she'd left Halifax.

She let the call go through, three times, before hanging up.

A short time later, her phone buzzed.

"Yeah, it's me," she answered.

"You're away?" the voice asked.

"Yeah."

"How did Moses Morris look?"

Straight to the point, Carma thought. "He looked fine. Took only scratches compared to the rest of us, but he healed pretty quick."

"And Kirk?"

She stared at a passing fence of snow-topped trees, unsure if she should say anything more. In the end, she did. Reports were reports. "Kirk healed completely. Lost an eye one night and woke up with it replaced."

The voice on the other end of the line paused for lengthy, thoughtful seconds, setting off Carma's suspicions.

"Thank you, warden."

"Anything else?"

"No."

"The others are still at Kirk's apartment. They'll be leaving when they're able."

Another solemn pause. "Good."

Carma thought of Janice being carried out in a body bag. She thought of Kirk. "Yeah."

The elder cut the connection.

The bus shifted gears as Carma closed the phone and

held it in a fist. Her fingers pinched at her lower lip in a pose of thought, and she looked out her window.

The frosty landscape sped by, hypnotizing.

*

At the other end of the broken connection, in a room swallowed whole by darkness, the elder lowered the smartphone to a knee and considered the warden's report.

Morris.

And Kirk.

The elder didn't dwell upon the pair of wardens, but he fumed at both of Bailey's failures. The *were* executioner deserved to die. The problem still remained, however. A problem that still needed correcting. It was time for more direct action.

The phone lifted and the elder punched in a number not frequently called, but one he knew.

Three rings went through before a voice answered.

About the Author

Keith C. Blackmore is the author of the Mountain Man, 131 Days, and Breeds series, among other horror, heroic fantasy, and crime novels. He lives on the island of Newfoundland in Canada. Visit his website at www.keithcblackmore.com.